SNOOPING AROUND . . .

Annie moved the flashlight slowly around the room. Jack Hogan had a taste for nubile babes. From somewhere, probably scrounged from the dump, he'd gotten several posters of half-nude women and pinned them on the wall.

He even had a mattress of sorts, covered with layers of filthy blankets. What a way to live. She almost felt sorry for him. Nearby was a small table with a pot containing the remains of his dinner. It looked and smelled like stewed rat. A lantern beside it, when she touched the shade with the back of her hand, was still warm.

Suddenly, hanging around seemed to be a really bad idea. She wouldn't stand a chance of getting away. He'd catch her before she made it down the stairs; and the implications of that didn't bear thinking about. She took a deep breath, eyes darting around, trying to see in all the corners of the room.

A dark shadow loomed in the doorway. . . .

Also by Ann Campbell

Wolf at the Door
An Annie O'Hara & Claudius Mystery

WOLF IN SHEEP'S CLOTHING

An Annie O'Hara & Claudius Mystery

Ann Campbell

A SIGNET BOOK

SIGNET
Published by New American Library, a division of
Penguin Putnam Inc., 375 Hudson Street,
New York, New York 10014, U.S.A.
Penguin Books Ltd, 27 Wrights Lane,
London W8 5TZ, England
Penguin Books Australia Ltd,
Ringwood, Victoria, Australia
Penguin Books Canada Ltd, 10 Alcorn Avenue,
Toronto, Ontario, Canada M4V 3B2
Penguin Books (N.Z.) Ltd, 182–190 Wairau Road,
Auckland 10, New Zealand

Penguin Books Ltd, Registered Offices:
Harmondsworth, Middlesex, England

First published by Signet, an imprint of New American Library,
a division of Penguin Putnam Inc.

First Printing, May 2001
10 9 8 7 6 5 4 3 2 1

ACKNOWLEDGMENTS

Many thanks to Joe Pittman, a wonderful editor with an eagle eye. Thanks also to my agent, Todd Keithley, who keeps me on the straight and narrow, and to all my friends, without whose suggestions and advice Annie and Claudius wouldn't have nearly been so much fun. Last but certainly not least, many, many thanks to Claudius—my dear friend.

CHAPTER

1

The Thurston Tavern, a rambling, slightly cockeyed example of New Hampshire eighteenth-century architecture, sat basking in the late afternoon autumn sunshine at the junction of Routes 155 and 152. The old barn stood by the west wing of the tavern, its roofline sagging a little beneath the accumulated weight of three hundred years of snowbound winters.

The white-painted house, two stories plus the cupola on top, had begun showing its age since Abraham Lincoln spent the night in the best bedroom one hundred and fifty years ago. The brick path through the herb garden was bumpy, due to last winter's frost heaves, and the perennial garden looked scraggly and uncared for because the tavern's present owner, Annie O'Hara, hadn't found time to weed it.

Still, the tavern was a splendid example of a country carpenter's expertise, and although the white paint on the facade was peeling, the proportions of the rambling building remained delightfully eccentric. Two side wings and two large chimneys were located at either end of the main block with its formidable paneled double front door. In profile the tavern meandered off rearward into a barn and stables with a series of open curving bays. Behind the barn lay a three acre cornfield, thick with rows of tassled stalks rustling in the breeze.

Every summer, the field was cut into a maze, this year

a skull and crossbones, complete with a stream and two bridges for viewing. It was a popular local diversion and the proceeds—$9.90 for adult admission and $5 for children under twelve—went to charity.

This warm Halloween afternoon, Annie was kneeling in one of the bays by a little octagonal-top table, cleaning it before putting it up for sale in her antique shop. She ignored the incessant barking coming from the side yard and started wiping down the legs with long, even strokes. Five hundred seemed reasonable for the table's sticker price. Then she might come down to three-fifty if the customer wanted to haggle. In her experience customers loved haggling and drove off with anything from cracked chamber pots to Victorian corsets, grinning ear to ear if she came down a little in price.

Three-fifty was as low as she cared to go. Of course, if the shop were over on Route 1, the old road north to Maine, where tourists were thick as fleas this time of year, what with the fall foliage, she could have gotten eight or nine hundred.

Momentarily, she savored nine hundred, which would go a long way toward a new stove and refrigerator. The present stove burned everything, and the refrigerator's idea of keeping food cold was to defrost all over the floor. She was sick of it, as were her two tenants, for that matter. And then there was the furnace, which didn't bear thinking about.

She needed a new one. Last winter, they'd made do with the wood stove in the kitchen, but it didn't heat the whole house; and she didn't want to rely on space heaters. They were dangerous.

The tabletop shone like satin. It was really a little gem. Wide-board mahogany, the original finish, and no one had bastardized it by cutting down the legs. Nine hundred—if the plumber offered a deal on a new furnace, she could get Ralph Goddard, a farmer up the road, to cut down the dead maple by the back door before it fell on the roof.

She gazed at the table with some complacency. She could get a thousand or even fifteen hundred if some rich New

Yorker came by with money to burn—which was about as likely as pigs learning to fly.

From the side yard, the barking halted momentarily, then started up again a little louder than before, as if making the point that if any rich tourist showed up, she could forget about conversational haggling until she took care of canine needs.

Annie brightened as a shiny black Geo tracker four-by-four pulled into the driveway and a blond-haired woman got out. It was not, however, a rich New Yorker. It was her soon to be ex-sister-in-law, Lydia—ordinarily the last person Annie longed to see, but not today.

Today, she'd come to pick up her dog. Thanks be to God.

"Hi," said Lydia, shaking back her glorious mass of long blond hair. The champagne color was almost natural—the actual shade more of a mousy brown—but she'd bleached it several shades lighter. Her skin glowed like a proverbial peach, and she was wearing black silky pants and a black cashmere sweater. Her full breasts bounced cheekily: 36 D if she was an inch.

Annie, whose figure was more along the lines of two fried eggs on an ironing board, reminded herself that Lydia's job as an up-and-coming interior decorator demanded that she make the most of her appearance. It hardly mattered that she could only take Lydia in small doses. Today, she was *very* glad to see her. Annie stood up and got straight to the point. "It'll take just a minute to get Claudius. He's in the backyard."

"I'm in no big hurry. It's been ages since I saw you. You got a new hairdo. Curls—looks good. Where'd you get the permanent?"

"I did it myself. It's cheaper that way." Not exactly the truth, but not a lie, either; and Annie didn't want to talk about it.

"Geez, don't I know," Lydia said, patting her blond coiffure. "I drop at least a hundred at the hairdresser's every two weeks. How was your trip to Arizona?"

"It was New Mexico, and it was okay." If you didn't count three murders and almost getting killed herself.

"At least you had a vacation and got out of this one-horse town." Lydia ambled around the bay. "How's my lambie-pie, Claudius?"

"The neighbors aren't too pleased with him."

"Why, what happened?"

"Harvey Billington down the street is obsessed with his lawn. Gives me the finger every time I walk Claudius by his house. He called the dog officer and claimed Claudius was a public nuisance, that I was deliberately letting him poop all over his yard. Which isn't true, by the way," said Annie, incensed even now. "The jerk. I told the dog officer that if he found elephant or whale poop on his lawn, he should come looking for me. Otherwise, the poop on his lawn had nothing to do with me or my dog!"

"Still, you'd better watch out. What if Billington is a nut? He might come over and burn the house down."

"You have a point," said Annie. "Anyone who crawls around on his lawn looking for weeds and leaves is crazy. He doesn't scare me, though. If he shows up, I'll sic Claudius on him."

Lydia, who never bothered about anything except herself very long, lost interest in Annie's problems as her eyes moved acquisitively over the jumble of furniture. "Hmm, nice bureau."

"It's from Maine. Original escutcheons."

"The feet are odd. Shaped like balls."

"That's the idea. They're ball feet."

"Oh." She picked up a small tin box. "What's this?"

"A box."

"Oh." She put it down, wiped her fingers on her pants, and looked around again with a moue of distaste. "Looks like a bunch of junk. You should better yourself, Annie. Get out more. Marry some guy with money this time. Not like your ex. Now there's a loser. You could have done a whole lot better than Lenny. Tom told me what a tightwad he was, working part time for a funeral home and bringing you wired flowers. Jesus, how dumb can you be? You had to go and marry the guy."

"Okay, so the marriage was a mistake. I never said I was perfect."

"Yeah, but still." Lydia smirked. "Hey, I hear the maze out back is a skull and crossbones this year. You must make plenty off that. Giving it all to charity, though, right?"

"Right."

"Last year didn't you have a witch on a broomstick? I remember Tom borrowed a tractor to cut the field. Took him a couple of days to get it finished. He worked his butt off. By the way, how is dear old Tom? I haven't seen him in weeks."

"My brother's fine." Drinking too much. Tom still hadn't gotten over Lydia, but Annie wasn't about to let her know that.

"I hope he's still got a job. I hate asking for alimony, but you know how it is. My job isn't all that secure. If I don't get a few wealthy clients soon, he'll have to fork over enough for my rent and then some."

Annie's hackles rose at the thought of Lydia taking her brother to the cleaners. "The court will decide about alimony."

"Sure, but tell him for me that if he lies about his income, he'll regret it to his dying day."

Enough of the small talk. Annie took a step toward the driveway and the side yard erupted once again in a cacophony of deep barks. Claudius had caught his beloved owner's scent.

Lydia placed a hand over her bosom. "Is that my baby?"

"None other." Annie was out in the driveway by now—Lydia trailing noticeably behind. Thirty feet more and they'd be in the home stretch, around the side of the barn and halfway to the fenced kennel area. In another five minutes, the good lord willing, Claudius would be on his way out her life forever.

Lydia, however, wasn't trailing behind anymore. In fact,

she'd veered off toward the front door, clutching her purse under her arm and looking purposeful.

Annie shot her a look of deep suspicion.

"I could do with a cup of tea. My throat is parched like you wouldn't believe." Lydia shrugged. "It was a long drive from Durham."

"I haven't been to the store. All I've got is decaf."

"Well, I'm easy. Decaf's fine with me."

In the kitchen, Lydia sat by the window and gazed disparagingly around the large, inconveniently-shaped room, with its wide fireplace and thirty-year-old appliances. "I wouldn't live in this dump if you paid me. I don't know how you stand it." She gave the wall by the fireplace a withering look. "Needs a coat of paint. Get one of the boarders to slap one on for you. That shrink, Deitrich. He isn't working steady. Make him pull his weight."

"I started repainting last spring," Annie said, letting her sister-in-law—soon to be ex—get to her and hating herself in the process. *Why the hell was she explaining anything to this stupid woman?* "The upstairs is done. I haven't had time to do the downstairs. As for Kirk Deitrich, who happens to be a psychologist and a college professor, he takes care of most of the upkeep. Rakes and mows the lawn. Last spring he put in a garden that supplied all our fresh vegetables. This fall he helped design the maze."

Lydia gave a snort of laughter. "So, it's not as if he's got a real job. That shrink stuff's just a sideline. He gets summers off, and what he does around here is probably . . . what? An hour or two every few weeks. Get him to finish painting the place. Not that it'd make much difference, though, seeing it's such a dump. It needs major work and it's so far off the beaten path it's a wonder you sell anything."

Annie frowned. "I do all right."

"Huh. I'll bet you barely make enough to pay the mortgage. You're out of your mind giving what you make from the maze to charity. The library, right? What did the library ever do for you?"

"I like to read and they need a new wing."

"Well," said Lydia, allowing a bored note to creep into her voice, "you couldn't afford to hire me to fix up this place. I was in Talbot's last week . . . that's where I got this outfit. A steal at one hundred and fifty, marked down from four hundred. Anyway, I was at the register, and two women behind me were talking about that antique shop on Main Street. Bluebird Antiques. The old man who owned it retired a few months ago, and a niece got everything. She moved in with her husband, and they're open for business again. Word is they're not staying, so the house will probably be on the market before long. A location like that should bring plenty." A fleeting expression of envy gleamed in her large, slightly protuberant blue eyes. "Not that it'll do me any good. Those two women in Talbot's were loaded—the kind of clients I'd kill for. Big houses, maids' quarters, four-car garages. The works. But guess how they hire a decorator, if you please—by the stars."

"You mean astrology?"

"Right. Both women said they always follow their horoscopes. For instance, if the stars say, 'Good things will come your way', it means they should go shopping." Lydia frowned. "I tried it, but it didn't work for me."

"Someone did your chart?"

"No, I checked my horoscope in the paper. I'm a Pisces, which means I have a generous nature. People are always trying to take advantage of me."

"That must be tough."

"You've no idea," Lydia said gloomily. Then her face brightened. "Still, think positive. Take this place. Forget it's a dump. It's a roof over your head, that's the main thing, and there's plenty of room. Speaking of which . . ." She put down her cup. "Something's come up. Unfortunately."

Annie's stomach tightened with foreboding. "Oh?"

"The landlord put his foot down. I can't take Claudius right now, so you'll have to keep him until I find a new place. In the meantime, here's a couple of dollars for some

Alpo." Talking fast, Lydia tossed a ten dollar bill on the table and headed for the back door. "You're lucky. You've got a home of your own. What I wouldn't give for that. No stupid neighbors sticking their noses where they don't belong. Not to mention bloodsucking landlords, upping the rent every time you turn around. Threatening eviction if you're the teeniest bit late with the rent. You know me. Live and let live, that's my motto. But with some people, you might as well ask for the moon." She shrugged. "The landlord said, absolutely no dogs. Period. Well, there's only one thing on his mind—sex. His girlfriend lives upstairs, and they go at it hot and heavy three, four nights a week. Naturally, it's okay for her to have a dog—one of those stupid little cockapoos—but not me." She drew an indignant breath and eyed Annie with an unnaturally innocent expression. "You'll just have to keep Claudius a little longer."

Annie was on her feet by now, furious with herself for underestimating her sister-in-law's duplicity. "On the phone last week you said you'd take him back . . . *you promised*."

"I know, and I'm really sorry."

No, she wasn't. Annie glared at her.

Lydia gave an airy shrug. "Hey, I'm not responsible for the landlord's being a creep. There's nothing I can do. Well, that's not true. He drools every time he looks at me. He'd sing a different tune if I blew his flute for him. In his dreams." Opening the door, she turned and waggled her fingers. "Give Claudius a kiss for me. I don't dare stop to see him. He'll break the fence down. You know how he adores me." A trill of laughter and she was out the door like greased lightning.

Annie stood there, seething, listening to the roar of the Geo's engine and the squeal of rubber as Lydia took off down the road.

She hated that woman.

CHAPTER

2

"I wouldn't put a thing past that one," said May Upton from the hallway. She came into the kitchen, put a skillet on the stove, and turned on the burner. In her late sixties, her white hair was styled in a fashionable frizz. Her plump face was tanned and glowed with health. She wore glasses with rose-colored frames, pedal pushers, and a Laura Ashley shirt in shades of green—the tan and pedal pushers souvenirs from a recent Florida vacation. Although May had lived in the United States for years, she'd been born in England and still spoke with a touch of an accent. "Do you believe in coincidence, Annie?"

"No."

"Neither do I. So when I see you looking upset and your sister-in-law driving off looking like the cat that swallowed the canary, I come to the reasonable conclusion that the two events are not unrelated. What's she done now?"

"Nothing." Ordinarily, Annie would have made polite conversation and asked May how her day had gone—she had a part-time job as caregiver for some of the town's house-bound elderly. But right now Annie was so mad, she could barely think.

May gave her a sidelong glance. "How come smoke's coming out of your ears?"

"Lydia drives me crazy. Tom filed for divorce. You probably already knew that."

"He mentioned it. As a matter of fact, I suspected Lydia was trouble the first time I set eyes on her."

"Exactly. She went to interior design school and got a degree in sleeping around. One of her girlfriends ratted on her. That's how Tom found out."

May got down two mugs. "She reminds me of Marilyn Monroe in that old film, *Some Like it Hot*. That scene on the train where she plays the ukelele, and everything jiggles."

"That was farce," Annie said. "This is serious. I was only supposed to keep Claudius for a week or two. Lydia promised to pick him up today."

"How about a cup of tea and a brownie?"

At the mention of chocolate, Annie perked up a bit. "Okay, but Lydia's not getting away with this."

"Correct me if I'm wrong," May said as she put a plate of brownies on the table. The kettle whistled, and she made tea. "Your sister-in-law's gone and the dog is still here."

Annie couldn't very well argue with that. Instead, she went outside and brought Claudius back indoors. He was a large, black husky-shepherd cross who, once off the lead, rushed around the kitchen, sniffing eagerly for traces of his beloved mistress. When he realized she was gone, he barked madly and scratched at the door.

"He'll be at this for hours," Annie said, dragging him away and giving him a biscuit. "Here. It's your favorite. Shut up."

He ignored the biscuit. His eyes glittered with contempt as he turned his back.

May burst out laughing. "He may be a pain in the neck, but he's loyal. Too bad he's chosen Lydia to adore—I like him."

"There's no accounting for taste," Annie said sourly.

"It's your own fault. You let Lydia off the hook. Have a brownie. You'll feel better."

Suddenly Annie was starving, and May's brownies always tasted wonderful. For some reason, the stove didn't burn whatever May baked. Annie took a bite and let it melt in her mouth. "I'd tell Tom to come get Claudius, but he has enough to worry about."

"It won't kill you to put up with the dog a while longer, and I don't mind taking him with me to visit my clients—they love him. You'd better face the fact that Lydia's not going to take him back. And if you can't keep him, there's always the pound. Someone might adopt him."

Highly unlikely, and they both knew it. People adopted cuddly beagles and spaniels, not dogs who looked like wolves.

"They'd put him down," Annie said. "I couldn't live with myself."

May shook her head. She'd lived upstairs in the Lincoln bedroom for the past year. Besides doing light housekeeping for the area's house-bound elderly, she wrote a weekly advice column for the local newspaper. She was "Uncommon Sense," dispensing wisdom and answering letters she received, mostly from locals. Lately, she'd taken up astrology as a hobby.

"Let me do your chart," May coaxed. "Maybe you'll find an answer to Claudius in the stars."

"I don't believe in the stars."

"Come on, all I need is your birth date and time."

"No, really. Thanks anyway."

"If you change your mind, let me know." May took the dishes to the sink and began to wash up.

Annie picked up a dish towel. "Where's Kirk?" Kirk Deitrich was her other boarder, a psychology professor at nearby Lester College.

"Running an experiment with his pigeons over at the college lab."

"Listen, you've been wonderful about Claudius," said Annie, putting the dried dishes away. "But you don't have to take him along on visits to your home-bound clients. It's too much to ask."

"Nonsense. Studies have shown wonderful results with

animal therapy. People in nursing homes and hospitals perk right up when volunteers bring their dogs along." Done with the dishes, May checked her watch. "Goodness, it's past three. I'm expecting a visitor."

"And I'd better get the Halloween decorations set up before the sun goes down and the trick-or-treaters arrive," Annie said. While May went upstairs, Annie headed for the barn to get the assortment of gray-painted cardboard tombstones, ghosts, and ghoulies, which she intended to arrange outside.

An hour later, she'd finished turning the lawn into a graveyard. Near the porch, three witches in black hats and capes stood around a large kettle. Eight or ten tombstones, painted to look old and lichen-covered, stood on the front lawn. They bore grim warnings, skeleton faces, and crossed bones. Ghosts made from sheets and yards of shredded cheesecloth were draped in the trees, and high in the branches, spiderwebs floated eerily in the wind.

While Annie was admiring her handiwork, a gleaming silver BMW with a vanity plate—OLDTHG—pulled into the driveway, presumably May's visitor.

From inside the tavern and right on cue, Claudius started barking, scaring off potential burglars. Unfortunately, he managed to frighten away most of her customers. Annie shook her fist at him as he glowered from the kitchen window. Even as she opened her mouth to yell at him, he ran off toward the living room—intending, no doubt, to while away the next few minutes chewing up the latest issue of *Antiques* magazine.

She seethed and counted to ten. At least he'd stopped barking.

Must be nice to be solvent, she thought as she watched May's friend, a well-dressed woman, get out of the BMW and head toward the front door. Money to burn . . . to spend on fast cars and lovely clothes. She waited until the woman disappeared around the side of the house, then walked over to check out the car. Hmm, a carton on the backseat with a silver candelabra sticking out of it. Eighteenth-century English and very nice, too.

Maybe she should open the shop. May's friend might be interested in that pewter plate she'd picked up last week. It wasn't in the same league as the silver candelabra, but it was an interesting piece. Eighteenth-century English, imported by John Hancock for the colonial trade.

The woman would have to pass right by the shop as she left, and if the lights were on, she might spot something she wanted to buy.

On the other hand, Annie assured herself, she wasn't that desperate for customers. And it would be silly, practically waylaying the woman on her way out the door. If she wanted to buy anything, she could look through the shop window and ask her to open up. No big deal.

That decided, she glanced at her watch. Almost four-thirty, time to feed the hell hound. She went to the kitchen, dumped dry dog food into his bowl, and added cottage cheese and yogurt. He looked at her, his expression a satirical sneer: Eat this junk? You've got to be kidding.

She gave in and told herself she'd never use the left-over chicken gravy in the refrigerator, took it out, and after dithering about how much to give him, dumped half in his bowl. At which point he agreed to eat.

She poured the rest in a smaller bowl, rinsed out the large gravy dish and washed her hands. The window over the sink overlooked the driveway and the silver BMWer still parked there. With a start of surprise she noticed a red sticker on the windshield. Annie had the same dump sticker on her own car.

So the woman lived in town.

Well, so what. Still, she couldn't help wondering who May's visitor was. Someone with money, of course; and there weren't many in town that she could think of off-hand. A federal judge with political connections and one or two construction company owners who hadn't gone bust a few years ago when the real estate market collapsed.

Townsfolk with old money didn't waste it on new cars. They drove around in dirty four-wheelers and dented pick-up trucks.

Claudius nudged his bowl, banging it against the stove. He wanted the rest of the gravy.

She handed it over. "That's all there is, so don't ask for more." He gazed at her, and she thought she saw a gleam of thanks in the depths of those dark eyes. But if it was there, it was only momentary.

The next twenty minutes she spent preparing dinner. The routine was that she cooked for whomever was home. Anyone coming in late fended for himself. As there were usually leftovers in the refrigerator, this wasn't a problem. The temperamental stove was another matter. Annie ran water in a large pot. If Kirk showed up, there'd be three to feed. Kirk, May, and herself. They'd have spaghetti with a fresh tomato sauce, meatballs, salad, and garlic bread. She washed a head of lettuce.

Just as she turned off the faucet, May's visitor came around the front of the house. She was slender, in her thirties. Without a glance at the antique shop, the woman crossed the driveway and got into the BMW, then drove off—a potential customer gone.

A second later, May came bustling in. "Good, you've started supper. Did you finish the Halloween decorations?"

"Yeah," Annie replied, brooding about lost opportunities.

"Do we need more tombstones? I could paint a few more—"

"No, we have plenty. Not to be nosy, but I wondered who your friend was."

"Abigail Woodruff. She and her husband live in that big old house on Main Street. Bluebird Antiques."

The shop Lydia had mentioned earlier. Expensive antiques, thought Annie, and unlike the Thurston Tavern, doing a roaring business. Maybe she should check it out again. "Mrs. Woodruff has a nice car. She must be doing well."

"It's her uncle's," May said. "Wallace Horne retired and moved to Arizona. Abigail took over the house and shop. Wallace's car was part of the arrangement. He and I became friends last year when he showed up at a few historical society meetings. You may not have seen the display at the library last spring. He lent a fascinating collection of antique mechanical card shark devices."

Annie nodded. "I remember it."

"He's not the easiest person to get along with, and his niece is a chip off the old block." May shrugged. "Wallace sold me a lovely old tea chest before he left for Arizona. Would you believe it? Abigail refused to hand it over. She offered me the fair market value instead. I said, no deal."

"Did she drop by to make you a better offer?"

"No, the tea chest is still over at her uncle's, well, now *her* antique shop. She refuses to part with it because she says it holds too many childhood memories."

"That could be true, I guess."

"Hogwash. That woman's got about as much sentiment as your average gallstone. She was born with a silver spoon in her mouth and a knife and fork in both hands. The better to carve up anyone who gets in her way." May's blue eyes narrowed. "Well, she's met her match this time. If she doesn't abide by the terms of the sale, I'll file suit."

"Lawyers are expensive."

May smiled. "I'll let you in on a secret. We started talking about astrology and numerology. Abigail told me her birth date and time, and I worked up her horoscope. I let her think her chart resembled Princess Diana's, and that Saturn is controlling her stars for the next six months, leading to a period of menace and danger she can avoid only through strictly ethical behavior."

"Very clever."

"Nasty, but Abigail deserved it."

*   *   *

The afternoon wore on. May went back upstairs to work on her newspaper column, and with the tomato sauce simmering on the stove, Annie became busy with a browser or two in the antique shop. A woman from Scarborough, Maine, bought a couple of wooden spoons and a glass honey pot for a net profit, after taxes, of $3.76.

Actually, she was lucky to sell anything, what with the racket Claudius made every time a strange car pulled up. He barked nonstop until the customers couldn't hear themselves think.

The only sensible thing to do was get a bark collar, which she could ill-afford even if she could get past her reservations about negative reinforcement. It was a moot point whether a bark collar could turn Claudius into a dog who knew how to keep his mouth shut. So she was in a gloomy state of mind as she closed up the shop and wandered back to the house.

A note from May lay on the kitchen counter: Sorry to let you know so late, but I have to go to Portsmouth to see my lawyer. If Tom drops by, tell him where I've gone. I'll call him tomorrow. See you later when I get in. May.

Lately, Annie's brother, Tom, and May had been thick as thieves. May had decided to get on the Internet with her self-help business, and he'd put together a computer system and set up a website. Annie didn't know the details, but the last time she'd talked to Tom, he'd said something about May's site being a potential gold mine.

Night fell and several young trick-or-treaters made their way through the fake graveyard and rang the back doorbell. There ensued the usual hassle while she hauled a loudly barking Claudius—his voice, like everything about him, rang with arrogance—to the downstairs bathroom and shut him in. Afterward, she let him out and discovered he'd eaten the toilet paper. Between groups of three-foot high witches, spacemen, devils, hockey players, and dinosaurs, dealing with Claudius, toilet paper all over the floor, and stashing the rest in the cupboard under the bathroom sink, she managed to set the table for supper.

At six-thirty, Claudius ran to the back door and started barking as Kirk Deitrich's gray Subaru roared up the driveway. The young psychology professor came in with a gust of cool night air. He was in his late twenties, tall and thin. His blond hair, ruffled by the wind, fell across his forehead. "Getting chilly out." He patted Claudius, busy sniffing his legs. "You smell the pigeons, don't you, boy? Hey, spaghetti and meatballs. Great, I'm starving. Just give me a minute to get cleaned up."

He disappeared upstairs while she tasted the marinara sauce and added a pinch of salt. A few minutes later, he came back. They sat down and ate.

"There's a dead branch on that maple tree by the back door," she said. She poured two glasses of Chianti. "We'd better cut it down before it breaks. We could use a ladder, but it'd be easier to reach from the roof. I'd like to save the tree if we can."

"I'll take care of it," Kirk said. "I was going to repair the flashing around the cupola tomorrow, so I'll be up on the roof, anyway. Oh, we need a can of roofing tar."

"I'll get some at the hardware store."

"Where's the dog?" Kirk glanced under the table. "He was here a minute ago. He's awfully quiet."

"I don't want to know." Please God, thought Annie. Make Lydia take her dog back. *Please. Please.*

"We did pretty well with the maze this year," Kirk said, helping himself to spaghetti. "Took in more than a thousand dollars. The skull-and-crossbones design was a brainstorm. Kids really loved it."

She nodded. "And it was easier to work out than last year's witch. Once we got the grid design on paper, it was just a matter of cutting the corn rows with the tractor."

Claudius trotted in and, adopting an air of complete disinterest, sauntered past the table. Having devoured his own dinner a good half hour ago, he'd have no compunction about eating whatever else was going. People food was much more desirable than chunky kibbles, and he was very fond of spaghetti and meatballs.

He sat down where he could keep an eye on the plates. Only his bright eyes and pricked ears betrayed his anticipation. There were sure to be leftovers, and he meant to get every bite.

"There was great publicity about the maze in the newspaper. Top right on the second page." Kirk handed her the paper. "Nice article. I'll bet we doubled the numbers from last year. Vita Charlemagne and the rest of the library board should be pleased. You'll have a fat check to hand to them."

She read the relevant paragraphs with interest. A brief history of the annual charity maze along with an aerial shot, probably taken last week. The skull and crossbones stretched out over three acres, with the two wooden bridges that allowed you to see most of the design from a good twenty feet up.

This year she hadn't passed out maps. People had paid at the entrance and spent the next hour or two walking around in the late autumn sunshine. If they failed to find the center of the maze, they'd eventually stumbled across one of the bridges, where they got their bearings and figured out where they were.

The tavern roof and cupola, along with the maple tree by the back door, were visible in the lower corner of the photograph. It was a big tree, at least two hundred years old, but seen from above, most of it looked dead.

Claudius stared at her plate with concern. She wasn't going to eat all that spaghetti, was she?

"How about trying sunflowers next year?" Kirk suggested. "Or we might cut a labyrinth in the field instead of a maze. What do you think?"

"Aren't they the same thing?"

"No. With a maze you get false passages that lead to dead ends. Tricks. A labyrinth is a single, winding path leading to the center. Concentric circles around something you place in the middle: a bench or a tree. Once you're on the path, you go in one direction, straight ahead. If you take the path backward, it always leads to the beginning. We could enlarge it to cover three acres."

Annie shook her head. "Kids wouldn't enjoy it as much. They like scary faces, witches, ghosts, skulls, and they like to be fooled. It's a game. If we turned it into a labyrinth, we wouldn't make as much money to give to charity." She grimaced and added, "Vita Charlemagne wouldn't be pleased, she'd accuse us of keeping half the profits. You know what she's like. May calls her the town witch. "

He eyed the empty chair. "God forbid. Speaking of May, where is she?"

"Portsmouth." By now it was clear that May wouldn't be back in time for dinner, and Annie was wondering if it was worthwhile to make up a plate for her to zap in the microwave later. She couldn't stand zapped spaghetti, herself. All the life went out of it.

He sipped his wine. "Who does May know in Portsmouth?"

"Her lawyer. Actually, I expected her back by now." Annie glanced at the windows. At the dark outside. The phone rang suddenly, and for some reason a sense of dread swept over her. She went to answer it, but no one was on the other end. "Must have been a wrong number. They hung up," she said, sitting back down at the table and noticing with surprise that her dinner was still there. Claudius hadn't made a mad dash to clear her plate. Well, Kirk's presence explained that.

But the phone call—she wondered, and her heart sank.

It could have been the police or a hospital reporting an accident. A vision of May, sprawled lifeless behind the wheel of her car floated before her eyes—blood matted on her white hair. Annie put down her fork, her appetite gone. "Why do you suppose she's so late?"

"There's probably nothing to worry about," said Kirk. "Though she seemed preoccupied yesterday. She had the newspaper under her arm and almost bit my head off when I asked if she was through reading it. I wondered if anything was wrong."

"I don't know." Annie remembered the conversation about Wallace Horne and the tea chest. But it didn't seem relevant, so she decided not to mention it. "May left me a note, but it just said she'd had to go to Portsmouth to see her lawyer."

The doorbell rang again, Claudius ran to the door, barking; and while Kirk got up to dole out the goodies, Annie dragged the dog off to the bathroom and thought about Kirk's comment that May had almost bitten his head off. It didn't fit. May was usually so calm and controlled.

A few minutes later, released from imprisonment, Claudius trotted in, a candy wrapper between his teeth. Kirk said, "That makes ten. The next bunch of little monsters at the door is yours."

The diminishing contents of the Chianti bottle began to do wonders for Annie's mood, and for once, the stove hadn't burned anything. The spaghetti was al dente, the meatballs delicious, the marinara sauce just right. On top of that, the salad greens were crunchy, the dressing tart and tingly on the tongue. A delicious meal.

By eight-thirty, they'd polished off the bottle and she was smiling benignly at the few swirls of spaghetti left on her plate. She couldn't eat another bite.

Claudius nudged her leg, and she gave up and put her plate on the floor. Licking sounds ensued.

It was a shock when, later, she glanced at her watch and discovered it was past ten. Aside from the glow of the porch light, it was pitch-black outside. There probably wouldn't be any more trick-or-treaters. In Lee, they rolled up the sidewalks after nine.

Kirk helped Annie clear the table and suggested they leave the porch light on for May. Annie agreed, and after deciding to leave the dishes to soak overnight, they said good night and went up to their respective bedrooms, Claudius at Annie's heels.

Outside, the night wind rattled the shutters, and as Annie closed her bedroom door, a gust of cool air touched the back of her neck. She pulled her sweater off and couldn't help glancing around to see if her resident ghosts were watching. It was an old house, filled with the presence of past lives.

The corner of the room lay in deep shadow. Claudius, who had plopped down in his usual spot, rose to his feet and stood staring at it, the ridge of fur along his backbone stiffening. But there was nothing there but an old wall cabinet.

The tavern's ghosts, nightcaps tied beneath their chins, were probably tucked up in their ghostly beds, she thought with a smile.

After another moment, Claudius yawned and flopped down on the rug again. She kicked off her sneakers and stripped off the rest of her clothes. She pulled on a long T-shirt and padded off to the bathroom to brush her teeth. When she came back, Claudius had made himself comfortable on the bed. "Off!" He didn't move, so she shoved him to the floor and told him to stay on the rug or else.

The last thing she saw before turning out the light was Claudius eyeing her beadily. There was a certain implied threat there that she didn't at all like.

When she woke up the next morning, the sky outside her window was imperceptibly November—pale, cold blue with a few puffy clouds. Something heavy was lying on her feet. The hell hound. "Dammit, get off!"

He did, but only after several wide yawns. Everything had to be his idea.

A half hour later, having showered and dressed, she went downstairs to let him out into the backyard. At the sight of May's car parked in the driveway, a profound feeling of relief came over her. Everything was all right. May had come home sometime in the night.

For some reason Claudius decided to alter his usual morning routine of maintaining law and order in the side yard, barking at squirrels and anything else that moved. He was determined to head toward the cornfield maze, barking, pulling, and jerking on the leash. Annie had a difficult time hauling him around to the side yard.

By now breathless and red in the face, she shoved him into the fenced kennel area, closed the gate, and locked it. "Stay there and keep your big mouth shut!"

He glowered at her and resumed barking at the top of his lungs. He was driving her crazy. Somehow she had to stop that racket.

A sure fire method was required. Quick . . . inhumane. On the other hand, if it worked quickly, it would be humane. He'd get the idea, and she wouldn't have to use it again.

A bark control collar. Electric-shock therapy. She hated the idea but was at her wits' end. What else could she do?

A few minutes later she was driving downtown to the hardware store to get roofing tar and thought, fifty bucks, maybe. Blessed silence . . . cheap at the price. She pulled into Overton Hardware's parking lot and went inside. Roofing tar, aisle five. She picked up a can and headed toward aisle two: doggy paraphernalia. Bowls, toys, leashes.

Ah, control collars. Everything from Pekinese size to bearlike, priced to match. Batteries required . . . electric shock therapy. She picked up the largest size, which came with a remote device. More than she could afford, but what the hell. Nothing worthwhile came cheap and you got what you paid for.

She paid for her purchases and drove home. As she got out of the car, she heard barking from the side yard. He was still at it. Well, not for much longer. It took only seconds to remove the collar and remote from the box and install the batteries.

She showed Claudius the collar, which he regarded with extreme disfavor. "This is for you." But he had other ideas. She got it on him, but just barely. He shook his head, growling and flattening his big ears.

She snapped on the leash and pulled him along past the maze. Claudius twisted his head, grumbling, clawing at the collar. "That comes off over my dead body," she told him. A moment later, she spotted Kirk on the roof and waved.

He'd already cut the branch off the maple tree, but unfortunately, it looked like the entire tree was dead. Kirk couldn't take the tree down by himself. It was just too big, and too close to the house. She'd have to hire a tree removal service.

Suddenly, the leash flew out of her hands as Claudius lunged forward, ducked his head, and stopped dead. The new collar flew off. "No you don't!" She snatched the collar and made a desperate grab for him. But he raced around, just out of reach, daring her to put that fiendish device on him again. He ducked as she took a swipe at him and missed. Inadvertently, she dropped the remote.

In a flash, he scooped it up in his teeth and ran into the maze. "Stop!" She ran after him, crashing through the six-foot-high dried stalks. There was no sign of him.

She raced down the rows, hoping to catch sight of him. No luck. She came to the first bridge, dashed up the wooden steps, and looked out over the skull-and-crossbones design. Bordered by a series of field-stone walls, it covered the entire three acres, complete with dark circles for eyes and a gaping maw.

Cornstalks swayed and rustled in the breeze. Suddenly, a flock of blackbirds by the mouth of the skull flew up into the air, cawing and flapping their wings. Aha, she thought. He was over there near the brook. Wasting no time, she raced off in that direction. This area was thick with shadows. The sound of her footsteps thudding on the earth carried on the cool November air.

He'd hear her coming.

He was clever, he was stubborn. It would be out of character for him to trot out of the cornstalks and go meekly back to the house with her. He was enjoying this.

Grimly, she ran down one row and up another, looking everywhere. Damn. She'd seen neither hide nor hair of him. There was no point in calling his name. He was notoriously good about ignoring her whenever he felt like it.

She stopped at the second bridge to get her bearings. Below the bridge was a small brook. Someone had dumped a couple of Coors' empties nearby. Great. She made a mental note to come back later and clean it all up.

She took a deep breath. *Where was he?*

No sound of him moving across the rows of dried cornstalks, no flash of his black fur. No sign of him at all.

She went down the bridge steps and noticed something in the water below. A black shadow.

Smiling, she darted beneath the bridge. He was there, all right, standing in the brook, laughing at her.

She splashed into the water and lunged after him, still holding the collar, which abruptly came to life. The current shocked in searing waves up her arm, her shoulder, until her jaw chattered. Her left side was numb. No, it *hurt*, she realized with horror.

She flailed around like Frankenstein's bride, moaning, knee-deep in the brook while Claudius raced up and down by the bridge steps, chewing on the remote. Tears of pain blurred her vision. She stumbled over a few rocks. Claudius kept chewing, and with each chomp of those big, white teeth on the remote, the collar between her fingers zinged to life.

Annie's legs went numb, and she toppled over.

The water was cold. By some stroke of good luck she'd dropped the collar. But it was the deluxe model and cost more than fifty dollars. She groped around among the rocks at the bottom of the brook, and by some miracle, found it. It was dark under the bridge. The sound of buzzing flies was loud in her ears. She could hardly see her hand in front of her face. She groped for one of the bridge supports and touched something peculiar. Firm and elongated, a leg of some sort. An animal, Oh, God, a deer must have wandered out of the woods and died in the brook. Nausea rose in her throat, all but choking her. She let go of the leg and wiped her hand on her wet jeans.

Claudius was staring fixedly at the shadows under the bridge. He growled, then began barking insistently.

Dear God, she had to get out of the brook.

Somehow, she clambered out. Her teeth chattered. "Quiet!" Then she turned her head to see what lay in the water, and her heart lurched. It wasn't an animal.

It was a woman.

"Oh, no!" It was May Upton, and she wasn't moving.

She was lying on her side in the shallows of the brook. She was dressed in a brown tweed suit. Water lapped against her face. Flies buzzed around her, landing on her cheek.

For some reason, God knows why, May had decided to come out to the maze last night. Probably she'd had a heart attack. The poor woman had fallen into the brook and died.

Annie grabbed May's shoulders and dragged her out of the water. She started CPR as Kirk noticed what was going on and yelled down from the roof, "What's wrong . . . My God, I'll call the ambulance!"

She kept hoping May would move, that air she was pumping into her lungs would bring her back to life. *Pinch the nose, blow into the mouth. Two, three, four. Again. Blow. Two, three, four. All she wanted was for May to move, for the color to come back to her pallid face. Two, three, four . . .*

Desperately, Annie kept up the CPR.

May didn't move.

Moments later, Kirk's feet thudded through the maze and he shouted that the ambulance was on the way. He took over CPR. "You're turning green, sit down. Don't faint on me."

"I'm okay." But she was trembling as she sank down on the grass. How could this have happened?

They were too late.

May was dead, there was nothing anyone could do. Now Annie saw sickeningly that there was blood on the side of May's head and a faint smear of reddish brown on the rocks by the side of the brook. *Not a heart attack, after all.* It looked as if May had walked under the bridge for some reason, fallen, hit her head, and drowned.

CHAPTER
3

Upon receiving the frantic 911 call from Kirk Deitrich, the police sent three patrol cars, an ambulance, and the coroner's wagon. The ambulance, its services unneeded as nothing would revive poor May Upton, was soon sent back to the firehouse. Meanwhile, the police photographer took a series of pictures of May's body from every conceivable angle.

More indignities. A detective stood and watched while May's sodden skirt was pushed up and her pantyhose rolled down so the coroner could slip a thermometer between her buttocks. He waited a minute or two, then removed the thermometer and inspected it. "Water temperature has to be taken into account, of course, but I'd say she's been dead for a good ten, twelve hours. Sometime around midnight. I'll know more once we get her downtown."

The attendants put May Upton's earthly remains in a rubber bag, zipped it up, and bundled her into the back of the coroner's station wagon.

Deafening barks erupted every time a police car arrived or departed. Annie had locked Claudius in the side kennel again—without the control collar, which in her mind would always be connected with May's death. She'd just have to figure out some other way to keep him quiet.

After changing out of her wet clothes, she went back to the maze to find another detective, this one burly and dark-haired, talking to Kirk. The detective's blue eyes gave her an all-encompassing look. He jotted a line or two in a notepad. "Gus Jackson, Ms. O'Hara. Too bad about this. Must have been quite a shock when you found her."

"Yes." Annie glanced at the shadows under the bridge and drew a shaky breath. "I thought she'd come home late last night. Her car was in the driveway this morning. I couldn't believe it when I found her."

He nodded. "Way things look, Mrs. Upton didn't make it as far as the house last night. She came out here for some reason, maybe dropped something and went under the bridge to pick it up and tumbled over a rock or maybe had a heart attack. Did she smoke?"

"No," said Annie. "Why?"

"We found a lighter in the brook. A Zippo with a road runner logo. Someone was standing on the bridge, smoking. Could have been Mrs. Upton, but maybe not. You know anyone with a lighter like that?"

Kirk shook his head and Annie did the same, barely keeping herself from gasping aloud. *Tom had a lighter like that.* Lydia had given it to him for his last birthday. And there had been empty beer cans in the maze. *He could have been out there when May died.*

Detective Jackson snapped his notepad shut. "Like I say, we'll know more after the autopsy."

Annie shuddered. The graphic image of a stainless steel table in a white-tiled room somewhere downtown, and poor May lying on the table, sliced open from stem to stern. Her eyes filled. She blinked hard and focused on the cop's face. Late thirties, laugh lines around his mouth. He had a nice smile and a nonthreatening manner that must have proved useful in investigating criminal matters. Not that Lee saw much of that. It was hardly a thriving metropolis, a few thousand inhabitants at most. And May's death wasn't a criminal matter. It was a terrible accident. She'd fallen, hit her head, and drowned. Unfortunate and sad, but there was nothing suspicious about it.

Kirk wiped his face on his sleeve and swatted at a late

mosquito while the detective moved away to have a few words with the coroner.

Wondering how in the world this had happened, Annie stared around at the rows of corn. The Halloween maze was a good hundred and fifty feet from the back of the house. There had been a full moon last night—presumably, May had been able to see well enough. On the other hand, if she'd been drinking, she might have stumbled and fallen. But so far, no one had said anything about alcohol, and as far as Annie knew, May hadn't been much of a drinker. It looked as if she'd simply decided to take a stroll through the maze before coming into the house. A tragic decision, as things turned out.

Kirk cleared his throat. "If only we'd heard the car last night. When she didn't come in right away, we'd have realized something was wrong and gone to look for her. She might still be alive."

"I know." Annie stared at the brook under the bridge, still barely able to take in what had happened. A few red maple leaves fluttered down to float on the water.

Momentarily, she wondered about the funeral. Did May have any living relatives? No children, but hadn't she mentioned a brother living in Seattle—Edgar Whittles, whom she'd said in passing that she didn't trust. May hadn't gone into detail, other than to say that he was a numbskull, all he cared about was money, and that she wouldn't live with him if her life depended on it.

Annie's gloomy thoughts were interrupted by a renewed spate of loud barking, and she realized she was being watched by the cop.

He moved closer, friendly public servant pose no longer in evidence. His bulk and presence warned that he was in charge and had a gun. "Can't you shut that dog up?"

"I could put him in the house, but he'd still bark."

"Better behind doors than out here." He gestured toward the tavern. "Take him inside, please. He's driving me nuts."

She complied, though Claudius had other ideas. He

showed every intention of dragging her back to the maze where the action was. She was forced to lure him indoors with the promise of a roast beef treat.

He weighed his options and, deciding that a slice of roast beef was worth a change in plan, trailed her indoors.

While he waited, drooling, she got out the roast beef, on sale at the Pick 'n Pay deli at $5.99 a pound, and which she'd planned for dinner. With a resigned sigh, she dumped it in his bowl. They'd eat vegetarian tonight.

"Enjoy."

He did just that while she stared out the kitchen window. Things were proceeding at a snail's pace in the maze, although Detective Jackson had joined two uniformed cops painstakingly searching the area around the bridge. Looking for God only knew what. As she watched, he took his notepad from his pocket again and began questioning Kirk.

No doubt she was next on the list. He'd want to know all about May's health, if she'd taken heart pills or was prone to fainting spells. The cops, Annie found herself thinking, wanted to have it both ways if a death occurred: Either the deceased was at fault for being elderly, careless, or infirm. Or some outside agent was to blame—lightning, an accident of some sort, or murder.

Claudius nudged her leg.

"There's no more roast beef."

He shot her a stony look, apparently suspecting she'd lied and was hogging the rest for herself, then yawned and trotted out to the living room to keep an eye on the cops from the window by the sofa. On impulse, Annie went upstairs to May's room to look for Edgar Whittles's address and phone number. Someone had to let him know his sister was dead.

Her bedroom door wasn't locked, so Annie, feeling decidedly guilty, went in. It was eerie to be alone in a room belonging to someone who'd just died. Meanwhile, downstairs in the living room, Claudius had started in again, taking umbrage at whatever the cops were doing. Wishing she were downstairs too, she hesitated just inside the door. Nuts. Someone had to do it. There wasn't anyone else.

The room was a reflection of May: neat, orderly, everything in its place. The books on the wall shelves stood straight, their spines even. Some were hardcover, but most were paperbacks: classics, thrillers, biographies, a few horror. She'd had an eclectic taste in reading, but a weakness for Stephen King. To the immediate right was the fireplace, a tall floor lamp, and May's favorite armchair with her wool cardigan tossed over the back. The cushions still retained the shape of her body. More than once Annie had looked in to find May fast asleep in that chair, her chest imperceptibly rising and falling with each breath, *The Shining* or *Misery* open on her lap, and an occasional faint snore escaping her parted lips.

"I'm sorry," Annie said. She gulped and started over, "If only we'd heard you come home and gone to check when you didn't come in right away. We didn't, and I'm so sorry."

Her whispered words barely penetrated the sunlit silence of the room, but for a moment she felt warm, as if May had put an arm around her shoulders in comfort.

Annie swallowed hard. Okay, where to start first. It seemed wrong to rummage through May's belongings, looking for her brother's phone number. May hadn't trusted him for some reason. But there was nothing else to do. As far as Annie knew, there were no other relatives.

The bedroom was furnished with the usual: a chest of drawers, wardrobe, and a writing desk in the corner. What May had lacked in family, she'd more than made up in friends. She'd kept up a voluminous correspondence with people all over the country.

The desk revealed pads and pens, and a number of standard white envelopes in slots. Bills mostly, all marked paid. May had been commendably prompt.

Feeling like a scavenger picking over the belongings of the dead, Annie stuffed the envelopes back in the slot.

Where would May keep her address book? She pulled open the desk drawers. Erasers, paper clips, tape, string, stamps. A day planner with appointments neatly jotted down. Annie flipped through this week's entries: dry cleaner's on Tuesday, Wednesday May had gone to the dentist, yesterday— an appointment with P. Cannell. Ten o'clock, psychic reading, $50.00.

What do you know, May had consulted a psychic. Annie wondered why. May hadn't ever professed a belief in psychic phenomena, but on the other hand, she'd never said she didn't believe in it.

Annie closed the day planner with a sense of frustration and hunted through the desk drawers again. No sign of an address book.

She eyed the bureau. A lace cloth on top, a silver brush set, a few cosmetics, and a hand mirror reflecting her own face. She put the mirror down.

The closet revealed an array of clothes. Wooly bathrobe, tweed suits, dresses, camel hair coat, Gore-Tex ski jacket, yellow slicker. The hangers rattled as she pushed them aside. The shelf above held sweaters and scarves. On the floor were several pairs of shoes and boots—Timberland and New Balance running shoes. May had loved to walk. Two pairs of high heels. One had fallen over. Annie placed it upright beside its mate. May had had small feet—size five and a half.

She backed out of the closet and shut the door. At the foot of the bed stood a small blanket chest. It contained a pink douvet and a stack of cooking magazines. *Gourmet*, *Bon Appetite*. At the bottom, her fingers touched something with hard edges. She dragged out the douvet and uncovered a writing case embossed with the letter M.

It held several pages of May's beige notepaper and the usual two or three sleeves for envelopes. The writing paper was blank. Turning to the other side, she poked her fingers in the pocket and felt paper. Several papers, actually. A greeting card and a business card with an attorney's name and address in Portsmouth. She tucked the business card back in the case and turned to the greeting card. Roses and daisies. A line of predictable doggerel expressing regrets, and at the bottom, a scrawled name: Edgar.

Her brother. Now if only May had kept the envelope. Always supposing Edgar had thought to put a return address on it—Ah, here it was. Kansas City, Missouri.

The last paper was folded in thirds. She stared at it, appalled. Good grief. It was a threatening letter. No signature, composed from letters clipped from a newspaper. According to the author, May was a bleeping whore who'd pay for the trouble she'd caused. She was a no good, bleeping bitch, sticking her nose where it didn't belong, and before he was done with her, she'd wish she was dead.

Above her harsh intake of breath, Annie heard a soft noise from out in the hall. A soft creaking. *Someone was coming.*

She fumbled with the writing case, pushed the card and letter deep in her jeans pocket, and dropped the case in the bottom of the chest.

The door swung open. Detective Jackson loomed in the doorway.

"What do you think you're doing?" he asked.

"Looking for May's brother's phone number." Her face was getting red, and there was nothing she could do about it.

"I see," he said. Silence. Evidently he'd exhausted his fund of small talk. There was a brisk click of nails on the stairs, and Claudius trotted into view. His eyes were dark and questioning as he stared from Annie to the detective.

All she needed at this point was for the dog to take an unreasonable dislike to authority figures. She grabbed him by the collar and dragged him behind her. "It's been a tough day. May was my friend."

"I'd say it was a tougher day for her. Of course, right now she's feeling no pain." Detective Jackson eyed Annie with a slight smile. "Seeing as she's dead."

You bastard, thought Annie. What was going on? Jackson's manner was a far cry from the friendly public servant she'd met twenty minutes ago. There was a hardness in his eyes now, an edge to his deep voice.

"I don't understand," she said, deciding not to demand what the hell he was getting at, not yet anyway. She took a step backward and hoped he wouldn't notice. He was crowding her, all but shoving his nose in her face.

"There's a problem," he said. "May Upton didn't decide to take a moonlit stroll through the maze. Footprints in the dirt indicate she ran for her life and lost, after first being attacked by the back door. So maybe what we've got is a case of homicide. Depending on what the coroner turns up in the autopsy."

Annie gaped at him, stunned. "I can't believe someone killed her. She didn't have any enemies."

"Okay, let me walk you through it. Downstairs."

Reluctantly, she traipsed downstairs and pushed Claudius into the bathroom, whereupon he shot her one of his characteristic "okay, you're gonna do this again" looks and swerved toward the toilet.

"I put the toilet paper in the cupboard under the sink, so there's no use looking for it."

He glared at her, and she closed the door with a feeling of satisfaction. Chalk one up for her side.

"These bushes by the back door are broken," Jackson said. "Didn't you notice?"

"My rhododendron bushes? No."

"Were the branches broken before last night?"

"I don't think so." She took a look out the door. You'd have to be blind as a bat not to see that something violent had happened there.

"We know she got this far," Jackson said. "Leaves from these bushes were caught in her hair. Rhododendron leaves."

"That doesn't prove anything. The brook is full of leaves

this time of year. Some of them could have come from these bushes. The wind blows them everywhere."

"You want the whole nine yards. Okay. Follow me, please." He took her back to the maze, down the rows of corn to the second bridge. Two cops were still searching among the shadows in the brook. Annie hoped they wouldn't notice her. They didn't, but the coroner, who was stripping off his rubber gloves, did. He raised his eyebrows.

Jackson said, "Ms. O'Hara needs convincing. Unzip the body bag, Charlie."

"Okay," grunted the coroner. "Sure."

He unzipped the bag, then stepped back. Jackson urged Annie closer to the gurney where the body lay, now half-uncovered. "Look at her hands and the sleeves of her jacket."

She looked. May's palms were deeply scratched, and rhododendron twigs were snagged in her jacket cuffs. "All right, she could have fallen in the bushes."

"Exactly. Another thing. Did she have family?"

"A brother, Edgar Whittles."

He nodded and made a note.

"What about her husband?"

"She'd been divorced for years," she said. He made another note, and she added, "I don't know where she'd want to be buried. She was born in England, but lived out west for a number of years. Oregon or maybe Kansas City." She cleared her throat and pulled the anonymous letter from her pocket. "I found this upstairs while I was looking for her brother's telephone number."

It didn't take him long to read it. Then he snapped, "Why didn't you give me this right away?"

"You startled me. I just stuck it in my pocket."

"That's no excuse. Do you know who wrote it?"

"No."

He heaved a sigh. "We'll check it out, but you've messed up any chance at fingerprints. In the meantime, the funeral will have to wait until we see where we stand." Whatever that meant.

"How long? Her brother will want to know."

"Earliest could be sometime next week. That's the best I can do for now."

She nodded, aware that he was watching her closely. "Thank you."

"We'll be talking to the brother sooner or later." There was a look in his eye she couldn't read as he asked, "Did she have any money—and if so, who gets it? Friends, other relatives? Kids?"

"No kids. She had a pension, some stocks and bonds. She wrote an advice column for the paper and volunteered at a home help agency in town. Her favorite charity was the Bide-a-Wee Humane Society over in West Lee. They never euthanize the animals. That was important to May."

Jackson took more notes. Finally, he said he had enough for the time being, which Annie took to mean that if he needed anything more, he knew where to find her.

The coroner zipped the body bag shut—a brutal sound she knew she'd hear in her nightmares for weeks. She'd caught one last glimpse of May's face. It wasn't her friend she saw, it was a face without life, a shell of a human being.

"What do you think killed her?"

Jackson shrugged. "It'll be in the final report."

She swallowed and said, "I have a right to know. She died in my maze."

"Okay, it looks like Mrs. Upton was hit on the head before she was put in the brook. That's what killed her." He shrugged again. "That's just my opinion. Which makes it murder."

"What are you going to do about it?"

"We'll find the killer. Make no mistake about that."

"I hope so." She couldn't help her tone of disbelief.

He bared his teeth at her in what passed for a smile,

then said, "Contrary to what you obviously think, Ms. O'Hara, we know what we're doing."

"Maybe, but we don't have much crime here in town, let alone murder."

"It's peaceful and law-abiding because the cops work hard to keep it that way. And I find it somewhat odd that you were home all evening yet claim you never heard a thing. Not even the racket by the back door when she was attacked. There must have been considerable noise. Didn't your dog bark?"

"I don't think so."

"That's strange. He's done nothing but bark the whole time we've been here. Yet you say nobody heard a thing. Too bad. The dead woman might have cried out, but we'll never know."

Annie watched as the attendants loaded the body bag into the coroner's wagon and slammed the door. She decided to take the bull by the horns. "If I didn't know better, detective, I'd almost think you suspected me of killing May."

"It's too early to rule anyone out," he said and strode off through the rows of corn to have a word with the coroner.

She went back to the house feeling frustrated and angry. The only thing she'd learned was that she was a suspect. Great. She picked up the phone and dialed information. After getting the number of Edgar Whittles in Kansas City, she dialed again and after a moment, a receptionist answered. "Whittles' Electric." Annie said she needed to speak to Edgar Whittles about a personal matter.

Unfortunately, he wasn't in his office. "If you'd like to leave your number," the secretary said in nasal tones, "I'll have him return your call."

Annie did so, emphasizing that her business was important and of a personal nature. The secretary didn't seem impressed, replying that he was extremely busy and she wasn't sure when he'd get back to her.

She hung up and stood by the window, watching the police pack up. After they'd left, the yellow plastic tape they'd strung around the edge of the maze flapped in the wind, proof that a crime had occurred. Murder.

Clouds gathered to the west. It began raining, spattering on the window.

Claudius, released from bathroom imprisonment, ran back and forth to the windows, barking at everything he saw. Tiredly, Annie told him to stop it, an order he ignored. Two joggers and a yellow Labrador retriever ran down the road, splashing through puddles, and he raised the decibel level. *Escaped convicts . . . Why didn't she call the cops, was she out of her mind?*

"They're just out for a run . . . for heaven's sake, forget the damn police training!"

He shot her a look of outraged disbelief and dashed off to the kitchen to keep an eye on what was going on outside. Every few minutes he gave an update, whether she wanted it or not.

She gave up and brewed herself a cup of tea and huddled in the wing chair in the library. A small room, which doubled as her office. She had a computer there, and it was cozy, and about as far from his racket as she could get. She lit a fire in the fireplace, tossed on a few logs, and watched the flames. Ordinarily, she would have booted up the computer and gone through the shop inventory, but not now. She didn't have the heart. Besides, customers were as few as hen's teeth; and though she had hopes that business would pick up soon, maybe it wouldn't.

She couldn't think about that now. Not while a murderer was loose.

CHAPTER

4

For Annie, the next few days passed quietly. All seemed normal on the surface, but beneath the layer of ordinary activities ran a river of unease. She stayed away from the maze and tried to avoid the broken rhododendron bushes where May had fallen, but the bushes were just a few feet from the back door.

She couldn't help seeing them every time she let Claudius in and out. He developed an inordinate interest in them, of course, and had to be dragged off to the backyard by force. Whatever happened there had left something he could sense: May's fear when her killer had chased her through the maze, and the terrible moment when he'd taken her life?

Why hadn't she cried out for help? Annie was sure she'd have heard something, and Claudius would have raised the alarm. Maybe it had happened too fast and there'd been no time to scream.

Someone had killed May, maybe the author of the anonymous letter . . .

That detective, Jackson, believed it, and somehow it was beginning to take root in Annie's mind as a certainty. But who would have had a motive to kill her? The very idea seemed ridiculous. Except May was dead, someone had hated her enough to have written that threatening note, and Jackson said she'd been murdered.

The cops took down the yellow tape and went away,

and though a number of cars slowed to a crawl as they drove by, only the local newspaper asked for an interview, which Annie gave with reluctance. It was printed several days later, and she read it hoping the reporter had kept to the facts. There was little sensationalism, if you didn't count the picture of the tavern under one of May, taken ten years earlier—and the implication that violent death was no stranger to the tavern.

By the time she finished the article, Annie was incensed. They'd said she and Kirk had been alone in the house at the time, leaving the reader to put two and two together and get six.

Other than that one reference, the body of the article was confined to the fact that she opened the maze each year for charity, and an accounting of the tavern's colorful history: a garbled mix of fact and fiction: A card game in the cupola in the 1860s, where a man caught cheating had been shot dead. Another man killed in a duel. And the occasion of Abraham Lincoln's overnight stay, when a drunken crowd had milled about in the street. According to eyewitness accounts, they'd complained more about the price of gin than the length of the war or the abolition of slavery.

So much for Thurston Tavern. The last two lines were a rehash of Detective Jackson's vague comment: They were investigating all possibilities and would issue a report in a few days.

But it's an ill wind that blows no good, and there was an initial increase of customers to the antique shop. Most were more interested in gossip than pine tables and bow-backed Windsor chairs, so the sales boomlet fizzled.

Vita Charlemagne called, reminding her of the Bargains in the Belfry meeting at the Unitarian Church. May had usually helped out, Vita said unctuously.

"Really." Annie sighed. She could see it coming, and she didn't have time.

"We're shorthanded." Vita waited, and when Annie

didn't respond, finally said, "The poor need our help. The Good Book says, 'The poor, they will be with ye always.' "

"Something's burning in the oven. I've got to go," Annie said hurriedly and hung up before Vita could bully her into helping out at the church.

A few nosy neighbors dropped by, expressing sudden interest in her welfare and safety—the Billingtons—hulking, bald Harvey, an electronics engineer obsessed with his lawn. And his plump wife, Faith, who taught junior high.

They stood over a bare spot in the lawn near the back door. Harvey glanced around. "Where's that damn dog?"

"In the house," Annie snapped. If Harvey became obnoxious, she had no qualms about retaliating. One crack about Claudius going to the bathroom on his lawn—which he never did because she made sure she walked him across the street—and she'd let him loose. Lee didn't have a leash law, so she was within her rights to let Claudius run anywhere he pleased.

"Good." Harvey scuffed the weed-ridden grass with his shoe. "Needs work. Lime, fertilizer, maybe some organic matter. You ought to reseed the whole lawn—it's infested with moss. Get a time-release weed killer—a spectracide. And a spreader."

"I like it the way it is."

He looked outraged. "You let the damn dog poop all over the place. Kills the grass. Burns it right down to the roots."

"Good, then there's less grass to mow."

"Heavens," Faith said hurriedly, sensing that battle lines had been drawn. "Isn't it dangerous, having that dead tree so close to the house?"

Annie nodded. "Ralph Goddard's taking it down."

Harvey considered that for a second. "Oh, yeah. He cuts the maze down every year. What's he gonna use? A cherry picker?"

"Maybe just a ladder and a saw," Annie said indifferently.

He frowned. "You don't understand what's involved. The tree could fall the wrong way and hit the house. Plus, bring one of those big jobs in here, it'll take months to get the tracks out."

Their voices had risen. Annie bit her tongue and changed her mind about telling him what he could do with his advice. Faith cleared her throat and changed the subject.

Although Annie knew perfectly well that speculation about May's death was rampant all over town, by mutual and silent agreement not a word was spoken about the possibility that she might have been murdered. After a desultory remark or two about heart attacks and deadly diets—Faith was of the school that said the real killer was America's dependence on meat and dairy products—Harvey kicked the grass again and said he thought Annie might have ledge problems, which could get expensive if she wanted the place to look decent.

Annie ignored this, she'd caught a glimpse of Claudius watching the goings on from the living room window. *The Manchester Union Leader* hung in shreds from his jaws. She heaved an angry sigh. She'd deal with him as soon as she got rid of the Billingtons.

Faith said pensively, "I always liked May, and I make it a point never to listen to spiteful gossip."

Spiteful gossip? "I wasn't aware there was any talk about May," said Annie.

Harvey gave Faith a nudge, which she ignored. "Oh, not talk, really. More of a rumor."

"Oh?" Annie still didn't get it.

"Goodness," Faith said, sorry she'd opened her big mouth but it was too late now. "You know how people are. There was a suicide a while back. There was talk that it had something to do with one of her columns. And she had that silly trouble with Wallace Horne a few months before he left for Arizona. Everyone said it was a lovers' quarrel."

"I don't think we should discuss this now," Harvey said

with a quick look at his watch. "I've got some raking to do, honey. Let's go home."

"In a minute. I'm talking about May. She couldn't have done the things they said. None of that was true."

None of what? "What's this all about?" asked Annie.

"Just a vicious rumor," put in Harvey hurriedly, so embarrassed he could hardly look her in the eye. "We wouldn't dream of dignifying it by repeating it." He grabbed his wife's arm and hustled her off to their car.

Two things struck Annie. One was Faith's apparently limitless capacity for denial—why in the world was she still married to that stupid man after all these years. She had to be as crazy as he was.

The second thing was that it was none of Annie's business.

She went back into the house, and approximately a half hour later, Ralph Goddard, whose farmhouse stood a mile or two up Route 155, arrived in his pickup truck. She didn't know him all that well, although he usually planted and harvested the cornfield maze. From time to time some of his sheep got loose and were found wandering in the maze. Annie had had to help round them up and drive them home.

Several large pumpkins and zucchinis were piled in the back of his pickup truck. "Had a bumper crop this fall," he said. "Thought you could use them." She accepted them with thanks. "Terrible thing," he went on, "that poor woman drowning in your brook. You won't open the Halloween maze next year, I suppose."

She shrugged and said she probably would. He looked as if he couldn't believe his ears.

"The maze stays," she said. "The money goes to charity. Actually, I wanted to talk to you about the dead maple by the back door." Kirk Deitrich had flown to New York for a day or two to lecture at CCNY, and she wanted that tree down as soon as possible. With her luck, the next brisk wind would topple it.

Ralph gave it the once over. "Carpenter ants. They eat the insides of these suckers before you know what's hit 'em. It'll cause one heck of a mess when it comes down on your roof."

"How about taking it down?"

"You want the firewood?"

Did he think she was crazy? The going price for a cord of hardwood was one hundred and fifty dollars. "Yes."

He looked disappointed. "I gotta harvest the north field, and there's a coupla other chores. I've gotta harvest your cornfield, too. Makes good winter feed. I dunno, maybe Friday. Fifty bucks, how's that sound?"

"Great."

The faint ring of the telephone came from the kitchen, and Claudius started barking. Annie excused herself and went into the house. After a brief tussle with him over the back door—he wanted out and lost—she picked up the receiver and gasped, "Thurston Tavern."

"Vita Charlemagne."

Annie raised her eyes to heaven. "Yes." God help her.

"I should have mentioned this the other day when I called," Vita said briskly. "May worked for our volunteer agency, Hands and Hearts. Her passing has been quite unfortunate."

"Tragic," Annie said. "A terrible shock."

"Exactly." Vita, organized to the teeth, had a tone of briskness in her voice, as if she was checking her watch and had alloted just so many minutes to this sad task. "It's caused a problem at the agency. May was an indefatigable worker, always willing to step in where needed."

"She loved her job," Annie said. "Staying active kept her young. She walked three miles a day. Frankly, I don't know how she did it all."

"Oh, that's so true! May was a bundle of energy, always on the go. And last week she brought a dog along on her client visits."

God, an apology was called for. Claudius had made a nuisance of himself.

"I'm sorry about that," Annie said hurriedly. "I wish there were something I could do. May seemed to think her clients would enjoy seeing a dog."

"Dear me, yes! He was a huge success! As a matter of fact, that's the reason I called." Vita's voice became extremely cordial. "May's death has caught us shorthanded. In fact, we're in a terrible bind. I was wondering if you'd help out."

"In what way? I'm quite busy with my antique shop."

"May prepared light meals and did a little housework for several clients in town. An afternoon here and there, nothing complicated. She didn't administer medicines. No drugs."

"Oh." Annie thought fast, but couldn't think of an excuse Vita was likely to believe. And the truth was she felt guilty about May's death. If she'd been awake, if she'd heard her, May might still be alive. Volunteering a few hours would help people who needed it, and she could do that for May.

"Your help will be a godsend," Vita said. "A few hours a week. I happen to know your shop is closed Mondays and Wednesdays, so it's perfect."

"We . . . ell—" Annie thought hard.

"It will make all the difference."

"I don't really have time."

"We're all busy, but under the circumstances—the untimely death of a dear friend carries obligations, responsibilities. And as far as the dog goes, we'd be delighted if you bring him along. It means so much to the elderly to interact with an animal. Jacob Gander and his brother, Isaac, both called and mentioned the dog. So did Iris Buchman. Oh, that's another thing. The Gander brothers are in their eighties, but in good health. You won't have to administer enemas or . . . that sort of thing. Jacob uses a cane and Isaac is a bit steadier on his feet. But Iris's husband, Steve . . .

it's so sad. He was fine until a few months ago, then there was a terrible automobile accident. His pickup truck turned over and he suffered a dreadful head injury. He doesn't always make sense and if he gets out, tends to wander. May kept an eye on him for Iris now and then. She likes her bingo nights. You and Iris can work something out, I'm sure."

"I don't know. It seems really—"

"Not to worry." Oozing genial sincerity now. "You'll do just fine, and it's only for a few weeks, until we get someone permanent. I'll drop the names and addresses in your mailbox tomorrow. And thanks again."

The phone went dead.

A few hours here and there, no big deal. Annie heaved a sigh. And she still believed in the tooth fairy. Right.

Vita was as good as her word. Bright and early the next morning, when Annie went out to get the paper, she found a list of names in her mailbox: Iris and Steven Buchman of Ivy Lane and Isaac and Jacob Gander on Main Street. Underneath, Vita had jotted the agency phone number. They were delighted she'd agreed to help out, and she was to call if she had any questions.

What happened to "make a few meals, a little light housework"? Fuming, Annie marched back toward the house. It was her own fault. If only she'd kept her mouth shut when Vita had brought up the subject of Claudius. Unfortunately, what's done was done. The only thing to do was make the best of things. The fact that she had an antique shop to run was, from Vita's point of view, completely irrelevant.

The last time Annie had volunteered for anything, she'd gotten stuck with Claudius, who was by any standard a royal pain. Even now he was barking loudly, announcing to all and sundry that he was furious because she'd gone to the mailbox without him. He glowered from the living room window, and she gave him a jaunty wave to show what a good time she was having outside without him.

Claudius had no sense of humor. Abruptly, he disappeared from the window and she started running.

God, what had she left out in the kitchen—toast, Cheerios, butter. By now she was racing toward the back door. But he got to the table first and was well into revenge. Cheerios all over the floor, and his head stuck in the box. She removed the box, and keeping her voice low—with a big dog lectures delivered in an even tone made more of an impact—said, "Thanks for getting into the cereal." Here her voice rose in spite of efforts to the contrary. *"Why do you do these things?"*

Unperturbed, he sat back and watched her sweep up the mess. As she dumped the last of the Cheerios into the garbage can under the sink, he yawned.

She tossed the pan and broom back into the closet and wondered how in the world to cope. From his point of view the problem was simple. He wasn't her dog, so why should he obey her? Living with her was preferable to the local pound, but just barely.

She mulled over his good points—a short list: single-minded loyalty. He was Lydia's, body and soul, and intended to remain that way.

His bad points were embarrassingly long. Nonstop barking, chewing, rudeness. She felt like tearing her hair out. Why couldn't they get along? Things would be so much better if he met her halfway. After all, he wasn't going to be here forever. Just until Lydia took him back, a few weeks, at worst a month or so. Surely, they could be friends. She sent him a pleading look. He gazed back stonily.

Slamming the broom closet door made her feel better, but failed to impress Claudius, who turned around and padded out of the kitchen.

Fine. From now on he'd get two squares a day and no biscuits, no treats. Either he toed the line, or else. What "or else" was, she had neither the time nor the energy to think about right now. It was almost ten; and she had to call May's clients to let them know she was coming and bringing Claudius.

A cup of tea. She turned the gas on under the kettle and got out a mug. By the time the kettle whistled, she'd calmed down. God knew it wasn't the Buchmans' or the Gander brothers' fault May was dead and they needed help. Life happened, you had to pick up the pieces and go on.

Hot tea and sitting more or less comatose for ten minutes helped. She even had a plan in mind that would facilitate taking care of May's clients: Kirk could keep an eye on the shop when and if he had time and she wasn't on the premises. The shop was closed on Mondays and Wednesdays, anyway. She'd fit the volunteer work around her schedule—it'd just be for a few weeks.

She called the Buchmans' first, and after three rings, a woman answered, "Hello?"

Annie spent the next few minutes explaining who she was and why she'd called.

"I see." There was a small silence. Iris Buchman began to unbend a bit. "Did Vita Charlemagne explain my husband's condition? He isn't safe to leave alone. He had an accident last spring and doesn't know where he is half the time. It's terrible."

Annie could well imagine. It couldn't be easy coping with a husband whose mind was so damaged. She made a sympathetic response, and Iris said, "Damn, he's heading for the door! Steve, no! You don't have to go to work. No!" Bang, down went the phone.

That seemed to be that. Annie dialed the Gander brothers, got no answer, and decided to try them later. She started loading the dishwasher, and at that point, a car came up the driveway. Claudius ran to the back door, barking like mad. She told him to shut up and glanced out the window as her brother, Tom, climbed out of his old red Hyundai. Looking preoccupied, he grabbed his backpack and headed for the house.

She let him in, and he gave her a quick hug. Tom was

dark-haired, about six feet tall, and too handsome for his own good.

A pack of cigarettes was in his shirt pocket. He'd started smoking again. He patted Claudius, who, to her surprise, didn't seem to care one way or another that Tom had arrived.

In fact, Claudius wandered off and flopped down on the rug while Tom observed that Lydia hadn't retrieved her dog yet, but what could you expect, she was a bitch. A muscle in his jaw twitched and he gave Annie a hard look. "Why didn't you call me? Damnit, May drops dead, and I have to read about it in the paper?"

"Sorry, but it's been a nightmare. May didn't exactly just drop dead." She sat him down and gave him a cup of coffee. "The cops think she was murdered in the maze. There are footprints in the field. She ran, trying to get away from whoever killed her."

"God, who'd want to kill May? The paper said her death was being investigated. Nothing about murder. The cops must be trying to flush out the killer."

"Looks like it. So, how are you? Still drinking?"

He shrugged. "May's death means the end of Uncommon Wisdom. I don't feel competent to hand out advice, at least not yet, though I think I could keep the business going if I had half a chance. What are you up to?"

She explained about taking on May's clients for a week or two, then said, "Someone sent her a threatening letter. The cops have it."

He let out a low whistle. "Once they find out who wrote it, they'll have the killer. That'll be a relief." He took out a cigarette and said, "Mind if I smoke?"

"Not if you do it outside."

He grimaced and stuck the cigarette back in the pack. "Don't bite my head off. Say, why don't we take off this afternoon. How about a hike up Mt. Washington?"

"I'm not feeling suicidal."

"You could do with the exercise. Claudius can come, too. The leaves are spectacular."

"It's probably zero up on top. We'll freeze to death."

"I'll call first. We can climb part way. If it gets too cold, we'll turn back. Come on, we'll work out the kinks, clear our heads." He gave her a beguiling smile. She felt herself weakening and knew she could have said no. She could have said she was busy, that taking Claudius anywhere was to be avoided at all cost.

But taking a hike might not be a bad idea—she wanted to talk to Tom. So she threw together a couple of sandwiches, and they took off in the Hyundai.

By the time they got on Route 16, heading north, they were barreling along. He gunned the engine and pulled around a Buick doing thirty-five. The white-haired old woman hunched over the wheel glared at them as they zoomed past.

Annie began to relax. Fresh air and exercise. Not a bad combination in spite of the fact that it was clouding up and looked like rain. They drove by black-shuttered white clapboard houses and fields of rolled hay. Standard New England scenery.

Tom had a laid-back driving style, one hand on the wheel, the other stretched along the back of the seat. Claudius pressed his nose against the side window. Every now and then he poked his head over the backseat, drooled down her neck, and was firmly told no.

"Same old Claudius," Tom said. "I thought you'd have taken him to the pound by now. The big sleep. You're crazy. He must be eating you out of house and home."

"Not yet." The topic of how and when to dispose of Claudius was distinctly irritating. Maybe she was an idiot, but damn it, she was still waiting for Lydia to keep her promise.

"Has he shown you his tricks from his days as Bruno, the prison guard dog?" Tom grinned. "The thing with the hands?"

"No, all he does is go berserk at the sight of joggers."

"Yeah, he thinks they're escaped convicts. But he does something else weird. Once in a while, if someone comes at him with his hands apart, he decides they should be in handcuffs and grabs 'em and takes 'em where he thinks they should go. But walk toward him with your hands together or behind your back, and he thinks you're manacled and leaves you alone."

"So far I've been spared that trick." She glanced at Claudius, who stared back with comprehension clear in his dark eyes. He understood every word.

She looked at Tom. "One thing surprises me."

"What?"

"Claudius didn't exactly give you a big welcome when he saw you. How come?"

"Lydia's the only person he ever cared about. So why do you still have him? Last I heard, she was supposed to pick him up."

"Her landlord won't let her have a dog."

"Maybe, but with Lydia you never know. She lies like a rug." A regretful look settled on his face. "One hell of a lover, though. Best sex I ever had."

"Do we have to talk about her?"

"What else do you want to discuss? The price of a six pack? May's murder?"

"Not funny."

"Sorry." They were at the intersection of Routes 11 and 75. He braked, then swung out into the thin trail of traffic headed north. Annie's side window was open, and a warm breeze whipped her hair. After a moment he went on, "Have you thought about the likely ramifications of May's death?"

"If you mean nobody's going to break down the door to rent a room in the tavern, yeah, that's occurred to me."

"Maybe it won't be that bad. It's not your fault she drowned in the brook in the maze. What I mean is, the cops can't prove anything."

She gave him a horrified glare. "I didn't kill her! For God's sake, she was a friend of mine!"

"Right. You didn't kill her. That's not—and hey, what I think doesn't matter. It's what the cops think that counts. Besides, if you had something against May, if you planned to murder her, you wouldn't do it in your own backyard."

She stared at him, speechless.

"Don't get mad," he said. "I'm only trying to help. Have the cops said anything?"

She swallowed hard. "They're running tests to find out why May died. They think it's suspicious that I was home and didn't hear anything, that Claudius didn't bark. I don't think they believe me. It doesn't matter that I had no motive for wanting her dead. They're capable of making up whatever suits them. If push comes to shove, they'll probably say I wrote the threatening letter."

"Jeez."

That summed up the situation in a word. She looked out the window. The air on her face smelled like rain, and it was getting colder.

"Hey, Annie, I'm sorry I brought it up. The cops won't find anything suspicious. You've got nothing to worry about." He cleared his throat. "The thing is, they asked me a few questions. They were just fishing, a lot of stuff about you. Tried to get me to say you might have had something against May. I told them they were nuts. If they tell you I thought you killed her, don't buy it. It's bull. You're not the type. Plus, you've always been lucky. If you wanted to kill someone, you'd do it right. You wouldn't get caught."

"Thanks for the vote of confidence."

"You're not perfect. You married the wrong guy, but forget Lenny. We all make mistakes; what I mean is, you have a way of doing okay in spite of the odds. Things fall apart, and you still make out okay. That's smart."

Considering his choice of the fair Lydia, Tom had a nerve criticizing her. "I try not to think about Lenny," she said evenly. "I was lucky to get out of the marriage with my back teeth." Lenny had been the human equivalent of fly paper, at least as far as her bank account was concerned. The day she left him—and while she was busy throwing clothes in a bag—he'd raced to the nearest ATM machine and cleaned out the account.

"I've never been lucky," Tom said, concentrating as usual on his own troubles. "May and I just get our business on track, and she ends up dead."

"Sticking your head in a bottle won't solve anything. It won't bring May back."

"Yeah, after last night, I've about decided to lay off the booze."

Her antennae quivered. "Why?"

His megawatt charmer grin was on full blast. "I had a few beers at Slat's. When I got home, the cops pulled in right behind me. They made a big deal out of a couple of drinks. I pointed out the fact that I was standing in my own driveway and not driving under the influence. That's when they said May was dead, that she died Friday night and how maybe you had something to do with it. I said that's ridiculous, you didn't have a violent bone in your body. Then they wanted to know where I was Friday night. Did I have an alibi, which I don't. Can't remember where I was. Must've passed out. I probably went to Slat's after work. I usually do. The only thing I know for sure is I woke up Saturday morning with a head like you wouldn't believe."

"Typical," Annie muttered under her breath. It was too much to hope that he'd laid off the sauce for five minutes.

A surreptitious rustling noise came from the backseat. She turned around to see Claudius chomping on what looked like his rawhide bone. But from the triumphant smirk he sent her way plus the bits of lettuce hanging from his jaws, she realized he was savoring the remains of their lunch.

"Hey!"

"What's wrong?" asked Tom.

"Claudius ate the sandwiches. There's only granola left, and there's not enough to keep a bird alive. I'm getting hungry."

"There's a campground with a general store a few miles up ahead. They probably have subs and sandwiches."

Having devoured everything worth eating, Claudius gave the water bottle a desultory sniff and stretched out in comfort.

A moment later, Tom glanced in the rearview mirror and frowned. "Damn!"

"What?"

"I should have guessed they'd do something like this. The cops are following us. Two cars back. I spotted him a few miles back, but didn't think anything of it. We turned off the highway, and he's still on our tail. The same cop who showed up at my place. A gray Ford Fairlane, it's got cop car written all over it."

"Come on, why would a cop be following us?"

"They practically accused me of killing May!"

"So slow down, see if he passes us," she said.

Tom checked in the mirror again, then took the next turn off toward Wolfeboro. They drove a few miles with the car he was certain was an unmarked cop car—a dark gray Ford Fairlane, staying right on their tail. A few miles more, and the Ford dropped back. They went around a curve, and Annie noticed a state trooper car in front, doing just under the speed limit. It started raining hard, slanting across the road in waves.

Claudius, who'd been snoozing in back as inert as a sack of potatoes, woke up, took one look at the state trooper car, and let out a tentative woof that half-deafened Annie.

"Cut that out!"

The state trooper's brake lights flashed as he came up to a stop sign. Tom had turned to shout at Claudius, who was still barking.

"Tom—stop!" she yelled.

His head whipped around. His eyes widened as he stomped on the brakes hard. Too late.

The Hyundai hit a patch of wet leaves and careened straight ahead. They crashed into the back of the cop car.

"God, just what I needed," Tom groaned.

The trooper got out. He didn't look happy. As he slammed his door, a piece of chrome trim fell off.

Claudius leaned out the window, tail wagging. As the trooper stalked up and glared at them, Claudius licked his hand, which for some reason, failed to improve matters. The trooper stepped back and got out his notebook.

"You folks okay?"

"Yes," Annie said brightly. "Fine."

"Er . . . sorry, officer," Tom said. "I hit some wet leaves."

"Failure to stop in time," said the trooper grimly. He wrote down Tom's plate number. "You got insurance?" Tom nodded. "Okay," the trooper wrote some more, then, "Step out of the car, please."

Traffic straggled past slowly, everyone gawking. A few laughing. Tom got out, and since it seemed like a good time to give Claudius a bathroom break, Annie got out, too, and took him over to the side of the road.

When he was done, she put him back in the Hyundai. By now the trooper had gone back to his car and was typing away on his computer, checking to see if Tom had any outstanding warrants, no doubt.

Just then, the gray Fairlane pulled up, and Detective Jackson got out.

"Well, what have we here?" he wanted to know.

"What does it look like?" she snapped.

"Like my prime suspects had themselves a traffic accident. Whose bright idea was it to run into a cop?"

That didn't deserve an answer. She decided to check under the Hyundai's hood for damage. No steam coming from the radiator, and when she looked underneath, nothing was leaking. But the front of the car was crumpled.

The bumper had buckled. In fact, it was wedged underneath the state trooper's back bumper.

She got in and started her up, but the car wouldn't move.

Jackson leaned in the driver's side window. "Too bad. Looks like front end damage. Need a ride home? The state cop's calling the wrecker. Lucky your brother's got Triple A."

"Are you heading back to Lee?" Annie asked. "You were following us, so this'll make your job that much easier."

He smiled.

"You got a point. Put your stuff in the back of my car."

While she was doing that, he strolled over to have a word with the state trooper. On the way back he eyed the Hyundai's front end, then put his large foot on the bumper and gave the Hyundai's hood a shove backward. The Hyundai popped free. The left headlight fell off with a loud clang.

Annie heaved a sigh. She was wet and cold and tired, and now they were dependent on Detective Jackson for a ride home. Of all the rotten luck.

Minutes later, formalities having been taken care of and the wrecker having arrived—the mechanic was busy cranking the Hyundai up on the flat bed—they were set to go. The rain had slowed to a drizzle, and it was icing up a little. Detective Jackson switched on the windshield defroster.

Tom was in the front passenger seat, Annie and Claudius in back.

Jackson pulled around the wrecker, eased up to the stop sign, and let the engine idle. The state trooper had already left.

"Going hiking in this rain?"

"Yeah," Tom said. "We don't mind getting wet."

Claudius was intently sniffing every inch of the backseat.

"Funny," said Jackson, eyeing Annie in the rear mirror. "I didn't take you for an exercise nut."

"Tom's the nut."

He slanted a look at Tom and aimed the Fairlane back toward Lee. "So it'd be comparatively easy for you to knock a sixty-year-old woman in the head and hold her under until she stopped breathing."

"Piece of cake," Tom said. "Only I didn't do it."

"Still, that insurance money's got to be looking real good right now, what with the accident. And your wife has expensive taste. We checked. Your credit cards are maxed out."

Annie had a sinking feeling. *Insurance*—what was that all about? She opened her mouth and closed it again. Anything she said would only make things worse.

"This isn't a police investigation," Tom snapped. "It's a witch-hunt."

Claudius's tail wagged. He leaned his muzzle on Detective Jackson's right shoulder. This was old home week. A cop car, cop smells. What more could a trained police dog want?

"Get the mutt off," Jackson said sourly.

"He loves you," Annie said.

"Get him off or I'll run you both in for obstructing an officer."

She yanked on the leash and Claudius lay down. But he kept his eyes on the man in the front seat.

CHAPTER
5

When they got to Lee's main drag, Detective Jackson slowed. A Burger King was just ahead on the right. "Hungry?"

"Yeah," Annie said. "Claudius ate our lunch."

They pulled into the drive-through, and Detective Jackson ordered four Whoppers, large fries, and coffee to go. He handed Annie two burgers and fries over the backseat and said, "Want to talk? By the way, the name's Gus."

There was a brief silence as Annie tried to think up something clever to say. He already knew her name. This was a sneaky way to get information. Not that she was surprised. Gus Jackson looked as if sneaky was his middle name.

All she could come up with was, "If you mean May's murder, I didn't do it, and neither did Tom."

"I need proof. Neither of you have a decent alibi."

"That's why you've been following us?"

He smiled. "Yeah."

Claudius gobbled up his Whopper and fries and looked longingly at Annie's. She gave him a handful.

"How about you, Tom," Gus said. "Feel like talking?"

"Nope."

Gus raised an eyebrow. "You're gonna make me do this the hard way?"

"Yeah, we are," Annie said. "Unless you're prepared to arrest us, just drive us home. I've had a bad day. The car wrecked, then standing around in the rain, getting soaked to the skin. Tom and I did our level best to answer your questions truthfully, and what's the thanks we get? You imply we're holding out on you."

Without further comment Gus drank his coffee and finished his Whopper and fries. He crumpled up the paper, stuffed the trash in the bin, and started up the engine. Ten minutes later, he dropped them off in her driveway and drove off with a smile that said they hadn't seen the last of him.

So what. He'd said it himself. He didn't have any real proof. And he wouldn't get any because she hadn't murdered May and neither had Tom.

It wasn't until she'd put Claudius in the backseat of the Volvo and they piled in front that Tom started groping in his jacket pockets. He frowned and dug through his pockets again.

"What's the matter?" she asked.

"Just looking for my lighter, the one Lydia gave me."

Annie remembered something. "What does the lighter look like?" *Please God, not a Zippo with a roadrunner logo. Not the one the police found under the bridge.*

"Silver. A Zippo with a roadrunner on it."

She closed her eyes. *The Coors' empties in the maze.*

He frowned. "What's wrong?"

"You had it the night you blacked out?"

"Yeah, probably. So what."

"The cops have it."

His face went pale. "Oh, no."

"You lost it under the bridge in the maze the night May was murdered."

"That's not funny."

"Do you see me laughing? You want the lighter back, ask Jackson for it."

"God." His face was ashen now.

She couldn't think of anything else to say, so she kept her mouth shut and started the engine.

After five minutes of driving toward Tom's apartment on the other side of town—Pondside Luxury Apartments—located next to a junkyard and overlooking the town swamp, she said, "Okay, you don't want to face it, but if your lighter is the same one the cops found—what do we do then?"

"Nothing. They can have it."

"That won't work. What if it comes out in the paper? Lydia might read about it and go to the police. I wouldn't put it past her, especially if she thinks there's a reward."

"She wouldn't—"

Annie bit her lip to keep from screaming. "Have it your way. Let's say she doesn't call the cops. That doesn't mean one of your bar pals won't read about it and drop a dime. It'd be better if you went to the cops voluntarily. Tell Jackson you lost it a couple of weeks ago and that you had nothing to do with her death."

"Damn," Tom muttered, "I can't remember what happened that night!"

"Look, why would you kill May? It makes no sense. You were in business together, you'd be cutting your own throat. You had every reason in the world to keep May healthy and making money." He didn't look convinced, so she tried another tack. "You're my brother, so Halloween night you decided to drop by and check out the maze. That's reasonable. You helped design and cut it. You walked out to the bridge, downed a few beers—I found the empties, by the way. Then you went home. You didn't do it."

"They won't care. They'll read me my rights and arrest me for murder. Does New Hampshire have the death penalty?"

"This is silly—"

"For God's sake, they'll have no trouble proving I tied one on at Slat's. Before long, they'll find out about the quarrel May and I had. No big deal—but they won't believe me. I put the system together and it crashed. May was sure the software had some damn virus from the Internet. She'd downloaded stuff and right after that it crashed big time. I told May I'd replace the mother board, but that afternoon, she freaked out over the phone. I couldn't make her see sense. Hey, it wasn't as if I didn't have money tied up in the business. We were partners. She needed a computer setup and web site, and I supplied both. If she didn't make out, neither did I. You heard Jackson. All he needs is proof. I had motive and opportunity. The lighter puts me at the scene of the crime."

Not to mention beer cans covered with his prints, she thought morosely. What a mess.

"What if I killed her?" Tom said. "It could have been an accident. I don't know how much I had to drink. If I fell, maybe she tried to help me up and somehow hit her head. But that doesn't explain how she ended up in the brook. *God, why can't I remember?*"

CHAPTER
6

It was nearly dark when they got to Tom's, and so far, they hadn't decided on a course of action. Annie had tried to persuade Tom to go to the police and come clean about the lighter, but he remained adamant that it would amount to cutting his own throat.

"Don't worry. I can handle things," he said.

"That's what I'm afraid of," she said darkly.

"There's just one other thing that might be trouble."

"What?"

He raked a hand through his hair. "Actually, it wasn't my idea. I didn't want to do it."

Annie wanted to grab him and shake him.

He eyed her nervously. "May . . . insisted we take out business insurance. Jackson mentioned it. The usual policy—one dies, the other collects enough to keep the business going."

Her heart sank. "How much?"

"One hundred and fifty thousand. I told her we didn't need it, but she said better safe than sorry. The cops must think this was my motive for killing her."

"Obviously," she said.

"Hey, I can't help that." He raked a hand through his hair. "Just one thing after another. I'll have to get another car if the Hyundai can't be fixed. Which means a car payment. The Hyundai might not look like much, but it's paid for."

Claudius whined uneasily and swung his head from Tom to her and back again. She scratched the dog's ears and managed to keep her voice on an even keel. "It's okay, Claudius. Just a few minutes. We're going home." He gave her a look of irony and shook himself all over as she said to Tom, "What are you going to do?"

"I gotta remember where I went that night. I'll call Mike, the bartender at Slat's, and find out if he knows anything. Christ, I can't believe they found my lighter in the maze. I don't even remember going there." He got out and said he'd be in touch.

She went home and for some reason wasn't the least surprised to see a cat carrier sitting on the back step. This was turning out to be a hell of a day. The carrier was occupied by a bad-tempered tomcat. A piece of paper tied to the handle had Lydia's writing on it: Pumpkin needed a home since that bastard of a landlord wouldn't let her keep him. Just temporary, until she got a decent apartment. Also, if Annie didn't want him to roam, he needed to be fixed, and she wasn't sure if he'd had all his shots. Annie might want to look into that. She—Lydia—used the vet over on Route 125. The part at the bottom where she thanked Annie a million with a little happy face was clearly an afterthought.

The orange cat stared through the bars of the carrier with narrowed eyes. He was emanating a peculiar rumbling noise, which Annie was pretty sure wasn't contentment. Claudius—Mr. Superior since he wasn't in a crate and that stupid cat was—came too close and received a slap on the muzzle for his trouble. "Meeoow!"

He jumped back and sat down, ears pricked, glowering. Annie picked up the carrier and lugged it into the house. Another nonpaying guest.

An old dishpan would do as the cat's litter box. After filling it with sand she kept for ice on the driveway, she plunked it down by the back door. Her mood grew blacker as she brooded about Tom's troubles. Would he have the sense to get a lawyer? And what did Detective Gus Jackson really make of the business insurance? She knew the answer to that one. One hundred fifty thousand tax-free dollars was a perfect motive for murder. Especially since Tom was more or less broke.

Out of the carrier, the cat stared about with narrowed eyes, then sniffed every inch of the kitchen. He walked with the athletic spring of a panther. He looked like the sort of cat mice would run screaming from, and the tip of his long tail twitched as he inspected the premises.

"If you're smart, you'll leave him alone," she told Claudius as she let him into the kitchen. He didn't take his eyes off the cat, now sitting on the counter by the sink. "I'll get cat food tomorrow. In the meantime—" pouring milk in a saucer and setting it on the counter, "Pumpkin can have a drink."

Claudius yawned, then shut his teeth with a horrible click. "Stop that!" In return, he cast her a look of boredom. She gave him a biscuit and said, "Leave the cat alone. There's plenty of food for both of you." In case that's what was bothering him. But she might as well have tried talking to a stone wall. He flopped down on the floor and stared at the cat with unblinking malevolence, all the while chomping his biscuit. Maybe Annie was losing her grip, but he wasn't.

She put the milk back in the refrigerator. "Fine. Learn the hard way. Go near that cat and he'll rearrange your face."

Claudius huffed and grumbled. *Cats were trouble, and this one was as nasty a specimen as he'd ever seen. She was out of her mind to give it house room.*

Annie made dinner, which she ate without tasting a bite. A half hour later, Kirk came in as she was washing the dishes. He looked tired.

"How was your day?" she asked.

"The usual, mind-numbing eight hours with several hundred sex-crazed college kids. My statistics course, and it's as boring as it sounds. No one wants to be there, least of all, me."

"There's chicken salad if you're hungry."

"I ate at the student union. A burned hamburger on a stale bun, but it's better than E-coli." He noticed the cat. "What the hell is that?"

"A loaner from Lydia. His name is Pumpkin."

"He's certainly orange." Kirk gave the cat a tentative pat. "What does Claudius think of him?"

"Not much."

Hearing his name, Claudius, now stretched out on a rag rug near the door where anyone coming or going was bound to trip over him, let out a perfunctory grunt and laid his head on his paws as if he'd spent a hard day guarding the house and needed a bit of well-earned peace and quiet. Presumably this was for Kirk's benefit. It worked, as he was given a biscuit and told what a good dog he was.

Annie said gloomily, "I've had a hell of a day—"

Just then, from the living room, came the sound of breaking glass. A hurricane lamp, one of a nice pair Annie had bought at an auction. The cat sat nearby on the arm of the sofa, watching as she swept up the mess. Claudius, exhibiting minor interest, strolled in and sat in the doorway.

She eyed the space between the sofa arm and the table. "The cat must have caught it with his tail as he jumped up. An accident."

They went back to the kitchen, and Kirk toasted an English muffin while she put the kettle on for hot chocolate. They'd just sat down, when there was a knock at the back door. The gray Fairlane stood in the driveway. Detective Jackson again. Terrific. Wondering what he wanted at this time of night—by now it was after eight o'clock—she let him in.

"Sorry to disturb you," he said. He didn't look sorry. In fact, his attitude appeared to be one of immense satisfaction. He put his hand in his pocket and drew out the Zippo lighter. "I thought you said you didn't know anyone who owned one like this."

"That's right."

Kirk sipped hot chocolate and tried to look invisible.

"Not your everyday lighter," Gus continued. "Someone had it made up special."

"Or ordered it from a Warner Brothers catalog. They sell all sorts of things with that logo."

"Maybe. But I asked around town. Your brother's got one just like it. I stopped at his place and he wasn't home. I thought I might find him here."

"I dropped him off a while ago. I don't know where he went. Without the Hyundai, he doesn't have wheels. He must have called one of his pals to pick him up."

"But he has a lighter like this one?"

She shrugged. "He doesn't smoke around me."

"Did you see your brother the night May Upton died?"

"No."

"So you don't know if he came by."

"I told you, I didn't see him."

"I see." Gus glanced around the kitchen. "Back from your trip?" This was aimed at Kirk, who nodded. "Business?" The detective's voice was casual.

"More or less. Among other things, I write. I flew back from New York and stopped in Boston to see my publisher."

"What kind of stuff do you write? Sexy novels?"

"Nothing so interesting or profitable. Psychology. *Behavioral Attitudes of the Adolescent, Living with Frustration.* That sort of thing."

Another loud crash from the living room. Annie snatched the broom from the closet and marched back down the hallway. The other hurricane lamp. Obviously, it hadn't fallen off the table by itself. She swept it up and dumped it in the trash. Something had to be done about the cat, now calmly washing his face.

She shook her finger under his nose. "Cut it out!" He gazed at her, slit-eyed. "I mean it!" His tail twitched and he stared her down.

Claudius sniffed the floor around the sofa. She had no

trouble reading his expression: This was her own fault. Against his advice, she'd taken in the cat. She deserved whatever happened. In other words, this was her baby and she could damn well rock it. "Easy for you to say," she snapped. "You don't have to clean up the mess."

When she returned to the kitchen, Kirk was holding forth about teaching and psychology. "With a large class, I give the sheep and goat lecture to start off the year. It gets their attention."

Gus raised an eyebrow. "Sheep and goats?"

"It's more of an experiment than a lecture. You've seen flash cards experts use to test psychic ability. Star, cross, square, and so on. I ask the class if they believe in psychic ability. The sheep say yes, the goats, no. Then I run the test, showing the cards. It's been around since the early part of this century. As a rule, psychologists don't believe in psychic phenomena. But whenever the lecture's given, there's a higher percentage of correct guesses for the sheep than there should be. In other words, it looks as if there might be something to psychic phenomena. And that was discovered way before the latest in quark theories."

"Oh," Gus said. "You're one of those psychic nuts?"

"No, I was just explaining the lecture—"

"Sounds like a bunch of bull."

Annie exchanged glances with Kirk.

Gus shot her a cold look. "I said something funny?"

"No." She coughed. "Frog in my throat."

He nodded. "There's a lot of flu around. Drink lots of orange juice." He put a card on the counter. "Here's my number. Give me a call if you hear from your brother. Tell him to drop by the station. We need to clear up the lighter. If he doesn't come by, it won't look good."

Annie showed him out, watching tensely as he backed the Fairlane down the driveway. Kirk said, "Charlie Chan he's not. I hope Tom knows a good lawyer."

Exactly what she was thinking. She dialed his number, barely noticing her own answer machine light blinking. For

twenty dollars it wasn't fancy. It had two volumes: loud
and off, which she'd discovered by mistake. No amenities
like date and time of incoming calls, so she had to remember to check it all the time—someone, despite the tavern's somewhat inconvenient location, might call looking
for a place to stay.

Tom didn't answer, so she hung up. There was nothing
else she could do. Kirk had already gone upstairs, saying
he had papers to correct, then planned to catch a rerun of
Masterpiece Theatre on PBS. Dickens's *Our Mutual Friend*.

She'd read it in school a long time ago. The plot was
hazy in her mind. Something about a corpse, robbers, murder, and money. Not exactly what she was in the mood for,
so she locked up the house and made sure the cat's food
was up high to foil Claudius, who was following her around
with a spurious air of innocence.

She turned off the kitchen light with a nagging feeling
of something left undone, but was so tired and worried that
it took a minute to remember. The answering machine. She
pushed the blinking red button. The tape whirred a few
seconds and beeped, then a man's voice said, "Ms. O'Hara,
it's Edgar Whittles. May's brother. I'll arrive in Boston late
next Friday afternoon, then rent a car and drive up. I plan
to stay at the tavern while I arrange my sister's funeral."

The machine beeped again and switched off. So Edgar
Whittles had found time to deal with his sister's inconvenient death. Who had informed him? The police, obviously.
His arrival meant complications—he'd demand an explanation. Unfortunately, she wasn't a good liar. How to say,
by the way, my brother happens to be the prime suspect
in your sister's murder . . .

Claudius padded by, heading toward the living room on
business of his own. Doubtless a stack of magazines he
hadn't chewed up yet, she thought somewhat distractedly.
What the hell. She went up to bed.

CHAPTER
7

Hearing a plaintive yowl the next morning, Annie ran downstairs, still pulling on her sweater. The cat wanted to go out. A cat door would be a good idea, but he was only temporary. Short term, like Claudius, who as luck would have it, watched in silent accusation as she let the cat out. She was consorting with the enemy. No good would come of this.

"I took you in when you had nowhere to go," she told him, and made a mental note not to go into the living room until she'd had coffee. There was bound to be a large pile of chewed up magazines and God knows what else.

Claudius curled his lip. He was nothing like the cat. They were not to be mentioned in the same breath.

Annie decided not to waste time arguing. It was almost six-thirty. Coffee. She shuffled to the kitchen with the dog at her heels. He stuck his head in the refrigerator while she took milk out. "Pardon me." He backed up six inches, and she shut the refrigerator door. "Thank you."

She made two egg sandwiches and handed him one. He gulped it down, then sauntered over and ate his usual dry dog food. As she chewed, she found herself thinking that this was getting to be a habit. Maybe, when Lydia reclaimed him, she'd get a dog of her own. Friendly, eager to please. A golden retriever or a poodle. They were supposed to be smart. On the other hand, dumb might be better. She'd had enough of smart.

A cold nose nudged her. She handed over the rest of her sandwich. It was Wednesday. By nine, she was supposed to be at the Gander brothers' house on Main Street. Her shop was closed on Wednesday, so the only thing she had to put off was her own housework.

On her way out the door, she noticed Gus Jackson's card on the kitchen counter where he'd left it. Mr. Big Shot Cop. She decided to call her best friend, Cary Goldberg. Cary worked as a dentist's receptionist, but her real talent was gossip. If anything was going on, she knew all about it.

"What's up?" Cary asked.

"You probably heard about May Upton's death—"

"Awful. Dr. Harris did a root canal for her. Who killed her?"

"I don't know, but there's this cop in charge of the investigation, Gus Jackson—"

"Yeah, he's new in town. Supposed to be a Boston homicide detective. Got shot up real bad and decided to move someplace quiet."

Annie cleared her throat. "Married?"

"No. He bought a fixer-upper at the lake. Doing the renovations himself. They say he's an okay guy. What's the matter, is he being a hard ass?"

"No, I just wondered."

"Well, that's all I know. He's only been in town a couple of months. Came in to have his teeth cleaned. He's got nice teeth."

Teeth aside, he was a cop. Which meant he was pushy and arrogant, two things Annie was allergic to in men. Nice teeth, broad shoulders, and lean hips weren't everything. They didn't begin to make up for pushy and arrogant.

Luckily, Annie wasn't interested in him.

After she hung up, she got in the car and drove over to the Gander brothers'. She was thinking. What a come-down, working in a one-horse town like Lee, living in a fixer-upper at the lake—a polite name for a fishing shack. Lee cops didn't make a whole heck of a lot. No wonder he was doing the renovations himself. He was hard-muscled. Hmm, when he wasn't on duty—no, forget it. He was a cop and she was a suspect in a murder investigation. That pretty much defined their relationship. Period.

After another five minutes of driving, she found herself on Main Street. Two blocks down, and there was the Gander brothers' big, white Victorian. She pulled over and parked, took Claudius firmly by the leash, and walked up the front steps. She rang the bell. She'd hardly taken her finger off the button when the door flew open. A tall man with white hair, a moustache, and piercing blue eyes stood there, leaning on a cane. Relief and welcome lit up his face as he gave Claudius a pat. "You're the O'Hara woman from the agency. Come in." He hauled her inside. "You're lettin' out the heat. Know what it costs to heat this place? We could live at the Ritz for what we spend. I suppose you didn't bring a vacuum cleaner." Annie admitted she hadn't. "Naturally," he snapped. "Young folks expect everything on a silver platter. In my day, we gave an honest day's work for an honest dollar. Not like today."

Considering she wasn't being paid, this was a bit hard to swallow. She smiled. "I do my best to oblige."

By now, Claudius was forging down the hall toward the back of the house. He already knew the way. Annie, on the other end of the leash, followed at a gallop with Jacob Gander tottering behind. He shouted, "Isaac is in the kitchen burning lunch."

A black cloud billowed from the oven. A cheese casserole, bubbling like a volcano and blackened at the edges, sat on the middle shelf. Isaac, who looked like Jacob except that he was shorter, fatter, and wore a goatee, flapped wildly with a dish towel.

"Damned stove never worked right. I told you a dozen times to call the repair man. This is all your fault!"

"I'd rather eat cold oatmeal than get cheated again," Jacob snapped. "Last time it was two hundred bucks be-

fore he got out of his truck. If I did everything you suggested, we'd be in the poor house. This is the home help.
Annie O'Hara."

"How do you do," Annie said, taking the dish towel
away from Isaac before it caught on fire. She picked up a
pair of oven mitts. "Let's get the casserole out first." This
she did, then turned off the oven. "Probably just needs a
good cleaning." She took off the oven mitts and turned
around. Two pairs of elderly blue eyes looked at her. The
Gander brothers were hungry. She sighed. "What's in the
refrigerator?"

"Leftover pizza," said Jacob. "Greasy as all get out."

"Chicken soup," said Isaac. "Jacob made it. He puts in
monosodium glutamate. Knows I'm allergic and puts it in
anyway. I could have a heart attack. We'll give the soup
to the dog."

Claudius, drooling at the prospect of free eats, wandered
around, hoping the soup would be good. Annie told him
to lie down, and he parked himself near the table. Since
half a loaf was better than none where getting him to obey
was concerned, she turned her attention to whipping up a
quick and nourishing meal: an omelette. She put a frying
pan on the stove, whipped eggs, added a dollop of cream,
salt, and pepper. Butter sizzled in the pan, then she dumped
in the eggs and added veggies from the refrigerator. In no
time, the brothers were wolfing down a hot lunch and
Claudius was wolfing down the despised, leftover soup.

She sat down. "Tell me what you want done. I might
not get to everything today, but in time we'll have the house
the way you want it."

Jacob nodded, busy eating. Isaac paused, fork in midair.
"May Upton was wonderful. Knew what needed doing without having to be told."

"Well, I'm new at this, so you'll have to be patient."

Isaac said, "I'm allergic to twenty-nine foods, plus I'm
marginally diabetic and become hypoglycemic at the drop
of a hat. My pills are in the cupboard by the telephone."

"He's a hypochondriac," said Jacob. "Calls the doctor five, six times a week. Last week he thought he had a brain tumor. We spent half the night at the emergency room before they sent him home. All he had was a headache. Eyestrain. I told him to wear his glasses, but he's as vain as all get out."

"So? You'd rather I dropped dead?" Isaac glared at his brother, his white hair all but standing on end with outrage.

Annie sighed. "Why don't you both go read the paper or take a nap while I clean up. I'll make banana bread for later." There were three very brown bananas in the refrigerator.

"That would be nice," said Isaac. "Don't use white flour. I'm allergic. We've got brown flour." He indicated the canister marked "flour" on the counter, and she said she thought she could find everything she needed.

The two brothers stumped off to the living room, Isaac complaining that he thought he was coming down with palpitations, and Jacob muttering something about seeing what was going on next door. Annie, busy running a sinkful of hot water and dumping in dirty dishes, paid no attention. They were obviously old hands at bickering.

After the dishes were washed, she cleaned the oven, made banana bread, and washed the floor. Then she went upstairs, made the beds, and cleaned the bathroom.

She was dying for a cup of tea and the floor was dry by now. When the water boiled, she filled the teapot, took the bread out of the oven and put three cups and saucers on a tray.

Isaac's response, when she took the tea tray into the living room, was to ask if she'd put walnuts in the bread. They gave him hives. She assured him she hadn't, and he accepted a piece. He inspected it, smelled it, and at last took a reluctant bite.

"Pretty good. Not as good as they make it in Maine, though. The women in our family all had a flair for cooking. My brother and I are from Maine, originally." He took another bite, then said, "We moved here thirty years ago. I'm not saying we wouldn't do it again. We made out all right, and Lee is a nice enough town, but it's not like home."

Jacob was peering out the window through binoculars. She assumed he was bird watching, but he soon informed her he was not occupied in anything so innocent. No, he was keeping a weather eye on the house next door, which happened to be Horne Antiques.

He gnawed on his moustache a moment, then said, "Funny, May up and died right after she asked me about consulting a lawyer."

"That's right," Isaac said. "She was driving us home from AARP. Said she was worried about something."

Jacob nodded. "It's as plain as the nose on your face. She knew the Woodruffs were crooks and planned to do something about it. We'd been talking to Howard Broughton. He's made big bucks from three car accidents—fifty thousand in three years. Slams the brakes on and gets rear-ended. Says his neck hurts. Whiplash. He got new aluminum siding for his house last year. Plus a new car and money in the bank. Tax free. Can't beat that."

At Annie's look of outrage, he huffed, "It's legal. Besides, how do they expect us to live these days on the pittance we get from Social Security? That's what's criminal! Anyway, Howard got himself a good lawyer. O'Boyle in Portsmouth. I told May to give him a call. Come to think of it, he might have joined some firm in Manchester—moved up to the big time. If he did, then just the partner's left in Portsmouth. Carrigan. Well, he's pretty sharp."

Conversation flagged. Annie poured tea.

"Terrible thing, May's dying in that maze behind your house," Isaac said. "Heart attack. She let things get to her. They don't call stress the silent killer for nothing."

"They're not sure what she died of," Annie said, thinking that under the circumstances, a white lie wouldn't hurt.

Isaac took another piece of bread. "Must have been a shock. Discovering her body like that."

"I don't think I'll ever get over it."

Jacob, who had been surreptitiously feeding Claudius, put down his cup. "Maybe it wasn't a heart attack. Maybe Horne's niece and nephew found out we were on to them and killed her."

"Who, May?" asked Annie, bewildered.

"That's right," Jacob said. "Took you by surprise, I can see that—hearing she was murdered. Maybe we oughta call the cops."

She frowned. "What for?"

"Get 'em to arrest her killers. Put 'em behind bars where they belong!"

"Who?" Her heart sank. Did they mean Tom?

"Wallace Horne's niece, Abigail, and her rat-faced husband." Jacob stumped back to the window. Claudius poked his nose over the windowsill to get a good look, too. Jacob adjusted the focus on the binoculars. "Son of a gun, they're at it again, and in broad daylight!"

Isaac grimaced. "Pay no attention. He spends all his time spying on the neighbors."

"I knew it!" muttered Jacob. "They're diggin' a grave in the backyard. The niece's husband is crazy, a homicidal maniac. Probably killed before. The state emptied the mental hospitals. The streets are full of crackpots."

Annie peered over his shoulder. The yard next door looked innocent enough. A terrace with a fountain. Beyond, lay the lawn, then brick steps winding up the hillside. An archway covered with roses. Several perennial beds. At the end of one stood Abigail Woodruff. She was waving a trowel and talking to a tall, dark-haired man, presumably her husband. He was engaged in back-breaking labor, double-digging the bed. He'd already dug down more than two feet, yet Abigail wasn't satisfied. She gestured with the trowel. It needed to be deeper.

Her husband threw down the shovel in disgust and

stomped off. Abigail held her hand up, shielding her eyes from the sun. She stared at the Gander house. She was frowning.

Claudius stared back at her. He growled.

"Take a good look, you cold-blooded killer!" grunted Jacob. "You won't get away with it, not if I have anything to say about it!"

"Have another cup of tea," Annie said, coaxing him from the window. Reluctantly, he resumed his seat on the couch. Claudius lay down at his feet.

"I'll tell you one thing," Jacob muttered. "I'm prepared. Keep a baseball bat by my bed, and my door's locked from when I retire for the night."

"If we have a fire, you'll burn to a cinder. Then you'll be sorry." Isaac opened a pill box and selected several pills of varying sizes and color. He said, "Forgot my antacid. Not that there was anything wrong with banana bread. But you never know these days, what with the additives and chemicals they put in things. Was it a mix?"

"No." Upon reflection, she decided not to mention that she'd put in more than half a cup of sugar. A little sugar wouldn't hurt Isaac.

Jacob rose and hurried back to the window. "The niece is a damn good-looking woman, I'll say that for her. Probably slept with half the town. Good lookers always sleep around."

"It's a woman's nature, I suppose," Annie said.

"You're darn tootin'."

"My brother wouldn't know a good looker if she kicked him in the arse," said Isaac. "Never had luck with the ladies. Naturally, he's bitter. Now myself, I've had many a fine-looking woman on my arm."

"Ha! Fanny Chadwick was as fat as they come, and that other one you ran around with had a wart on her nose," said Jacob. He leaned closer to the window. "Huh, she's got a bag of bulbs. That's a laugh. Once it's dark, they'll plant their victim. They don't fool me."

"The only thing they're planting are tulips," snorted Isaac.

Annie tried to change the subject, but neither brother would be diverted from their incessant quarreling. She set down her cup and got to her feet. "I've got to go. I'll fix something for dinner that you can warm up in the oven."

Isaac, involved with recounting his pills, muttered, "Eh?"

She went to the kitchen and threw together a chicken pot pie, which she put in the oven. Against her better judgment, and praying they wouldn't burn the house down, she wrote out cooking instructions: fifty to sixty minutes at 350 degrees.

She started a list, staples: milk, eggs, butter. A fire extinguisher topped the list.

When she was done, she clipped on Claudius's leash, told the brothers she'd see them in a couple of days, and that if they had any problems they could reach her at the Thurston Tavern.

They barely acknowledged her departure.

After stopping at the store and arranging to have groceries delivered to the Gander brothers, she drove over to the Buchmans'. Thirty-nine Ivy Lane—a winding road ten minutes from the highway. The houses in this neighborhood were spacious and set back from the road on two and three acre lots.

Thirty-nine was at the end of the road. She parked and took Claudius for a quick walk, looking over the house. It was actually two barns joined together. An herb bed by the side door was bursting with sage, thyme, and marjoram, and a hummingbird feeder hung in front of the kitchen window.

When Iris Buchman opened the door, Annie was gazing at the herb bed. "It's lovely," she said.

Iris was a pretty woman, early forties. Her ash-blonde hair was caught back in a black ribbon. Her skin was smooth and there were only a few laugh lines around her blue eyes.

"Bring your dog in. May did. My husband likes him."

So Annie stepped inside, hoping Claudius would behave.

"You should have seen the place when we first bought it," Iris said. "Snakes in the basement, roof caving in. It was a disaster." She led the way to the kitchen.

Gleaming copper pots—the real thing, antique, very French and very expensive—were hung on a brick wall. A pine farm table as a center island. A brass chandelier hung over the table, and a hooked rug lay on the floor.

"The chandelier came from a New Orleans whorehouse. I wasn't sure it would look okay. Well, I wanted everything to be perfect. Then I realized we had to compromise, or it'd be just a matter of time before Fred and I killed ourselves or went broke, or both. Fred was my first husband. He died last year." She waved a hand at the table. "Sit down. How about a cup of coffee?" She switched on the stove—a Viking—which Annie figured must have set her back eight or ten thousand.

"Coffee's fine," Annie said.

"I was so sorry about May's death. It said in the paper that you found her in the maze in the field behind the tavern."

"Yes, it was awful."

"We're never ready for death. When Fred died, I was devastated. I never expected to fall in love again, but I met Steve. He was a carpenter. He swept me off my feet." Iris poured coffee and said, "Then he slammed his truck into a telephone pole. It left him brain-damaged, which is why I need help." Clearing her throat, she changed the subject. "May told me about your wonderful old tavern. And you have an antique shop?"

"Yes."

"Sounds marvelous."

"I'll never get rich."

"You're off the beaten track. Move closer to Boston or New York, that's where the real money is."

"Maybe you're right."

"Oh, here's Steve," Iris said, turning as faltering footsteps came downstairs.

Tail wagging, Claudius trotted out into the hall. Annie, of two minds whether to grab him, decided to let him go. Seconds later he came back, leading a dazed-looking man dressed in jeans and a sweatshirt. His medium brown hair was tousled. He seemed to be a few years younger than Iris. He was very handsome.

Iris spoke soothingly to her husband. He must be hungry. She'd make him a sandwich. Or would he prefer a bowl of chowder? Steve Buchman sat down at the table as if he wasn't sure where he was, while Iris continued to talk to him as if he understood every word.

Annie suspected he didn't and was glad she'd agreed to help out. She was doing something worthwhile, and it was only for a week or so until Vita found someone permanent.

Iris place the bowl of warm soup before her husband. "Clam chowder, dear. It's good for you."

He gazed at her in a strange, puppylike way. "I . . . didn't get the framing done before it started raining."

"That's all right," she said. "It's not a problem." He lowered his head and began eating, and she turned to Annie. "The main thing is to keep him calm and not let him roam outside. We're on a bad curve. Our dog, Caesar, was hit by a car a month ago. Steve was almost killed. The driver never saw him."

"Oh, no," Annie said, wondering if she was really up to this, but Iris deserved a break.

Steve had spilled soup on his shirt. Iris mopped him up, telling him teasingly what a lot of trouble he was. "How about carrot cake?"

He nodded like a child, grinning as she cut him a piece. He dug in.

Just then the phone rang, and Iris went to answer it. Steve was still eating cake—cramming it into his mouth, and Annie wondered if he had problems with choking.

"Are they here?" he asked suddenly.

"Uh, no, not yet," she said.

His eyes gleamed with sly knowledge. "Is it screwed in nice and tight?"

"Yes." She frowned. Iris said he'd been a carpenter, so it would be normal for him to talk about his work. But that wasn't what his eyes were saying. Damn, he must have injured that part of his brain that controlled the libido.

"That's the way women like it." His voice lowered. "It's how I always do it."

Just what she needed—a horny two-year-old.

Iris came back and gave her a narrow-eyed look. "Getting acquainted?"

"Yes," Annie said with a quick smile. "Maybe you could fill me in on a few more things?"

They went out to the front hall, and Iris folded her arms across her chest. "Having second thoughts?"

"I need to know what to expect."

"He's a child. A very big one."

There was no point in mincing words. "What about sex?"

"That's none of your business."

"It is when your husband makes a pass at me."

"You must have misunderstood. He's not like that."

It was obvious Iris Buchman was in complete denial about her husband's uncontrolled sexual behavior. At least she didn't let him run around loose. Still, Annie decided, looking at Iris's tired face, she needed a break.

"Maybe I was wrong."

"Of course you were." Iris patted her shoulder with a look of relief. "Steve may not be the way he was, but he's always a perfect gentleman." She opened the door and the fading daylight fell on her face, revealing lines of exhaustion and strain. "We were married for such a short time before his accident, barely past our honeymoon. I'd be grateful if you'd give me a few nights a week. Just a few hours. I got addicted to bingo, of all things. Don't laugh. It keeps me out of trouble and makes the time pass more quickly."

Saying she'd be glad to help, Annie left with Claudius and drove home. When she got there, she turned off the engine and stared at the tavern. Comparisons with Iris Buchman's home were inevitable. The Thurston Tavern, with a background of evergreens and scraggly hydrangea bushes, looked a little rundown. Maybe she should move someplace else, closer to Boston. Or New York. Why was she living in a house that was all but falling down around her ears.

She liked it. So it wasn't perfect. She needed a new hot water tank and a new roof. She'd manage somehow.

Even before she got out of the car, Kirk came rushing from the carriage house. He looked worried, and her heart sank. More trouble.

"Thank goodness you're back! I know the shop's usually closed on Wednesdays, but I had a couple of hours free and thought, what the heck. Why not open up for the afternoon? And we had a flood of customers! I sold that pie safe and the blue willow dishes, plus the Federal mirror with the broken pediment. I came down a little in price, not much, ten percent or so. I hope you don't mind."

"I'm ecstatic! We can get a new water heater."

It was hard to think of the local plumber as an historian, but David Kelleher of Kelleher Plumbing and Heating would have put Herodotus to shame. For the two hours it took him to install the water heater on Friday morning, he treated Annie to numerous stories of local characters and legends. "For years, Othello was the only black slave in town—belonged to Ezekial Putnam, rich as Croesus and twice as stingy. The old man bought him in South Carolina. Othello walked behind him holding a parasol. He was eighty-five when he died, and the minister decided to bury him in the graveyard with proper folk. Ezekial Putnam's got the biggest tombstone, the one with the angel. You can't miss it. Othello's got a little bitty stone—like one you'd have for your dog." He tightened the brass fittings one more time. "That oughta do it."

He handed her the bill. "Too bad about May Upton. Drowning's a tough way to go. My uncle drowned one winter. Ice fishing. He'd been drinking, fell in and got trapped under the ice. By the time they found him it was too late. 'Course, right now it's too early for ice to be a problem." He patted Claudius, who was sitting at the foot of the stairs, eyeing the new water heater. "Place as old as this has seen a lot of people die over the years. Still, you don't want a reputation as a house of death. You'd get no paying customers. Er . . . May Upton did drown, didn't she? The paper said she was found in the brook in the Halloween maze."

"They're doing an autopsy," Annie muttered and winced as she read the total at the bottom of the bill.

He packed up his tools. "For a small town, we get more than our share of accidental deaths. Last year Fred Cohen burned to death, camping up north. Careless smoking. Must have fallen asleep. Iris, that's his wife, she didn't have much luck with her second husband. Steve Buchman. He bought a new truck and damn near killed himself. Speeding. Don't think he had more'n a couple of beers, but he ended up brain damaged. Doesn't know where he is half the time."

Only half-listening, Annie wrote a check that amounted to most of the shop's recent profits. As the plumber drove off, she acknowledged with a sigh that she was financially back to square one.

Meanwhile, Pumpkin, adjusting nicely to his new quarters, was busy sharpening his claws on the bannisters as Claudius sniffed the new water heater, decided it was acceptable, and marched back upstairs. Time for a snack.

Fifteen minutes later, both Claudius and the cat had been fed assorted goodies, and Tom arrived. "How's it goin' Annie?"

"Fine. How'd you get here?"

"I borrowed Marty's car." Wonderful, the obliging bartender.

"That detective, Jackson, stopped by the other night. Looking for you. He knows the lighter is yours. He said it'd be better if you went down to the station on your own. Want me to go with you?"

"No, I'll go down this afternoon. Hey, where's Ralph Goddard? He left a message on my answering machine. Said he needed help taking down the dead maple by your back door."

"He's supposed to show up this morning. We can't count on Kirk—he went to the lab." Hardly were the words out of her mouth when Goddard's truck roared up in a cloud of blue exhaust.

"Speak of the devil," Tom said, and they went outside.

"It's a big one," Goddard said, looking up at the towering maple by the back door.

Annie squinted upward. "How long will it take to bring it down?"

"An hour or two." Goddard unloaded a power saw and several coils of rope from the back of his truck. "We'll need three or four lengths of rope."

Tom was told to get the extension ladder from the barn so he could attach one of the ropes to a nearby tree. Annie was sent to the barn for a small wooden ladder. "Tie a second rope to that oak over there," Goddard said. "I'll do the same with one of those trees." He indicated a stand of smaller trees in the front yard. "Once we get the other ends tied to the maple, I'll climb her, make an initial cut, then lop off the top. We'll take it in stages, to control how she falls."

Leaving Goddard to get the saw ready and put on his leather belt with metal climbing clips, Annie hurried off to get the wooden ladder while Tom propped the extension ladder against the oak. It was obvious Goddard knew what he was doing. He'd put business cards advertising brush and tree removal on the bulletin board at the supermarket. He usually had more business than he could handle.

He was very particular about placing the ladders. The aluminum extension had to be a good ten feet higher, so the rope would be tied nearer that crotch, and Annie's wooden ladder was leaning against the wrong tree. They had to rearrange everything three times before he was satisfied.

"Hand me the other end of the ropes when I tell you," he said, hitching his belt higher. The chain saw, filled and ready to go, hung from one of the belt clips. He looked awkward as he climbed, pulling himself upward, the heavy chainsaw swinging at his side. Annie watched with interest. With a hard hat and cleats on his work boots, he looked like a telephone lineman.

About thirty feet up, he stopped and said, "Okay, Tom, toss me the first rope."

Tom heaved up the rope and stood back. "Anything else?"

"Make sure the rope's tight before throwing me the second one. Sometimes they loosen up."

"You got it," Tom yelled and, with Annie trailing after him feeling like a fifth wheel, proceeded to check all three ropes as Tom tossed them up, and Goddard fastened the loose ends to the towering maple. "Okay," Tom shouted. "You're all set."

Just as Goddard swung the chain saw into position and switched it on, Claudius, watching from the living room window, began barking his head off. Tom yelled, "Damn it, that dog's enough to wake the dead. Annie, go shut him up."

She opened the back door. She never saw him—just felt the blow to her knees as he bolted out the door. "Hey! Come back here!"

He did nothing of the sort. He dashed around, sniffing the ladders and getting in the way. Just then Goddard, high in the dead maple, yelled, "Timber!"

Tom made a lunge for Claudius, and missed. "For God's sake, Annie, what'd you let him out for?"

"I didn't—"

Horribly, with one gigantic cracking sound, the top two-thirds of the maple tree fell, crashed into another tree, then hit the lawn with a thunderous roar that shook the earth. Somehow they'd misjudged where it would fall. Annie's heart seemed to stop, and Tom, stared, white-faced. It had taken down the tree where he'd been standing just moments before. "Oh, my God!" she gasped.

Ralph Goddard, still halfway up the dead maple, yelled, "Jeez, you okay? What the hell happened?" Then he clambered down, mumbling curses under his breath. He'd told Tom to get away from that aluminum ladder and stand by the wooden one, but Tom had wandered all over the yard and almost got himself killed. "Goddamn it," Goddard shouted. "This is the last time I'll accept help from idiots!" Red-faced and furious, he ordered them both into the house while he finished the job.

They went.

Claudius, sniffing the fallen maple, lost interest and ambled back to the house. Tom grabbed his collar and hauled him indoors. After which, he glared at Annie, who'd collapsed in a kitchen chair, shaking. "Damn dog!" he shouted. "Look what almost happened! If you'd watched what you were doing when you opened the door, he wouldn't have gotten out."

Her eyes filled with tears. "I'm sorry."

"No harm done, thank God." He stared out the window at the remains of aluminum ladder crushed beneath the fallen maple. Broken branches lay everywhere. Goddard had already taken down the rest of the main trunk and, grim-faced, was cutting it up in ten foot lengths.

Annie got up and joined Tom at the window. "The lawn's wrecked. I'll have to reseed it."

"No thanks to you, I'll be around to see it come up," he retorted, still angry.

She shivered. It had happened so fast—like a bolt of lightning. She was too upset to think straight, and Claudius, taking advantage of this, placed his front paws on the kitchen counter and looked around.

There ought to be something worth eating. Tuna fish in the cat's dish. Ordinarily, he didn't care much for fish, but he decided to make an exception. He gulped it down. Maybe the cat would take the hint and leave.

Annie opened her mouth to yell at him, but Tom grabbed her arm. "Forget the damn dog, I could use a drink—"

"All I've got is coffee." She refused to fuel his alcoholic blackouts.

"Okay, better than nothing. I'll go see if Goddard needs a hand. I can't get into trouble, dragging branches off the lawn."

Annie made coffee and brought it outside, a peace offering, which Ralph Goddard accepted with muttered thanks. He stripped off his work gloves.

"Rest of the job won't take more than an afternoon. Sorry your grass is a mess. I didn't expect it to land where it did. Should have hit the driveway—wouldn't have done any harm there."

Annie gave him a tight smile. There wasn't much else to say other than a miss was as good as a mile, but she didn't think he'd appreciate that.

She spent the next two days in a flurry of activity, organizing her life. She cut expenses to the bone on the theory that if she watched the pennies, the dollars would take care of themselves. She hung out a vacancy sign and advertised in the newspaper. Not that she intended to rent May's old room—the cops would have something to say about that—but there was another bedroom, unfortunately overlooking Claudius's fenced-in area. She wouldn't get what she'd gotten for May's room, which was bigger and located at the front of the house, far from Claudius's incessant barking. But even with fifty less a month, she'd be better off than she was now. She also found time to cut prices in the antique shop and hang out her usual sale sign a month early.

When Gus Jackson called and told her they'd searched May's car, looking for her purse, and that it was missing—along with her key to the tavern—Annie decided to invest in a burglar alarm and new locks on all the doors. By the following Wednesday afternoon, when the locksmith left, she felt as if she was in complete charge of her life again.

She was headed upstairs when the phone rang. It was Tom. "I just got back from the police station. I told Jackson what I knew, which was nothing. I don't think he believes I had a blackout, but it's the truth. I didn't kill May."

"What about the lighter?"

"I told him I must have dropped it in the brook a couple of days before she died. He can't prove I didn't."

"Did you call a lawyer?"

"Yeah, some guy Marty recommended. The line was busy. I'll try him again later. By the way, I told Jackson I'd take a lie detector test any time." He laughed. "They didn't expect that."

Logic said that Gus Jackson was giving Tom just enough rope to hang himself. They probably knew all about his quarrel with May. Her heart sank. Well, they were bound to hear about it anyway. One of Tom's drinking pals would undoubtedly rat on him.

"Well," he said cheerily, "gotta get back to work. Don't worry. I'm off the hook. The cops'll go after the real killer."

She suggested again that he get a good criminal lawyer, not some guy Marty the bartender recommended, but Tom knew best. Finally, having run out of stupid things to say, he hung up and she was free to go upstairs and finish cleaning the bedrooms.

But there was still some unfinished business. The tea chest May had bought from Abigail Woodruff. May had said she planned to consult a lawyer in Portsmouth—in doubtedly where she'd gone the night she died. Annie dug out the lawyer's card and decided to call him.

She dialed and got his receptionist, who said that he'd just come in.

"What can I do for you?" he asked.

"I'd like an appointment. Tonight. It's an emergency."

"Sorry, I'm busy—"

"It's about May Upton." The tone of her voice was hard.

He hesitated a few seconds, probably wondering what new trouble had just reared its ugly head. He knew May was dead. It was all over the news.

"Okay, I can see you for a few minutes. The office is on Front Street. Come after six." He hung up.

She wore her best black suit. It looked as if it had cost a fortune. Half price at Frugal Fannie's. The skirt almost covered her knees—just as well since they were a little knobby. Sheer stockings, black heels, and a white silk blouse. She eyed her reflection and decided she looked pretty good. If Andrew Carrigan was even half a man, it was bound to work to her advantage. If, say, he was reluctant to reveal details of his conversation with May, he'd see that she looked like a successful executive and tell her whatever she wanted to know.

It was well after six when she got to Portsmouth and knocked on his office door. He called out that it was open. "Come in."

She did and closed the door behind her. The outer office was deserted, but she could see that Andrew Carrigan was doing quite well for himself. A sleek wooden desk with the usual computer, phone, rollodex, and jar of hard candy. A grandfather clock ticked in the corner. Off to one side was a conference room: wall-to-wall law books, polished brass, and thick carpeting. The receptionist had already left for the day.

"Be with you in a minute," Carrigan called from the inner office. "I'm on the phone."

She sat down on a black leather fake Eames chair and

waited. And waited. Ten minutes later he came out and said, "I heard about Mrs. Upton's death. I'm sorry. I didn't know her well, although she'd consulted me recently about several matters. She seemed to be a fine person."

"She was," Annie said and followed him through to his office. "I was wondering why she consulted you."

Carrigan sat down behind his desk. She sat in the armchair opposite.

"I don't have to talk to you," he said with his professional lawyer's smile. He was in his thirties, pale-skinned, with fair hair, blue eyes, and a red mouth. He looked like an extra from a Bela Lugosi movie and wouldn't have cared if she'd shown up naked.

Anger, boiling away beneath the surface since May's death, bubbled up and spilled over. This self-satisfied little man had information that might provide the clue to why May had died and who'd killed her.

"I work with the Lee police department," she said. "I can make a call to the attorney general's office. Life will get very difficult."

"What's that supposed to mean?"

"What do you think?"

He narrowed his pale blue eyes. "Sounds like a threat. I don't like threats."

"I don't care what you like."

He leaned back and studied her suit for a second. He made up his mind. "I take it you're handling Mrs. Upton's affairs?"

"In a manner of speaking."

"Well, seeing as she's dead, I suppose it won't matter if I talk to you." He rearranged the pens in the tray on his desk. "Mrs. Upton consulted me about a recent problem. She'd bought an antique, and the seller refused to hand it over."

"Wallace Horne sold her a tea chest before retiring to Arizona. The niece, now in possession of the shop, wouldn't give it to her."

"Exactly. I take it that in general terms you're familiar with her wishes in the matter?"

She nodded. Strictly speaking, of course, this wasn't true, but what Andrew Carrigan didn't know wouldn't hurt him.

"The niece didn't have a legal leg to stand on. It was a straightforward sales agreement, dated six weeks ago, shortly before Wallace Horne moved away."

"Six weeks?"

He pursed his lips. "More or less. That's all we talked about." He paused, then said, "There was something else."

"What was that?"

He smirked. "Sorry, can't oblige. She said she'd call me in a couple of days. As things turned out, she didn't have the time."

Annie nodded thoughtfully. Whatever else May had wanted to talk to him about probably had nothing to do with her death. Or did it?

CHAPTER
8

Annie paid a visit to Horne Antiques the very next morning.

It specialized in early American antique furniture. Everything beautifully maintained. The front hallway was tiled in white and black marble squares. A discreet sign warned that food or drink was not allowed and that there were no rest rooms. A lovely old French Aubusson rug covered the floor in the room to the right, which was filled with expensive, authentic antiques.

There were no other customers, although Annie knew the shop did a roaring business. A woman was sitting at a tea table in the corner. Her ash blond hair was drawn back in a chignon. Her gray dress was silk. She oozed success, money. She looked up from a pad on which she'd been writing. It was Abigail Woodruff.

"Were you looking for something in particular?"

"Just browsing," said Annie. She was wearing her black suit again this morning. The idea being to look as if she could afford to buy something.

"Everything is on sale. Fifteen percent. The shop is closing permanently in a few weeks. Everything has to go."

"That's too bad. For you, I mean. For your customers, though, it's great." Annie gestured at the roomful of expensive furniture. "Bargain prices."

Abigail gave a thin smile. "Not quite. Until recently, the shop was owned by my uncle. When he retired, I took it over. I don't plan to live in Lee. We have a place in the Bahamas."

"How nice. Palm trees, warm ocean breezes, no snow to shovel."

"Exactly." Abigail glanced back at the pad she'd been working on. It looked like a list of figures with lots of 0s. She was adding up their assets.

Annie walked around the room, pretending an interest in a chair or lamp. The white tags all bore prices that were way out of her league. On a tiger maple bureau sat what looked to be May's tea chest. Mahogany, with scrolled teak inlay and a tiny brass lock. It would fetch close to three thousand. The sale tag on it read thirty-five hundred. Abigail was out for all she could get.

Out of the corner of her eye Annie watched the proprietress, who had returned to her figuring.

A cozy chat was in order.

Annie sauntered over in her direction. Sounding a little pushy even to herself, she explained that she lived in town. The shop had such lovely things, and the house was a local landmark. Wonderful architecture and that lovely garden. Wallace Horne's roses had always taken first prize at the flower show in July.

Abigail looked up with a frown. "Oh, yes. My uncle is quite a gardener."

"Such a satisfying hobby," said Annie, babbling. "He always kept busy. I'd drive by and see that open sign on the front door."

Abigail shrugged. "His whole life was the shop. He never went anywhere. Except to auctions."

"If the house is going on the market, I might be interested. I've always been very fond of this place."

"Oh?" She shot Annie a speculative look. "We haven't put it up for sale yet. My husband and I haven't decided on a price. We've had it appraised at a million and a half, but the market for old houses is red hot. We could easily get two million or more."

"I see." Annie tried to look as if this was pocket change.

"Whatever the market will bear," Abigail said with a hint of mockery in her eyes.

The thought of going on with the masquerade made Annie uncomfortable, but it was the only way she could think of to gain access to the house and backyard. Yesterday, Abigail and her husband had been digging away in the flower bed again—supposedly planting bulbs. Jacob said he'd been at it all week. But Annie didn't believe it. They'd been up to something—what, she didn't know yet. But she intended to find out if it killed her.

To prime the pump, she oohed and aahed over a tiny oriental prayer rug, which could be had for two hundred dollars. She promptly wrote out a check on her personal account, which would bounce if she didn't remember to transfer some money from the shop account.

Meanwhile, Abigail got busy rolling the rug up in tissue, tying it with a piece of string. Her manner was now less standoffish, so Annie took a chance and invented a rich background. "My grandmother in Boston died a few years ago and left me the lot. I was surprised because she didn't approve of me. No ambition. I'm the black sheep of the family."

"I know how that feels," Abigail muttered. "My uncle disapproves of my husband. Nathan—he isn't rich enough, didn't come from the right family, didn't go to the best schools. Well, I married him, anyway." She paused, then said, "I never thought I'd take over my uncle's house and shop. It was a real surprise when he asked if I'd be interested."

"Abigail?" A man's voice spoke from the doorway. It was Nathan Woodruff. Seen from a distance, from the second floor window of the Gander brothers' house, he hadn't looked very prepossessing. Tall and dark, with a slim build. But seen closer, Annie noticed a bitter twist to his mouth. His eyes were hard. No doubt about it, he was a calculating son of a bitch. No wonder Wallace Horne hadn't approved.

Abigail made the introductions, and Annie repeated the fiction that she was interested in buying the house. If it wasn't too much trouble, would they mind if she strolled around a bit?

Nathan produced a prospectus of the house and grounds and got down to business. The twenty-three room house on its five acre lot was pictured in living color and appraised at one and a half million. Taxes were ten thousand a year. There were six full bathrooms, eight bedrooms, and assorted other rooms for doing whatever took your fancy.

This was tricky. Annie read it and tried to look interested. "I see it has a new heating system."

"My wife's uncle had it put in before he moved to Arizona." Nathan nodded. "New wiring, all new appliances. The old boy spent more than fifty thousand modernizing it. When it goes on the market, it'll be snapped up in no time."

Annie didn't doubt it for a minute.

Abigail said to her husband, "I have some work to do and need to keep an eye on the shop. Why don't you give Ann a guided tour of the house and grounds?"

So they traipsed upstairs and downstairs, Nathan Woodruff in the lead and Annie trailing a few feet behind. He kept up a stream of patter about the house and its three hundred year history. That it had been a stop on the Underground Railroad and its chimneys still bore the black stripe that was the signal to frightened runaway slaves only added to the hefty price tag.

Annie said it was her understanding that several houses in town had sheltered runaway slaves, Lee having been a hotbed of abolitionists before and during the Civil War.

"Could be," Nathan replied disinterestedly as he pushed open the door to yet another bathroom. By her count, this was number five. Only one more to go.

"My, the tub is lovely. Green."

Nathan looked bored. Perhaps she hadn't sounded enthusiastic enough. She opened the medicine cabinet and tried to look thrilled at the empty glass shelves. "Your wife's uncle did a wonderful job renovating the house."

"Took him more than five years. Five layers of asbestos shingles on the roof. That had to come off. Floors a mess, everything had to be stripped and repainted. Labor alone ran into the thousands." Nathan frowned as if resenting those lost dollars.

"The garden is lovely," Annie enthused. The bathroom window overlooked the rose garden and terrace below.

He checked his watch. "There's just the cellars and the third floor ballroom and a few storage rooms, but we can skip all that. Stairs are murder, anyway. Treads so narrow you almost have to crawl up on your hands and knees. Servants lived up there years ago."

"Well, I'd like to see the grounds. If you're busy, I can walk around by myself."

After a moment's thought, he decided it was safe to leave her to her own devices, and they trooped back downstairs. He showed her out the back door, then pointed up the hill where rows of apple trees indicated a small orchard. "Stick to the paths, you can't get lost. The greenhouse is on the east side of the house. Wallace loved old roses. He had more than fifty varieties. They're not blooming now, but you can see the garden layout."

"I'll be fine," she said. He flashed her an insincere smile —he'd already decided she was just looking—and closed the back door. She was on her own.

From here she had a bird's-eye view of the grounds. Perennial beds, stiff and dead at this time of year, although an occasional flame of red and orange indicated a surviving chrysanthemum. To the north and west lay a fieldstone wall. In the middle the hillside had been terraced and tamed with winding brick and stone paths. On the eastern side of the house, she noticed the greenhouse—a nice old Victorian model in white, like a small wedding cake.

Beyond the lilac hedge loomed the house next door, the Gander brothers'. Light winked from an upstairs window.

Jacob was at it again.

She heard the sound of the window opening and started to walk away up the hill toward the rose beds. Too late, Jacob had recognized her.

"Hey, Annie!"

"Quiet!" She cast a nervous backward look at the Horne mansion. The drapes had been pulled across most of the windows. The house looked unoccupied. Hopefully, Abigail and her husband were hard at it in the front room, counting their chickens. "I'm doing a little snooping."

"Well, get on with it!" ordered Jacob, with an impatient wave in the direction of the bed of newly turned earth. "They buried someone in there or I'm a monkey's uncle."

"I'll go up there right now."

"Okay, I'll leave you to it," he shouted and shut the window with a crash.

She plodded uphill, past flower beds overgrown with weeds. Although fall was well advanced, no one had bothered to mulch the beds or hill up the rose bushes. It was too bad, but if they had a typical New Hampshire winter, most of the plants would die.

Around a bend in the path she came upon the piece de resistance of Wallace Horne's garden: a topiary bed. But unless the Woodruffs found a buyer with deep pockets and an eye for topiary, the mix of fanciful animals was doomed. The largest clipped bush looked like an octopus, while lions and bears stalked about menacingly at the ends of the long bed. Not her thing, but that's what made life interesting.

The bed the Woodruffs had been digging lay near a line of spruce and white pines. It yawned blackly, at least four feet deep—much deeper than recommended for tulips, or anything else Annie could think of. A bag of bulbs had been tossed nearby, half obscured by the lower branches of a large blue spruce. They hadn't bothered with bulb food.

She looked down into the pit, frowning.

Jacob was right about one thing. They'd either been burying something or digging it up. Nathan Woodruff wasn't into manual labor, and Abigail wasn't the type to ruin her manicure for nothing, so whatever they'd been up to, it had been well worth their while.

Wondering what she'd do if she hit something solid, and praying she wouldn't, Annie picked up a stick and jabbed down hard into the damp wormy depths. Suppose there really was a body down there, and they just hadn't had time or energy to fill in the hole. Suppose for their own crazy reasons, Nathan and Abigail Woodruff had killed someone the authorities didn't even know was dead. A macabre thought. She couldn't get it out of her mind. The body rotting, flies buzzing, worms crawling all over it. Maggots. Ugh.

With renewed determination, she poked around some more, but hit only rocks. New Hampshire had very rocky soil.

"Did you drop something down there?" Nathan Woodruff asked suavely, creeping up behind her on cat feet and startling her into almost falling into the pit. "Are you all right? You look pale."

"I'm f . . . fine," she managed. "Just wondered how deep it was."

"More than three feet. Too deep for the tulips, but my wife thinks anything less and we'll have rodent problems. Tulips are her favorite flower." He had a drink in his hand. It looked like scotch, and it smelled like Chivas Regal.

"That's too bad. I like tulips."

"I can take 'em or leave 'em," he said, waving his drink around. "Topiaries are more to my taste. Shall we go back?" Put like that, there wasn't much she could say, and gentleman that he was, he let her proceed him down the hill back to the house. A momentary shaft of light from the upstairs window in the Gander house next door indicated that Jacob was still watching. Doubtless he thought she had things under control and had found out something damning. Which, of course, she hadn't—other than the fact that Abigail had what amounted to a mania for tulips and Nathan had a taste for expensive scotch.

It took a few minutes to extricate herself from the Woodruffs' clutches. Even if Nathan no longer believed her a serious prospect, Abigail did and was determined to wangle a deposit from her. Annie explained that, what with the market being so volatile, she had to move some funds around and would be in touch. She thanked them cheerfully, picked up the prayer rug she'd bought, and left.

When she got into her car, her heart began to slow down to normal. She couldn't wait to get away from that house.

A half hour later, after she'd gone home to change clothes and fetch Claudius—he'd been shut up in the house all day and needed a walk—she drove back to the Gander brothers' and parked discreetly around the corner.

Jacob let her in, patted Claudius, and fumed impatiently while she explained what she'd seen next door. There was a deep pit, but it was empty.

"Empty, my foot! That Woodruff's a slick talker. He made a jackass out of you."

"I don't see you asking him any awkward questions."

He gave her a look that said for two cents he'd be over there like a shot, and Isaac said, "Don't give him ideas. What's for lunch?"

"Beef vegetable soup and a tossed salad," she said. "With bread pudding for dessert."

"I hate bread pudding," snapped Jacob, still annoyed with what he saw as her lack of initiative. She'd blown an opportunity to discover exactly what nefarious business the Woodruffs were up to.

"I'll make brownies."

"No walnuts," Isaac said. "I'm allergic."

Claudius, lounging on the floor behind the sofa, perked up his ears. They were talking about food. That was more like it.

Waving the binoculars at the window, Jacob said, "Maybe that woman's an imposter, and they killed the real Abigail Woodruff. They didn't show up until after Wallace left town. If he left town, which I seriously doubt. I think they killed the old boy."

"Not that again," Isaac snapped.

"What if I'm right?" Jacob said with grim relish. "Wallace had a lot of money. The niece has possession of everything."

Isaac sputtered, "You're nuts." Then again, louder. "Nuts! For the sake of argument, let's say Abigail Woodruff isn't the real niece. Where's her body? According to Annie, the flower bed is empty."

"Hunh," muttered Jacob. "She didn't really dig down very far. They could have buried an elephant and she'd be none the wiser."

"You think you can do better?" Annie demanded.

"Darn tootin'! Not much gets past these old eyes. I should've been a detective. Had the knack, even as a kid. Used to size people up with one look and I was never wrong."

"Funny the way people die," Isaac said thoughtfully. "Family that owned that house before Wallace Horne bought it . . . well, today, experts would call them dysfunctional. They fought like cats and dogs. The father drank. Beat the mother. The older son ran away. Joined the navy. The younger one committed suicide in the garage. Hanged himself. Then the mother just up and died. Leukemia. I always thought it was a broken heart."

Feeling a little sick, Annie went out to the kitchen and started making lunch.

CHAPTER
9

Later that afternoon, Annie dropped Claudius at the groomer's for a bath and nail clip. She told the proprietor, a small woman with firm hands and a piercing gaze, that she might need to muzzle him since he tended to be difficult. At that, Claudius shot Annie a look of disgust and turned his back. The groomer said with a smile that she thought she could handle him, and Annie drove off with a sense of profound relief.

May Upton's appointment with the psychic the day before she died wasn't much of a lead, but the cops were zeroing in on Tom as the likely murderer and other than the threatening letter, which she'd given to Detective Jackson, the diary notation was all Annie had. She'd already checked the phone book. P. Cannell was listed as living on Main Street.

P. Cannell was Prudence Cannell. There was a listing for psychic readings in the yellow pages. The address was a shop on Main Street, Heavenly Illuminations, which turned out to be easy to find, with plenty of parking out back since the lot was all but empty. The shop was located in a block of old houses converted into stores. The building next door was, unfortunately, typical of the seedier end of Lee's commercial district: a CD-comic book establishment replete with deafening music and posters in the front window that hinted darkly of right-wing fanaticism.

Prudence Cannell's house had two wide front windows.

A sign in one urged patrons to strengthen their "Psychic Journey" with positive thinking and "Emollients by Fiona." Beneath this, another sign indicated that pets were welcome as a manifestation of "whole earth energy, harmony, and the magical powers of the animal kingdom."

The bell tinkled as she went inside. A glance around revealed a dozen racks and shelves of New Age ephemera. A faint fragrance of sandalwood hung in the air.

The wispy-looking dark-haired woman behind the cash register was presumably Prudence Cannell. Her photograph was strategically placed nearby—dressed in a Druid cape, expression soulful, the suggestion of heavenly clouds in the background, the psychic on a higher plane of consciousness. A small sign indicated to interested patrons that readings were $50 per hour.

While Annie pretended to examine a crystal that came with an audio cassette and promised to "banish negative thoughts and fears, thereby freeing the mind to its full potential," she mulled over phrases likely to elicit information about May Upton. Just then, a well-dressed, gray-haired matron with a Pekinese on a leash entered and struck up a conversation with Prudence Cannell.

Annie, skulking by a book rack, put the crystal back. She snatched up a pamphlet on scrying for beginners. Every once in a while the psychic sent an intense stare her way. Evidently, shoplifters were something of a problem.

Putting the pamphlet back, she examined a crystal gazing ball, a steal at $79.95. Moments later, she pricked up her ears. After scolding the Pekinese to "be a good boy and stop humping Mummy's foot," the woman said, "I stopped by last week, but you were closed."

"I took a few days off," the psychic said. "I've been very stressed lately."

"Believe me," the woman replied, "I know how it is. And May Upton's dying like that—dreadful. They say she was found in the Halloween maze behind the Thurston Tavern."

"I sensed malevolent influences," Prudence said. "But nothing was clear."

"I heard it was murder," said the woman, lowering her voice.

Prudence sighed and looked at the ceiling. "If I'd used the crystal . . ."

Annie edged closer to the counter and found herself facing rows of unguents touting the efficacies of aromatherapy. For the mere price of $19.95, one could "discover the uniqueness of self, tap the universal healing power, and connect with a spiritual guide waiting to serve you." She was almost tempted.

By now Prudence was admitting that she'd had a similar experience when she'd been unable to warn someone of malevolent forces. "I was tormented by recurring visions of the letter D," she said sadly. "A black Mercedes crashing in a tunnel. A premonition of death. Days later, Princess Diana died. Well, I did what I could. I asked my clients if they knew anyone with a black Mercedes."

"You can't save everyone," the customer murmured sympathetically. "Look at your own brother's suicide. It must have been terrible. My heart went out to you when I read about it in the paper."

The psychic's face closed up. "It was difficult. There were other factors, outside forces I couldn't fight. I tried, but Joe refused help." She paused, sent another sharp-eyed glance at Annie, then added in a low voice, "If I'd tried harder to reach my spiritual guide, Manoush, I might have received a more definite message. I might have stopped him."

"It wouldn't have done any good," the woman said firmly. "Some people just don't listen. Jeanne Dixon told President Kennedy not to go to Dallas, but he went anyway."

At that point, they began chatting about mundane matters, and Annie pretended an interest in a box of unpleasant looking salve until the woman left. Then she introduced herself and asked if she could possibly get a reading without an appointment.

Prudence eyed her up and down. "Well, I am rather busy." Annie put two twenties and a ten on the counter and Prudence said, "On the other hand, I could close the shop for a while. Just let me lock up." It took only seconds to hang a "closed" sign on the door, then she led the way upstairs.

Prudence Cannell's apartment was large and airy and smelled of lavender. The furniture was sleek and minimal, mostly steel and glass. An overstuffed, flowered sofa was the only comfortable piece in the room. Beyond it, a bay window framed by green curtains looked across an alley to the expanse of buildings on the next street.

Along one wall was a hutch with knickknacks and what looked suspiciously like several stuffed cats. A gray tiger-striped, two gray Persians, and a black with yellow eyes. A white Persian, also stuffed, was curled up in a rocking chair. The chair rocked slowly back and forth. Electrified. Prudence Cannell loved cats, dead ones anyway. Annie hadn't seen any trace of live ones.

"Interesting," she said, raising her voice slightly as a loud thumping erupted from the CD establishment next door.

"Have a seat," shouted Prudence. "Would you like a cup of tea?"

"That would be nice."

"Herbal, raspberry, and peach. Or Earl Grey?"

"Earl Grey."

Prudence disappeared down the hall, and in between the bass notes, Annie heard her filling the kettle in the kitchen.

There were no ashtrays in sight and no sign of a man's presence. No large Lazy-Boy chair in front of a wide-screen TV. In fact, no TV. Just the cats and the rocking chair.

Annie took a seat at the table and gave the room another once-over. Two rickety tables at either end of the sofa with several New Age type magazines right at hand. A suitcase stood by the hutch. The whole place reeked of flowery incense.

Prudence returned with a tray of tea things, which she set on the table. She placed an oven timer by her cup and turned it on. "I need something of yours to hold." Her manner was brisk. Small talk wasn't part of the deal.

"Like what?"

"Anything, a book, gloves, your purse."

Annie handed over a pen she'd rescued from Claudius, who'd chewed off the cap.

"Do you want an hour or a half hour reading?"

"Half an hour." Annie doubted she could stand much more of ten or twelve pairs of glass eyes staring at her.

Holding the pen between her hands, Prudence breathed deeply. She closed her eyes. "I seek my spiritual guide, Manoush. My inner voice calls out to him." Silence. She heaved another deep breath and said, "You have stress in your life." This was hardly news. Annie remained silent.

"I see pieces of the past, present, and future."

"Everything?"

She opened her eyes and gazed intently at Annie. They were a bright blue, although somewhat bloodshot, and reminded Annie of Tom's, which was a shame because she immediately wondered if the psychic had a drinking problem.

"Impressions and flashes come to me from beyond. Manoush isn't always direct. Sometimes it's a clear vision, sometimes it's jumbled. I can only tell you what I see."

"Like what?"

"You're intelligent as well as stubborn. That means conflict. Your marriage was a mistake." Bulls-eye. But Prudence could have picked up the fact of her failed marriage from her interview with May. Who knows what they'd talked about before getting down to brass tacks.

"Okay, that's my past. What about the present?"

Prudence got up and pulled the shade down, plunging the room into eerie darkness. The silence was broken only by the creak of the electric rocker in the corner. "Do you want a long or short answer?"

"The short answer."

"Watch your back." She said this in a matter-of-fact voice.

"What's that supposed to mean?"

"It's not clear. I'm getting several impressions. Conflict, a strong will that won't be denied. A tall tree, water . . . darkness, death. There are negative forces. I see shadows. People, two people." The psychic gazed ahead unseeingly, as if her vision was focused on something beyond the room. Annie waited. Several seconds of tense silence, then the psychic said, "You must avoid those with dark auras." And how in God's name was she supposed to do that?

"How do I avoid people with dark auras? I'm not psychic." When Prudence didn't answer, she said, "Okay, forget that. What about my future?"

The psychic continued to stare straight ahead, saying nothing.

"My future?" Annie repeated.

"It's cloudy."

"What's that supposed to mean?"

"Difficult to say." Prudence frowned, as if trying to look into the ether. "I caught a glimpse of a romance, a dark, curly-haired stranger, but it's not clear. I'm sorry, I can only tell you what I see. It's not promising."

Ever the optimist, Annie concentrated on the first part. Romance. A dark, curly-haired stranger. Gus Jackson had dark hair. Hmm. She frowned. "Wait a minute, I thought psychics weren't supposed to tell you anything really bad. Do you mean I have no future? You can't get much worse than that." She plunked another twenty down on the table. "What about May Upton, did you see a future for her the day before she died?"

Prudence raised a disapproving eyebrow. "I don't discuss my clients' private readings."

"May's dead. The police think someone killed her. Did you tell her she had no future?"

Something happened to the psychic's face. She didn't seem as tense as she had been a moment ago. As if she'd been waiting for an accusation, and not hearing it, relaxed.

"You're right. I try not to give anyone bad news. May Upton's aura was pale. It was just a matter of time."

"So, what did you tell her?"

"I told her she should see a doctor. That's the least I could do." She picked up the twenty and stood up. After a second's hesitation, she scribbled a few words on a piece of paper, folded it, and handed it to Annie. "Don't read this now. Read it in seven days. As for May Upton, I didn't tell you the truth. I did see her future. In fact, I had one of the strongest visions I've ever had. I saw her lying in water, drowned. It was quite upsetting." She straightened her shoulders. "The reading is over."

After leaving Heavenly Illuminations, Annie picked up Claudius at the groomer's. He looked uncommonly festive. His black fur shone, and a green bandana with yellow and black turkeys on it had been tied around his neck.

"My, don't we look like the cat's meow," said Annie.

His expression indicated just what she could do with that witticism. He got in the car and pretended to fall asleep in the backseat. Fine, two could play that game.

She drove back downtown listening to NPR on the radio: A woman originally residing in suburbia had chucked it all and moved to the wilds of Vermont to raise sheep. She'd bought an Australian sheepdog, who, as it turned out, was allergic to grass and therefore completely useless.

Claudius jumped in the front seat with every indication of interest. He'd discarded the despised bandana.

She'd planned to go home, but suddenly remembered an account in the local paper of a suicide some months ago. Probably Prudence Cannell's brother, now that she thought about it.

She swung the car around, pulled in, and parked behind Heavenly Illuminations, and, taking Claudius along, reentered the shop, which was again open for business.

"Oh, you're back," Prudence said in surprise, glancing up from a psychic magazine. She'd been making out an order for a nude Tai Chi video.

"My dog needs to discover the uniqueness of his inner self."

Prudence said frostily, "There are dog treats in aisle two that strengthen mental acuity."

Claudius sniffed his way down the aisle, and Annie, after he'd made his choice, took a box of beef-basted yummies promising a pleasant state of awareness, allowing one to experience life without distortion, back to the counter.

"He likes this."

Prudence rang up the sale. "They're quite popular. All natural. The beef are raised on meadow grasses. Ordinarily, the shop is strictly vegetarian, but some pets are carnivorous."

Claudius, bored, wandered around to the back of the counter as Annie got out her wallet. She decided to do a little probing.

"I was sorry to hear about your brother's death."

A nerve twitched in Prudence's cheek. "Joe made his own choices. He suffered from depression. His death was a terrible waste." Her hand shook as she made change. "I don't mean to sound melodramatic. His death was preventable. It's simple. I failed him. I hardly saw him from one month to the next."

"I hope he didn't suffer."

"He locked the garage and turned the car on. Carbon monoxide. They say it's painless."

There was a sudden metallic clatter from behind the far end of the counter. Claudius had knocked over a wastebasket. "I'm so sorry," Annie said, stooping to help pick everything up. Crumpled pieces of paper, filmy packaging, more torn paper with bits of lettering pasted on them. Words, phrases.

Prudence's face was red and blotchy, her eyes cold. She snatched the paper scraps from Annie and stuffed them back in the wastebasket. "Thank you. I'm closing now. You'll have to leave."

CHAPTER
10

Talk about here's your hat, what's your hurry, thought Annie as she got into the Volvo. She stared back at the shop. *Torn up pieces of paper with pasted-on letters. . . . The anonymous letter she'd found in May's room had been composed of letters cut from newspapers and magazines.*

Maybe the psychic had written those threatening letters. Then, when May had been murdered, the necessity for writing them gone, she'd discarded her latest effort.

Or maybe the letters hadn't been just a cruel prank, maybe Prudence Cannell had killed May, then torn up that last letter.

Unfortunately, a motive was required and for the life of her, Annie couldn't think of one off hand. She tried to remember what had been on the letter she'd given to the police. Rambling threats, curses. An expression of a troubled mind.

Those torn-up bits of paper back in the shop—if only Prudence hadn't grabbed them. Let's see . . . *something, something you'd better get it if you know . . . or else . . . you won't . . . around to be sorry.*

That sounded like a threat.

None of it made sense. Why would Prudence Cannell threaten May? Other than that one consultation, they'd hardly known one another. Of course, May's newspaper advice column had been published weekly. The psychic could have been a devoted reader.

Or maybe not.

On the other hand, there were all those cats. Maybe Prudence didn't need a motive to kill someone.

Annie turned toward home feeling she'd missed something important.

She'd hardly driven half a mile when she spotted Lee's resident tramp, Jack Hogan. He camped out in a shelter rigged up at the old mill about a mile down the road from the tavern.

May had insisted he was harmless.

Annie didn't know about that. Sometimes he popped up like a jack-in-the-box, frightening joggers or people out for a walk.

Often he held up signs by the road while trading insults with people coming or going to work. Mostly, the signs dealt with Biblical warnings or ecological concerns. He termed himself a naturalist and was intensely proud of his dropped-out lifestyle.

He hunted small game: squirrels, chipmunks, rabbits. If he'd lived closer to the tavern, Annie might have thought about him more—firing off his rifle at all hours of the day or night at God knows what. He wore a moth-eaten fox hide over his shoulders as he held up his sign.

Most were self-evident: "Drop dead!" "God gave man dominion over animals." Others murkier: "The Wrath of God!" "He Sees All!"

He'd been arrested once, although Annie was vague about the details—something to do with a raccoon. Whatever. For that transgression, he'd spent six months in the house of correction.

This afternoon a cigarette hung from his mouth. He was filthy and unshaven, scratching himself and holding up a sign: "The Angel of Death is Nigh."

He shook his fist as she drove past. Claudius stood up and growled. Then, deciding he wasn't worth bothering about, the dog lay down again.

The Angel of Death is Nigh. Well, he was a little late

with that one if he had May in mind, she thought, glancing in the rearview mirror. Something shiny glinted on his hand.

She looked again. He was walking across the road. Smoking like a chimney, of course. From the little May had said about him, he wasn't picky about his booze. She'd tried to talk him into going to AA. Annie had told her she was nuts. What did she know about him other than the obvious fact that he was a drunk and a sociopath?

He gave her the finger in the mirror and shouted something, probably another obscenity. Annie kept on going.

Past the red brick library, past the sign declaring a town meeting at the school gym, past the green and the old horse trough. As a rule, the garden club kept it filled with seasonal flowers. Just now it contained nothing but dead petunias. There was a silver Mercedes parked in front with the trunk open, and Iris Buchman was taking flats of chrysanthemums from the trunk.

Annie took another look as Jack Hogan approached Iris and said something. Whatever he'd said had an effect as she put the flat down, took her wallet out, and gave him a couple of dollars.

It wasn't until Annie was well up the hill that she realized what she'd seen on his finger: an amethyst ring.

No one in his right mind would give Jack an expensive piece of jewelry. He didn't have a job, no money. He'd probably broken into some house while the owners were off at work.

Annie took a last look in the mirror. Jack Hogan was making for the bench. He was downing a beer. He didn't care who the hell saw him.

She drove home feeling unaccountably annoyed. Claudius didn't help, of course—watching her with that expression on his face that gave nothing away.

If she forgot and gave him a friendly pat, he'd jerk his head away. Who did she think she was, Lydia?

Most dog books said it took an average dog six weeks

or so to become acclimated to a new home. Not that hers was permanent, of course. But still. Through no fault of hers other than a misplaced sense of compassion, it was his home for the time being. A cruel fact of life, perhaps, but there it was. The least he could do was make an effort, for heaven's sake.

He'd made himself at home and knew the routine, the fact that he wasn't supposed to sleep on her bed and did, anyway. Their twice daily walks, the fenced kennel area.

In the midst of all this brooding, Annie forgot about Jack Hogan and the purple ring. It wasn't until she got home and opened the shop and sold the little octagonal-top table to a woman from Massachusetts for $500 that she remembered. And connected it with something else.

May had worn a ring like that, a large amethyst set in a golden rose. It had been her mother's. She never took it off.

But Annie couldn't remember seeing it on May's hand when she pulled her out of the brook. She thought back. Surely she'd have felt it. Those stiff fingers . . . no, there'd been no ring.

If she'd worn it, the police would have it with the rest of her personal effects. Annie decided to call downtown and ask. Presumably, Detective Jackson would be willing to divulge whether or not May had worn an amethyst ring the night she died.

She dialed the police. Not 911, but the number reserved for questions of a nonemergency nature, complaints about noisy neighbors and straying farm animals.

The dispatcher answered. She wasn't very helpful. Sorry, Detective Jackson wasn't in. She'd take the message and have him call her back.

Annie hung up, dissatisfied. She'd been lucky to find a live body at the other end of the line. Lately, what with budget constraints, the town closed the police station by noon and switched calls electronically to the three police cars on patrol.

Claudius nudged her leg, and she gave him a biscuit, which he sniffed with suspicion before deciding it was edible. She put him in the house and went back across the driveway to the shop, where she spent the next few hours taking inventory. By the time she closed at five, several customers had dropped in. It had been a good day. Besides the octagonal-top table, she'd sold some pewter plates she'd picked up last spring at an auction in Maine.

Gus Jackson didn't call.

Later on, when she told Kirk about Jack Hogan and May's ring, he didn't seem to put much stock in her suspicions. He barely listened. He was sharpening a hatchet with a whetstone. Ralph Goddard had left a pile of wood that needed splitting for kindling.

"Well," she demanded, "what do you think I should do?"

"About what?"

"May's ring. I called the police, but Jackson wasn't there. They said he'd call back."

"So wait until he calls." Simple enough, but Annie was impatient. She wanted action and Tom's name cleared. If Jack Hogan had May's ring, maybe he'd killed her.

"Something else," she said, remembering the threatening letter and the torn up paper in the psychic's wastebasket. She told Kirk about her visit, the cats, and Prudence Cannell's nervousness. "Her brother committed suicide a while ago. She's still uptight about it."

"She's probably suffering from a sense of guilt. Families blame themselves for not seeing warning signs in time or not taking them seriously, when the truth is there's probably nothing they could have done."

"That's sad."

"True, but people generally don't kill themselves on a whim. Something causes a breakdown. Loss of a job, stress, illness, mental or physical. They suffer from a sense of hopelessness that makes facing life unthinkable." Satisfied the hatchet was sharp enough, he put it on the kitchen floor.

"In the case of Prudence Cannell's brother, his wife had left him and filed for divorce."

"Really?" It was always a surprise how much Kirk seemed to know about what went on in town. He said it was a simple matter of keeping your mouth shut and your ears open, but she wasn't so sure. He volunteered two nights a week at the Samaritan's hotline.

Maybe Prudence Cannell's brother had called him late one night when the devils were eating at his soul.

"Did he ever call the hotline?"

Kirk shrugged. "I never talked to him, but that doesn't mean he didn't call. He was arrested for spousal abuse. Beat the hell out of his wife. Finally she went to a shelter and filed for divorce. That's when he killed himself."

"I don't get it. If he hated his wife, why commit suicide? It'd make more sense if he'd killed her."

"He might have, but the shelter is in a secret location. He was a classic abuser. People commit suicide because they're angry. They want to make other people suffer. The funny thing is they don't realize they won't be around to enjoy it." He shrugged again. "On the other hand, if his wife hadn't left, he might have killed her and their two kids, as well. There's an article about suicide in the current issue of *Psychology Today* if you're interested."

She grimaced. "No, I don't think so."

"Maybe you should be. You said Prudence Cannell acted nervous when she found out who you were. Why would that bother her?"

"People get jumpy when they—"

"When what?"

"Well, when they get involved with murder. I think she knew why I was really there, and it wasn't to have my fortune told. I asked what she'd told May."

"And?"

"She said May's aura was off. She was afraid May was sick. That's what she said at first, then just before I left she said she saw a vision of May dead in the water. Oddly enough, I believed that part. The rest of what she told me is probably the usual psychic baloney."

"Maybe Prudence Cannell killed May."

"Maybe." Annie eyed him thoughtfully. "What else do you know about the brother?"

"Joe was the younger brother. The older one, Mike, runs an auto body repair shop in town. He has a nasty temper."

"What makes you say that?"

Kirk smiled. "If you used the paper for something other than wrapping breakables in the shop, you'd know as much or more than I do." She grimaced. There was a certain amount of truth to what he said, although to be fair, most mornings, Claudius got to the paper first. When he did, there wasn't much left to read.

Maybe Kirk had a point. Where there was smoke, you generally found fire. She was tempted to go downtown and look through back issues of the paper. There just might be more to this suicide than at first glance.

When Annie walked in the front door of *The Lee Enterprise* early the next morning, she felt almost furtive. It was just after nine and it was raining hard. She took off her raincoat and shook it out, then stopped by the front desk and asked to see back issues of the paper for the past year.

"It's all computerized," said the receptionist, a motherly looking woman. "Back issues are a dollar apiece. Something in particular you're looking for?"

"No," Annie lied. "Just the past year or so." If you told one person in town, pretty soon everyone knew your private affairs.

"Setup's easy. Click back twelve months."

"Thanks." She sat down in front of a nearby computer and went through the menu, clicking on the prompt for the past year. She scrolled through January and February without finding much of interest other than the fact that the police had been called to 54 Butterworth Road more than once. The wife had refused to press charges so there had been little they could do. That went on for a few weeks, then in March, they'd arrested Joseph Cannell. Court proceedings for the next week indicated he'd been arraigned on domestic abuse charges and released on bail.

Probably soaked his sister and brother for the bail money, Annie thought. She scrolled through the rest of March and almost missed it among articles of local news and gardening advice.

There it was, May's column. Well-written, thoughtful, and all about domestic violence. A reader had sent her a disturbing letter. May hadn't reprinted it word for word, but she'd included enough. The woman had two kids. Her husband had been arrested for beating her and was out on bail. Terrified, she'd taken the kids and was staying with a friend. She didn't know what to do. Her husband said it wouldn't happen again; but that's what he always said. Over the years he'd broken her nose, a couple of ribs, and knocked out her teeth. So far, all he'd done to the kids was slap them around a little, but what if it got worse? She was tired of living like this. With no money and few friends, she was helpless.

May had devoted an entire column to answering the letter. Pointing out that not only was the woman's own safety at stake, but also that of her children. Her husband's behavior was not to be tolerated. She was exposing her children to violence on a daily basis, forcing them to endure both her pain and their father's drunken abuse. Children who grew up in these conditions often repeated such behavior as adults. Lack of money and friends was no excuse for staying with him. There were safe houses, shelters. People who could help. May had listed several phone numbers.

Ann made a copy of the column, paid at the desk, and left; but on the way home wondered if she'd wasted her time checking out Prudence Cannell's brother.

Maybe it was a dead end. Maybe she had it backward

and the psychic had received threatening letters like May. It was pretty nebulous, all she had to go on was a few torn pieces of paper, which no doubt no longer existed. The sensible thing to do would be to concentrate on Jack Hogan and that ring.

The more she thought about it, the more she was certain she was right. And there was another thing—Gus Jackson hadn't returned her phone call. Well, he was busy. Doubtless, he thought whatever she wanted to talk about wasn't important. But it made more sense than pinning a murder on Tom just because he'd dropped a lighter in her maze.

She picked up the phone and dialed the police as soon as she got home. "I'd like to speak to Detective Jackson."

"Who's calling?" said the dispatcher. Behind her was the faint crackle of a police radio.

"Ann O'Hara." Then, thinking they wouldn't know who she was, "I live at the old Thurston Tavern."

There was a pregnant pause while she listened to more static, then Gus said, "Annie, what can I do for you?"

"I called the other day about a ring of May Upton's. I didn't see it when I found her body."

"And?"

"You have everything she was wearing. Was there a gold and amethyst ring?"

Another pause, then, "No, she had on a wristwatch and a pearl necklace, that's all." Annie was conscious of a note of boredom in his voice. He was a busy man with better things to do than take calls from meddling idiots. A sense of injustice stiffened her resolve. So what if she was meddling, she'd do anything it took to keep Tom from being framed for murder.

"May always wore that ring. It was her mother's. It meant the world to her."

"Maybe the stone was loose and she took it to the jeweler's."

"Was there a jeweler's receipt in her purse?"

A longer pause. "Actually, we didn't find her purse. It's missing."

Her heart thudded as she remembered. Maybe that meant they thought Tom was in the clear, after all. She swallowed. "Then it could have been a robbery gone bad?"

"The case is still under investigation. Look, Annie, I'm really busy. I don't have time—"

"But I saw someone wearing that ring."

"Christ, will you do something for me? Forget about May Upton's death, okay? Leave the investigating to me. Now, you got that? I've gotta go."

Annie informed him icily that she had, indeed, got that, and banged the phone down. If she hadn't been so mad, she would have told Gus Jackson what an idiot he was. But as things stood, she had a long day ahead of her, what with the shop to open and her two home help appointments. Kirk had promised to keep an eye on the shop after four so she could go over to the Gander brothers' and do some light housekeeping. And it was Iris Buchman's Bingo night, so she'd be stuck there until nine or so.

And there was something else she wanted to do, a visit to Jack Hogan's place at the old mill.

She'd just have to drop by there on her way home. Jack Hogan wouldn't be around. It was town meeting night, and, much to the selectmen's chagrin, he always showed up. They regretted bitterly that he couldn't be kept out, but he knew his rights and stated them loudly and often.

By the time she got to the mill it would be well after dark, but that couldn't be helped. Besides, she had a flashlight in the car.

When Kirk arrived, she loaded Claudius in the car and left for the Gander brothers'. Remembering Isaac's allergies, she stopped at the supermarket and picked up ingredients for a vegetarian quiche and an apple pie. If he complained about that, he could fix himself something else. Jacob was easier to please and as far as she knew, wasn't flirting with vegetarianism, so she threw a small flank steak in the shopping cart.

The meal was a success. Isaac declared the quiche to be passable and the pie okay. Jacob dug into his steak with every evidence of enjoyment, while mumbling how difficult it was, having to live cheek by jowl with Lee's criminal element.

That's when Annie made the mistake of sympathizing with him. What was the world coming to when you didn't feel safe in your own home. Immediately, he wanted to know if she'd reported their suspicions about the Woodruffs to the police.

"Well, no."

"Why not? For some ridiculous reason the police said they needed corroboration. Another witness. As if I'm not credible. It's critical that you file a report!"

She sighed. "It isn't a good time for me to report anything to the cops. May was found in my maze."

"You mean you're a suspect?" Jacob snorted. "Preposterous. I've kept a close eye on what's been going on next door. We need to strike while the iron's hot. What if they skip town?"

"The Woodruffs may not be ideal neighbors," Isaac said drily, "but they have rights."

The brothers were bickering over the last of the pie when she left.

Iris Buchman's house lay at the end of a long, winding driveway. It got dark early now. Just past five, and Iris had turned on the front light for her. A basket of bright yellow chrysanthemums stood by the door. If Annie hadn't been in such a foul mood, she'd have sat and admired it for a moment or two after parking and turning off the engine. As it was, she sat for a moment and brooded about the chances of really finding out who'd killed May.

Gus Jackson had told her to leave the investigation to the professionals. Good advice, except that they seemed to have decided that Tom was the one they were after. Annie had seen enough TV cop shows. They'd turn over every rock in Tom's life until they found enough circumstantial evidence to cobble together a conviction.

Gus Jackson wanted Tom to talk, all right. Talk his way into jail.

She wished she were better at judging character. This investigation business wasn't as easy as it seemed on the surface. Going around, asking questions, putting facts together in some kind of order that made sense, trying to discover motives sufficient to drive people to violence and murder.

Claudius whined from the shadows of the backseat. *Was she going to sit here all night?*

"Wait a minute." She glanced at her watch and saw with surprise that it was almost six. She'd been sitting here for a good twenty minutes. Accomplishing nothing.

Claudius snuffled in her ear. He had to go. *Now.*

She spent a few minutes walking him by the edge of the driveway. Fifty yards of grassy meadow separated the road from thick woods, and she pulled her sweater tighter about her as a cold wind whipped through the trees.

She turned Claudius back toward the house as Iris peered impatiently through the living room window. The front light was on, she'd been expecting her to come in all this time.

"Sorry," Annie apologized as Iris opened the door. "The dog needed a quick walk."

"I'm running a bit late," Iris said. She snatched up her purse. "Steve's gone up to bed. I have my key, just lock the door when I go. That way, if Steve comes downstairs, he can't get out. If he does get up and he's hungry, there's broccoli soup in the fridge." She smiled. "He loves it."

After Iris left, Annie made herself a cup of coffee and settled down with a book she found in the living room. *The White Mountains:* views of rushing streams, stands of birch and pine, wildflower meadows. Photographs interspersed with essays by New England naturalists.

Time passed, and she became engrossed in the book.

Halfway through it, she turned a page and came upon a photograph almost indescribable in horror. The aftermath of a fire. Charred, twisted stumps of trees, rocks blackened and scarred by the heat. A collapsed ruin of a trailside hut, all but unrecognizable.

Terrible. And who knew how many animals had died. According to the article, the fire had been the result of a lightning strike. But others were caused every year by careless disposal of cigarettes and camp fires. The book was riveting. Even after she finished it and looked through the paper, she picked up the book again and browsed through stunning autumn views of the mountains. Later, she checked on Steve, but he was fast asleep, so she went back downstairs and watched TV.

Claudius padded to the back door and barked as headlights swept up the driveway.

"Home at last," Iris said, smiling as she came in. "Didn't win anything, but I had fun. Did Steve get up?"

"He never stirred." Annie pulled on her sweater and tried to snap on Claudius's leash.

"Oh, dear," Iris said, "there's apple crisp in the fridge. I forgot to tell you. Did you find it?"

"No, I made coffee. It was fine." Annie took advantage of Claudius's inattention—at the mention of food, he'd focused completely on Iris—and got the leash on at last.

"I feel terrible. You should have made yourself at home. Had a sandwich or some soup."

"Really, everything was fine. Steve slept like a baby." Which was just as well because if he'd gotten up and started hitting on her, she'd have had to deal with it. Who knows where that would have led? Nowhere, of course. Iris was obviously in terminal denial about what her husband was capable of.

"Good." Iris thanked her for coming and made arrangements for her to come again later in the week. "I'm addicted to bingo. I ought to have my head examined."

"It's nice to get out of the house. It must be difficult for you."

"I'm not the first to be in this position, and I won't be the last. It's not easy. I try and take things one day at a time."

Annie let herself out, reflecting on the ironies of life as she started the car and turned down the driveway. The last sight she'd had of Iris as she glanced back through the front window—the woman had been standing by a table. She'd looked very unhappy.

Annie drew a deep breath and dismissed Iris from her mind. She had other fish to fry, and it was still the shank of the evening. Not yet ten o'clock, plenty of time to take a stroll down by the old mill.

The moon had risen. A hunter's moon.

CHAPTER

11

It was, Annie decided, dangerous to allow herself to think about exactly what she was doing: heading over to the abandoned mill, the pied-à-terre of the town's resident weirdo.

If she had a brain in her head, she'd wait until daylight. But the town meeting would go on for hours, and Jack Hogan would be there with bells on. They were meat and drink to him. He always showed up, holding one of his signs, ranting and raving. He wasn't above a little pan-handling. He liked a captive audience.

The selectmen generally dealt with this distasteful situation by having him stand in the back of the gym, but he had little trouble circumventing this by yelling at the top of his lungs. He fancied himself a budding poet, spouting doggerel along the lines of "June, moon, screw, you."

God, the very thought of him made her tired. Never mind, while he was safely occupied downtown, she'd search the mill. It wouldn't take long, half an hour, tops. She'd just poke her head in, look around for anything to connect him to May's murder, and leave.

What did she have to worry about? She had Claudius along in the car, protection of a sort . . . if he happened to be in the mood. One look at him and even a brute like Jack Hogan would think twice about trying anything.

Her tires crunched over gravel as she lurched through yawning potholes in the mill driveway. When she opened the door, the sound of rushing water was loud in her ears. The river behind the mill was down a foot or two. Recent rain hadn't made up for the dry summer they'd experienced, but the river still rushed on in the autumn night.

The air was cold. She shivered a little and pulled her jacket closer. The mill looked deserted. No sign of life. No glow of a fire or light shining through the broken windows. She listened to the sound of water and the intake of her own breath. Nearby trees stood tall and dark, like silent sentinels, and the moon cast an eerie bluish white glow on the road. Long ago, a back section of the mill roof had collapsed, leaving it a shambles; and she was just wondering if it was really safe to go inside, when she heard something else: a faint sound, like shuffling footsteps. No, more like a tree branch scraping, or the wind.

She took a deep breath. Jack Hogan couldn't be in two places at once. He was down at the high school auditorium, holding up one of his ridiculous signs.

That decided, she let Claudius out with a warning to be quiet, and he shot her a look of disbelief before lifting his leg by the left rear tire. *There was a dummy here, all right, and he knew it wasn't him.*

She told him to heel and slowly walked toward what had once been the front entrance. Her flashlight illuminated the faded sign mounted over the sagging door: Hansen's Feed and Grain. Cash and Carry.

Something cracked behind her, like a twig breaking underfoot.

She turned around and didn't see anything, but that didn't mean someone wasn't there. Even with the flashlight she could hardly see her hand in front of her face. Another visitor to the mill? At this hour?

It couldn't be Jack Hogan. The meeting was just getting under way, and when it was over, hours from now, it'd take him a good half hour to make it back home. And no self-respecting burglar would be caught dead in the vicinity of the mill. There was nothing here worth stealing.

It had to be some small night creature, a field mouse scavenging for food.

Just as her heart rate dropped somewhere near normal, the door to the mill creaked open, banging in the wind. She froze. If it hadn't been the wind, then there was someone inside. While she dithered—should she turn around and run straight back to the car, Claudius growled low in his throat.

"Quiet!" She grabbed his collar and waited. No one came through the doorway, obviously it had been the wind. Nothing to worry about. Nothing at all.

Taking a deep breath, she told herself she wasn't scared—a big fat lie she didn't believe for one minute. There were a hundred good reasons she could think of for not going inside and only one for doing it: Tom was in trouble. If she didn't dig up some other credible suspect in May's murder, he'd probably end up in jail for the next thirty years. A brief image of May, dead in the maze, flashed through her mind, followed by another just as strong, this one of Jack Hogan shouting threats in her rearview mirror. She tried to forget the brutality in his face. He could have had a bad day. Everyone had one of those once in a while, and May had sworn he was gentle at heart. A few months ago, she'd started saving things she thought he could use and had him come by the Unitarian Church on alternate Saturdays, when they held Bargains in the Belfry, handing out secondhand clothing, food, and odds and ends to the needy.

According to May, Jack Hogan had helped himself to a number of things: an overcoat, boots, a lamp, and in magpie fashion, small, shiny objects.

He'd helped himself to the contents of her purse, as well, and when she caught him, he'd flown into a rage. They'd argued, and he said he'd see her dead before admitting he'd stolen anything. In the end, May had retrieved her wallet, but he'd stomped off, muttering threats. May had been sure he'd just been blowing off steam, but it was an odd coincidence that a week later, she'd turned up dead.

All of which didn't make searching the mill any easier, even if Jack Hogan was miles away.

Claudius, of course, was no help. Suddenly he got it into his head that going back to the car was what he wanted to do, and no matter how hard she hauled on the leash, he was going while the getting was good. Frantic commands of "Good boy, heel!" got her nowhere. He was hell-bent on returning to the car. She resorted to threats.

"Obey or else!" He pulled all the harder. Her feet skidded as she dug her heels in the gravel. Her arms were all but yanked from their sockets. *"What's the matter with you?"*

There was a moment of loaded silence while she caught her breath and he eyed her stonily. She decided he was saying that he wasn't crazy, he didn't like dark, spooky places. She gave him the benefit of the doubt. Okay, he wasn't a coward. He was being sensible.

Which left the question of what she was up for grabs, and she was careful not to examine that one. When she opened the car door, he jumped in and lay down in the backseat as if he didn't have a care in the world. He stretched out, yawning widely.

"What if something terrible happens to me and there's no one to drive you home, what are you going to do then?"

He eyed her dispassionately.

"Fine, stay here if you want. I'm going inside."

He yawned again.

Okay, if that's how he wanted it. See how he'd like it if he ever needed help. She was damned if she'd make a move to save his hide. The ingrate. As if this wasn't bad enough, tension made her abdomen cramp painfully. She winced. God, why now of all times did she feel as if she had to go to the bathroom? She waited a few seconds, and luckily, it went away.

Clouds floated across the face of the moon, a couple of bats flitted by, and it grew darker. She aimed the flashlight so the beam streamed across the front door.

It was wide open now.

It hadn't been open that wide a minute ago, had it? A little bit, maybe, a crack. But not like this.

God, wasn't there some hoary tale about the night watchman dying here more than a hundred years ago? Something about his falling down a flight of stairs. Supposedly, he still walked the dark corridors, shining his lantern.

Maybe he opened doors, too.

"Hello?" She stared at the door and nearly passed out with relief when no one answered. Everything was as still as the grave. It had been the wind, that's all.

The rotting front steps creaked under foot as she went inside. A quick look around revealed a deserted interior stretching gloomily down a barren hallway. A delapidated stairway sagged on the left. Cobwebs everywhere. Peeling paint. Whatever else Jack Hogan was, he was no threat to Martha Stewart.

Everywhere the overpowering smell of dust, mold, decay. She tried not to breathe.

The floor was littered with garbage. A metal sign had been rigged across the bottom of the stairs, looped over a broken bannister: "Keep Out" in red, underlined—professional looking. In small letters underneath: "Trespassers will be prosecuted." Hardly Jack Hogan's handiwork, which would have been along the lines of "Get out or die."

Her hand was sweating on the cold barrel of the flashlight. She clutched it harder and peered upward through the dust-laden air. The beam barely penetrated the inky blackness. Okay, she'd search the ground floor, then upstairs. If she got lucky, she'd find something, exactly what she didn't know, before having to climb those rickety stairs, which would doubtless collapse under her weight, leaving her dead in the cellar. Or worse, trapped and alive for Jack Hogan to find when he came home.

She was being silly. Searching the place wouldn't take long. And if by some horrible stroke of fate, Jack Hogan showed up, she'd adopt Plan A and simply tell him she was a neighbor collecting for charity. Cancer or Heart disease. She had pamphlets for both in her pocket.

Naturally, if he went bonkers and decided for his own crazy reasons to attack her, there wasn't much she could do but fall back to Plan B and run.

It wouldn't happen, she thought, trying to look on the bright side. Jack Hogan was down at the school gym, annoying the hell out of everyone.

Her footsteps echoed hollowly on the old floorboards. Heart pounding, she went through the downstairs rooms. Everywhere were piles of old boxes and junk, stacked up bricks and old mill wreckage. The aftermath of years of neglect and disuse. Only the acrid smell of urine indicated recent human habitation.

Upstairs, in one of the back rooms, which once seemed to have served as a store room, she found a tent of blue plastic rigged up as a makeshift shelter with old blankets draped over rope tied to the wall. Jack Hogan's lair.

She moved the flashlight slowly around the room. He had a taste for nubile babes. From somewhere, probably scrounged from the dump, he'd gotten several posters of half-nude women and pinned them on the wall.

He even had a mattress of sorts, covered with layers of filthy blankets. What a way to live. She almost felt sorry for him. Nearby was a small table with a pot containing the remains of his dinner. It looked and smelled like stewed rat. A lantern beside it, when she touched the shade with the back of her hand, was still warm. As if Jack Hogan had left for the gym mere moments ago. Or was still here somewhere.

Watching her.

Suddenly, hanging around seemed to be a really bad idea. She wouldn't stand a chance of getting away, he'd catch her before she made it down the stairs; and the implications of that didn't bear thinking about. Okay, one last look, and she'd go. She took a deep breath, eyes darting around, trying to see in all the corners of the room.

There were more creaking noises, ominously like footsteps out in the hallway. A dark shadow loomed in the doorway: Not the night watchman's ghost, however. Her worst nightmare, Jack Hogan. His large hands hung from his too short jacket. His shoulders were massive, his neck thick as a tree trunk. She swallowed hard.

His hands tightened into hamlike fists

"Hey! What the hell you doin' here?"

She dug in her pocket and took out the cancer brochure.

"Hello, sorry to bother you—" Oh, God, it was no good. She couldn't think of anything vaguely believable. Cancer wouldn't fly—clearly Jack Hogan wouldn't be the least bit interested in the seven warning signs. Or heart disease, for that matter. Her voice trailed off into miserable silence.

A strange, haunted look came into his eye as he stared at her. "Some deny what the devil sees. He knows what darkness hides. Forged in flames, the demon's cries fade to silence night."

She frowned. This was some of his vaunted poetry. His speech was slurred, and he was having trouble standing upright. The moth-eaten fox hide was slung around his neck, its eyes stared glassily at her.

"Well," she said, her heart in her mouth, "you've fixed up the mill. It looks really nice, homey." No one in his right mind would believe a word of this, but Hogan wasn't exactly *compos mentis.*

Eyes glazing, he grinned boozily, losing track of what she'd said or maybe he wasn't interested in home decorating.

"I've come at a bad time," she said, edging toward the door. "There's no point in our having this conversation now."

"She mocked Beelzebub," he intoned suddenly. "The day of atonement cometh. Avenging angels riding on steeds of fire. 'Yield to me,' they cry, demon voices shrieking in the night. Water flows on, deep and dark as the grave."

His poetry was drivel or a bizarre form of chanting. No rhyming. Was he capable of rational thought? Somehow, she didn't think so. She eyed the distance to the door again.

He stared at her, still somewhat vacant-eyed. A vein in his forehead throbbed. He took a wavering step forward and she took a hasty step backward.

"I'm not sure exactly what you mean by 'avenging angels,' " she said. Poets liked talking about their work. Maybe he could be lured into polite chitchat.

"Fools," he said, gesturing wildly. "Like clouds before the wind they fly. Dark and evil thoughts like writhing snakes, a snarling succubus, witches beckoning with bony fingers."

Speaking of which—she stared at his hands. *He was wearing the ring.* Now, how to bring it up as a subject of light conversation? No particular interest, merely a passing comment.

"My, isn't that a pretty ring you're wearing."

He held up one of his signs.

The roughly painted words jumped at Annie: "Seven times seven they tested her will. She wouldn't give nor yield. She suffered not, but lay quite still. Water flowed over her face."

He tossed the sign aside and from his jacket pocket produced a fifth of whiskey, which he opened and swilled down with apparent pleasure. He waved the bottle. "Nobody listens, no one believes."

"I believe you," she said with great cunning. "Was that ring May Upton's? Did she give it to you the night she died?" Even before the words were out of her mouth, she knew she'd made a terrible mistake.

Conversation, such as it was, ground to a halt. With a defiant glare, he collapsed onto the room's only chair. Now the only light in the room came from her flashlight as the moon had slipped behind a cloud. All she could see of Hogan was a hulking black outline.

Discretion was clearly the better part of valor. She inched sideways, closer to the door. "This has been really interesting, but . . . it's getting late. I have to be going."

He sat there in a drunken stupor, seeming to see or hear nothing. Then suddenly, he roused himself. "Lies!" he bellowed, almost giving her a heart attack. "Lies! Think I don' know, but I do. I sit at Beelzebub's right hand. He tells me secrets. I'll live forever."

There wasn't much she could say to that. "No kidding," might be indelicate, and "You're crazy," although true, was potentially dangerous.

While she was mulling over what, if anything, to say, he muttered, "Go 'way, leave me 'lone." His large head nodded, he belched once or twice, then fell silent. His breathing slowed, his head drooped on his chest. Replete with a tasty rat stew washed down with the tipple of his choice, he'd dropped off to sleep.

That, apparently, was that. She'd get no more information from him tonight. Her heart in her mouth in case he woke up, she raced downstairs and outside.

Claudius eyed her dispassionately when she jumped in the car. She started the engine, nearly dying with relief when it started. When she'd jounced the car back onto the road and roared off toward home, he sniffed her arm, then sat down again with a wide yawn of boredom. He didn't fool her one bit. He was dying to know what had gone on in the mill. Too bad. She refused to give him the satisfaction of telling him anything. If he'd cared, he'd have gone with her.

He started snoring as she drove the few miles home. She had plenty to think about. That had been close, she'd escaped by the skin of her teeth. *That ring was May's.* She'd bet her life on it. Which meant either Jack Hogan had been given the ring, or he'd taken it. And what about his strange sign? "Water flowed over her face" sounded like Ophelia . . . *or a description of May's body.*

More to the point: How would he have known so many details? *Unless he'd been there.* In which case, either he'd killed May, himself, or he knew who had.

CHAPTER
12

All Annie had so far was speculation, nothing in the way of real proof. Maybe Gus Jackson was right and she should leave the investigation to professionals. When she really thought about what she'd done tonight, it was frightening. Anything could have happened and almost had. And why? Because Tom was in trouble. Her faithless brother, who, a few days ago, had implied in so many words that he thought *she'd* killed May.

Damnit, he didn't deserve her help, the ingrate.

Headlights flashed by and a horn blared as a car passed going the other way, and she swerved to the right. God, she was all over the road, a sure way to get herself killed.

She was still shaking by the time she got home, and like a tongue probing a sore tooth, her mind had reverted to topic A: Somehow, she had to find out who'd murdered May. Nobody else seemed to care, certainly not Detective Jackson, who doubtless planned to pick up Tom as soon as he could figure out how to make the charges stick.

God, what a mess.

She parked by the barn and took Claudius for a quick walk by the fence, where he chased tree frogs in the grass and she lurched around at the other end of the leash, deep in thought.

If May hadn't rented a room and gone into business with Tom, he might not have turned up drunk the night she was killed. So drunk he didn't have the foggiest notion of where he'd been. He wouldn't have dropped his lighter in the brook to be found by the police. And May, God rest her soul, might not have been murdered by person or persons unknown, or perhaps it might have happened somewhere else. Anywhere else.

Annie noticed Claudius standing in front of her, glowering. He'd been set to go indoors a good five minutes ago.

She took him in the house and while he checked his food dish to see if she'd refilled it yet, Annie, in a feeble attempt to make herself feel better, thought, *Well, things could be worse.* Her mother could have been here on one of those month-long visits when she did nothing but count her daily dose of pills and complain about her aches and pains. That stomach ache must be a hernia. Her cough, the big C. As light entertainment, she was fond of tossing around grim adages as if they were fact: Bad luck came in three's. Or in this case, disaster.

Annie frowned. You couldn't really call getting murdered bad luck. May's murder was a disaster, and it was a definite one. Two had to be Tom's being the prime suspect. And three? Obviously three was right around the corner.

Or maybe three had been tonight's confrontation with Jack Hogan, which had accomplished nothing. That was another thing: She had to convince the police to take a serious look at Hogan. Somehow, she had to prove he'd been at the pond the night May died and that if he hadn't killed her, he knew who the murderer was.

Claudius strolled over to the cat's dish, polished off what was there, and licked his chops, then, hoping she'd relent and take something decent out of the refrigerator, followed her down the hall to the telephone. The red light on the answering machine was blinking insistently: two messages. She pressed the button, and Tom's voice said with a geniality that she immediately found suspect, "Annie. Good news!" She gave an inward groan. He usually gave her bad news in a garrulous, breezy way, as if he, personally, wasn't responsible.

"Guess what?" he went on chattily. "Lydia and I are going to give it another try. Total honesty's the only way, so I told her about the insurance money, and she admitted she loves me! We'll take it slow, work things out. It won't be easy, but we'll make it. She's moving back in with me this weekend."

She grimaced. Lydia and Tom together again? It didn't stand a snowball's chance in hell.

"Did you hear that?" she asked Claudius, who yawned and seemed to take the news in stride. "You might be moving back in with Lydia before long."

His big ears twitched. He eyed her for a moment, then turned around abruptly and headed back to his favorite spot on the hall rug, where he flopped down for a quiet snooze.

She pressed the button again and was rewarded by the nasal tones of May's brother, Edgar Whittles. His flight had landed. He was calling from Logan Airport, in Boston. He'd rent a car and be there in an hour or so.

He'd called about eight-thirty. It was now after ten.

She stared at the answering machine. Maybe her mother was wrong and disaster came in four's. Well, there wasn't much she could do to keep Edgar Whittles from coming. He was already on the way. With a sense of impending doom, she went upstairs to make sure the bathroom next to the back bedroom on the second floor had fresh towels and soap.

When she came downstairs again, Kirk was in the kitchen, making tea. He poured them both a cup. "You look tired, Annie. Anything wrong?"

Wrong? What on earth could be wrong? She gave him the short version. "May's brother is arriving tonight. Edgar Whittles. I'm putting him in the back bedroom."

"Sounds good."

"I'd like your advice on something."

"Okay, shoot."

"Tom called. He and Lydia are getting back together."

"So?"

"It's not going to work out!"

"So?"

Goaded by Kirk's indifference, she started waving her arms. "Tom lost his mind and told Lydia about the insurance check. That's the only reason she wants him back."

"Hmm, maybe this calls for something stronger than tea. How about cooking sherry?" Kirk got the bottle out, poured two glasses, and handed her one. "Much as I like your brother, he's never struck me as having much common sense."

She drained her glass to the dregs and felt herself begin to relax. Maybe things would work out. Maybe Lydia would get hit by a truck. "Tom's lack of common sense is not the point."

"Oh, then what is?"

"Lydia doesn't care about him, she never has. She's a shark." Annie heaved an angry breath and hiccuped. "She's not capable of loving anyone but herself."

"That doesn't matter. Stay out of it."

"Please. Every time he gets into trouble, I get dragged into it."

"It's your own fault. Once he has to live with the consequences of his own stupidity, he'll wise up."

"So I'm supposed to stand by while he makes a complete fool of himself. Again."

"Yes. Unfortunately, your brother happens to be one of those people who has to learn the hard way."

Much as she hated to admit it, Kirk was right. He finished the last of his sherry and put the glass in the sink. "If you feel like talking, I'll be around."

"Thanks," she said morosely.

Through the window, she saw headlights sweep up the driveway.

It had to be Edgar Whittles.

It was.

Any hopes Annie had been harboring that Edgar Whittles would be understanding about May's death and the awkwardness of her position in all this died the moment he walked through the front door. He made no effort to hide his arrogance. He was fair-haired, balding, and sixtyish with a paunch his three-thousand-dollar suit failed to conceal. What hair he had left on the top of his head was swept into a ridiculous pompadour—evidently, he was sensitive about his lack of inches. He was about five foot eight.

Kirk came back downstairs at that point and she performed introductions, and tried to convey to Edgar how sorry she was about May's death. Whereupon, he dumped his suitcase on the floor, raised his voice over the considerable racket coming from the bathroom down the hall, and dismissed her fumbling expressions of sympathy.

"What *is* that?" he demanded with alarm.

"My dog."

Claudius broke into an ear-splitting howl.

"My God," Edgar muttered, blanching. "Is he part wolf?"

The howl intensified. Exasperated, she said, "Actually, I don't know his exact breeding heritage. If you're not comfortable here, there's a Holiday Inn downtown or the Marriot out near the highway."

"I already tried both places. They're full up." Edgar's lip curled with distaste as he glanced around. "Unfortunately."

She'd taken an instant dislike to him from the moment he'd walked through the door. He was a boor and an ignoramus, but he was also May's brother. At the very least, she owed him courtesy. She kept her voice even.

"There are other motels in the area."

"I tried them all. Not a room to be had in the whole damn state. I left Missouri at eight this morning. It's been a long day. I'd like to go to my room, such as it is. My God, I can't stand that noise one minute longer. Make that animal shut up!"

She'd shut Claudius in the downstairs bathroom before letting Edgar in. After an initial spate of barking, he'd fallen silent, which Annie had hoped indicated that he'd fallen asleep or lost his voice. However, it seemed he'd merely caught his second wind and now demanded to know what was going on. She yelled at him to be quiet. One good thing, she'd had the forethought to put the toilet paper in the cupboard beneath the sink. There'd be no mess to clean up.

"We'll try to make your stay as comfortable as possible, under the circumstances," she said.

Kirk picked up Edgar's suitcase. It looked heavy, as if Edgar planned to stay more than a few days.

Great.

"Hmmph," said Edgar, looking around and finding little to his liking. "Let me be brutally frank. I run a thirty-million-dollar company. If I had a choice in the matter I wouldn't set foot in a place like this."

Annie cleared her throat. "Well, we're . . . in the middle of renovations. I wasn't really expecting anyone."

"Nonsense, there's a vacancy sign out front." He smiled nastily. "As a matter of fact, May sent me one of your brochures. It says you provide for your guests' every possible need, including late-night suppers."

"Uh, well, yes, we do. You know, May was such a lovely person. The police are working day and night to find out who did this terrible thing."

"They'd better. Or I'll know the reason why." He turned to Kirk. "There's another bag in the car."

Kirk nodded and went out to get it.

"I'm hungry," said Edgar. His voice held a taunting note. "What they serve on planes wouldn't keep a mouse alive." Obviously, he expected her to whip up a three-course meal.

She had plenty of eggs and the soup de jour was bean and vegetable—left over from yesterday, but what Edgar didn't know wouldn't hurt him. "How about a Spanish omelette and soup?"

He made a face. "I suppose that will have to do."

While Kirk lugged both suitcases up to the back bedroom, Edgar brought up the rear, making loud, pointed remarks about the deplorable lack of accommodations. His nasal voice faded. A few seconds later the bedroom door slammed shut.

Annoyed, she banged pots and pans around and heated the soup. She was just sliding the omelette onto a heated plate when Kirk came back downstairs and informed her that Edgar preferred to eat in his room.

"Thank God. He's about as unpleasant as they come."

"He tipped me a quarter."

"Lucky you."

It was hard to think fondly of a dog who barked his head off and reduced toilet paper to confetti—somehow he'd managed to get into the cupboard under the sink—but later on as she was washing the dishes, Annie found herself contemplating Claudius with affection. At the moment, he was the only bright spot in her life—an indication of just how dreadful things were.

He'd made it perfectly clear, when released from imprisonment, that Edgar Whittles was a suspicious character. She'd narrowly averted disaster by grabbing him when he lunged for the stairs—Edgar had appeared on the landing long enough to announce that in the morning he wished to be awakened at seven sharp. He expected *The Wall Street Journal* with breakfast, and in the meantime did not wish to be disturbed.

However, worries over Dow Jones were forgotten the instant Claudius made his intentions clear. Edgar shrieked, and Annie shouted—over frenzied barking—that the dog was really quite gentle—once he got to know you. This fabrication did not deceive Edgar, who, when she tried to tell him about keeping his hands together when approaching the dog so as to make it appear as if he were manacled, dashed back to his room and slammed the door.

In the morning, Edgar came downstairs, sneezed, looked around with trepidation, and glared at Annie, who'd just let the dog out. He sneezed again and pointed at the cat, busily sharpening his claws on the scatter rug.

"What's that cat doing here?" he demanded.

"He lives here, temporarily."

"I'm allergic to dog and cat hair."

"Oh, dear, then you have a problem."

"No, *you* have a problem. I am paying through the nose for the privilege of sleeping in what amounts to a closet."

"Why that room has quite a history. In fact, Madame Blavatsky slept there." Unfortunately, this cut no ice with Edgar.

"If you happen to be from Cambodia, you might think that room acceptable. If you're from the civilized world, absolutely not. Get that animal out of here!"

Annie did as he requested, but Pumpkin, the cat, did not take kindly to being removed from the scatter rug. Ignoring his self-righteous yowling, she put him outdoors in the herb garden. There was a patch of what she suspected was catnip, since neighborhood cats had been known to chew the leaves and stagger into the nearby raspberry bushes to sleep it off.

As for the rest of the morning, Annie was thankful for small mercies. After informing her of his destination, which happened to be the police station, and she could make what she wanted of that, Edgar made himself scarce.

She washed the breakfast dishes in a state of near panic. You didn't need to be a psychic like Prudence Cannell to figure out what would happen at the police station. Once the formalities were dispensed with, the question of the prime suspect was bound to come up, and if Detective Jackson named names, it would be Tom's. At which point all hell would break loose and Edgar Whittles would storm back to the tavern demanding blood.

Suddenly, staying inside doing nothing was more than she could stand. Somehow, she had to keep herself occupied with something useful.

May's journal. Maybe there was something there she'd missed.

Quickly, she ran upstairs and got it from the desk. Flip-

ping through the pages, she came upon an interesting entry.
Every other week, May went over to the Unitarian Church
to sort donations for the Bargains in the Belfry. Well, Vita
had said as much when she'd called and tried to bully her
into volunteering.

Now that she thought about it, she remembered that it
was one of Jack Hogan's haunts. May had said he came
around, looking for free stuff—anything he could use or
hock.

Today was the day Bargains in the Belfry was open.

He was bound to show up. She could talk to him again
and find out for sure where he'd gotten May's ring. The
more she thought about it, the better the idea seemed. She'd
have no trouble weaseling her way in—the Bargains in the
Belfry committee was always looking for recruits. Vita had
made that point abundantly clear. More importantly, there
was safety in numbers. The rest of the committee would
be there. This would not be a repeat of last night's scary
scene at the mill.

You had to hand it to Vita, Annie thought an hour or so
later. She was a pain in the backside but she got things
done. Fifteen minutes after her arrival at the church, Vita,
as chairperson, had organized everyone into a team. Annie,
since she wasn't a regular and therefore presumed to be
ignorant if not downright incompetent, was designated to
open up boxes left over from last month's clothing drive
while the rest of the committee went through the piles of
new stuff.

"One thing more, Annie," Vita said with a kindly smile.
"We appreciate your stepping in like this and helping us
out. You're a great help." She waved a hand at the mess
of cartons and bags dumped in the back corner. "That's already been looked over, but I'm sure there are still some
useful things. We can't let anything go to waste."

"Of course," Annie said, opening up the first carton at

hand, which seemed to be full of stuff left over from a garage sale.

"Good." Vita inspected a wrinkled old barn jacket. "We can't put this out. It's missing a button."

Vita delighted in fussing over details no one in his right mind would care about. They weren't selling the clothes, although monetary donations were always welcome. If the clientele of Bargains in the Belfry couldn't be bothered to wield a needle and thread on their own behalf, then too bad.

"The question is," Faith Billington said, "whether we put the shoes and boots in the box up front for them to paw over, or keep them in back by the balcony door."

Vita, who had a well-earned reputation of snapping up the best stuff for herself, had already decided where the shoes and boots were going. She pointed to the bell tower stairs. "Over there is perfect. Out of the way, and the box gives them something to look through as they come upstairs." She turned to Sandy Stephanopolous, the mousy-looking wife of the elementary school principal. "Is there anything you want before we open up?"

"Well," Sandy said, "I had my eye on that blue sweater with the snowflakes, but I guess it's already taken."

"First come, first served," snapped Vita. "I opened up."

"We couldn't get in," Sandy pointed out feebly. "You had the only key."

"As the committee chairperson, naturally, I have the key. However, that's neither here nor there. If you really want the sweater"—as if said garment were a rag—"then take it."

"No, no, I only thought, if you didn't want it."

"It might just do for my daughter." Vita shrugged dismissively. "I tell you what, if it doesn't fit Rachel, I'll let you have it."

"Oh, thank you," Sandy gushed.

Ginger Broughton bustled in and got right down to sorting stuff into piles.

Annie was glad to see her. Plump and motherly, she was

kind and caring, with none of the petty-mindedness some of the other committee members seemed afflicted with.

"I brought down last winter's woolens from the attic," Ginger was saying to Faith Billington. "I haven't had time to go through everything, but when I do, I'll donate what we can't use."

"Harvey's bringing over two boxes of woolens from my sister, Begonia, up in Ontario. Every year she sends us clothes. You'd think we were on welfare." Faith gave a self-deprecating chuckle. "I don't know why she bothers. Nothing ever fits."

"That's too bad," said Annie, busy sorting through broken toasters of pre–World War II vintage and an assortment of frayed extension cords tangled up with a mass of mildewed children's mittens. There appeared to be a great many orphaned mittens.

Vita held up a black raincoat, noticed the Saks label, decided it looked as good as new, and tucked it under her purse with the blue sweater.

"Could you," said Ginger to her sweetly, "just move the rest of that pile over here? We'd all like to look through it." The pile in question had been donated by Abigail Woodruff, evidently some of the things she was throwing out before putting the house on the market. Most of the donated clothing had belonged to Wallace Horne's late wife, Edna, a woman of taste and elegance. When she'd died three years ago, he'd left her things as they were. Now that he'd retired and moved to Arizona, it seemed Abigail was cleaning everything out.

"Was that black raincoat a size thirteen?" Faith asked Vita hopefully.

"It's a nine," Vita retorted, lying without compunction.

Most of the ladies had come intending to grab anything remotely wearable, and few were prepared to waste their time sorting through what they privately referred to as "junk."

"Honestly," said Ginger. She had her own agenda, which

included being on the lookout for a nice winter jacket for her thirteen-year-old granddaughter. She watched the goings on with dismay and wondered how to stop Vita from taking everything worth taking. "Last month you took all the dresses and slacks. There wasn't a stitch left for anyone else."

"The early bird gets the worm," Vita pointed out unarguably. There was a stiff silence, while Ginger and Sandy exchanged glances and brooded about the advantages of power.

Annie rummaged through several brown paper bags of jeans and flannel shirts. They looked to be in fairly decent condition and wouldn't need repair or cleaning. She dumped them on the table near the front. Then, finding a box of junk jewelry, she picked out anything with vague traces of gold or silver, and put them in a pile. Something to catch Jack Hogan's eye if he showed up—May had said he was a magpie.

There was an old mirror on one wall for the convenience of the clientele—after all, who wanted a pig in a poke. Sandy held up a navy blue dress under her chin and eyed herself in the mirror. It was about two sizes too small.

"You'd look like a stuffed sausage," Vita told her smugly.

"Just my luck. Nothing fits. Everything's too small. It's the sizing. They don't make clothes like they used to." With a wistful sigh, Sandy put it back on the table, and a moment later, Annie noticed Vita add it to her pile of loot.

"Middle-aged spread, Sandy," Vita said, exuding false sympathy. "You're getting old."

Ignoring this jibe, Sandy glanced at her wristwatch and shrieked, "Almost eleven, and we don't have all this sorted. They'll charge in like a herd of buffalo and grab everything in five minutes flat."

"Isn't that the idea?" asked Annie. "That's why we're here."

"That's as may be," sniffed Sandy, disillusioned with helping the poor and downtrodden. "All I'm saying is I'd like to see a modicum of civilized behavior from these people. Just because you're poor doesn't mean you can't be polite. You'd think they'd never seen clean clothes before."

"Most of them haven't," Vita said with a shudder. "That dreadful Jack Hogan, for instance. He hasn't bathed in months. I hope he doesn't come. He smells to high heaven." She glanced out the window and gave a horrified gasp, "Oh, no! There he is!"

Annie, whose only reason for being here at all was the hope of waylaying Jack Hogan, said, "I feel sorry for him. He was probably a productive member of society at one time." She looked over Sandy's shoulder. Jack Hogan was down there all right, large as life, dirty as ever, and carrying one of his weird signs. This one bore the scrawled message: "Demons two, black as night. They slew her without mercy. Water failed to purify her sins!"

A car had stopped down below in the street. Annie could just see the front of the hood, the rest of the car was behind the side of the Fellowship building. But the driver must have called out to Jack Hogan because he went over to the car.

Vita pursed her lips, anger emanating from her every pore. "That man is a menace!"

From down below came the muted slam of a door and the sound of shuffling footsteps on the tower stairs.

"I hate this," said Faith worriedly as more cars pulled into the church parking lot. "Here they come, and Sandy's right. We don't have everything sorted."

"Hmm, a Mercedes, no less," commented Vita, calming down somewhat since Jack Hogan seemed to have lost interest in entering the church. "Who is it?"

Annie immediately recognized the swanky clothes and beautifully coiffed head. "It's Abigail Woodruff. Looks like she's bringing more stuff."

Indeed, as they watched, Abigail took a large carton from the trunk of her shiny Mercedes. She slammed the door and headed for the entrance.

And right behind her came the shambling figure of Jack Hogan.

The Bargains in the Belfry Ladies Committee collectively squared their shoulders and unlocked the door.

CHAPTER

13

"I hate it when Vita does that," grumbled Sandy as she and Annie watched Vita rearrange a pile of sweaters on a nearby table. The pile had been just fine. Vita simply had to assert her authority over everything.

By three o'clock, things at the church bell tower were in full swing. Ten or fifteen customers were milling around tables of assorted clothing and household goods. Jack Hogan, after casing the joint, sauntered over to Annie's table.

He smelled as bad as he looked. His ratty fox hide hung limp around his scrawny, dirty neck. If he remembered seeing her last night, he gave no sign of it, barely glancing at her as he poked through the box of necklaces and rings. She'd set out a basket for monetary donations, which he shoved aside.

Sandy whispered, "Vita says if he acts up, we're to call the police."

"I can handle him," said Annie, staring at Jack's right hand where May's ring glittered like an evil eye. How had he gotten it? May wouldn't have parted with it, not if she'd been alive.

"Don't turn your back on him," Sandy hissed. "He'll steal your purse."

"Forewarned is forearmed," said Ginger, coming over with an armful of children's snowsuits. She hung them on the rack behind the table.

Jack looked around, very much the dissatisfied customer. "Got any watches?"

"No," Sandy said icily.

Vita, by now chatting with Abigail Woodruff across the room, took a look at what was going on and chirped, "Yoo hoo, ladies! Mrs. Woodruff's brought in some wonderful coats. Help me sort through them."

"Ah, the master's voice." Ginger sighed and said, "Be right there." Grabbing Sandy, she hurried across the room. At that point, several more people came in: Iris Buchman with last year's summer things and Prudence Cannell with two winter coats that smelled overpoweringly of moth balls. The Gander brothers turned up empty-handed, but clearly weren't intending to leave that way. Jacob had his eyes on a pair of wooly long underwear, and Isaac needed a muffler.

Annie nodded at Prudence Cannell, who stared back, the color rising in her face. She glanced around, her mouth moving as if she were saying something under her breath. Then she dumped the coats and darted down the stairs as if the hounds of hell were at her heels.

Well, wasn't that interesting.

Annie turned back to Jack Hogan and showed him a pair of silver cuff links. "These are nice. Not as nice as your ring, though. Where'd you get it?"

He quickly shoved his hand in his pocket. "None of your business."

"Did May give it to you?"

He pretended he hadn't heard and poked through a stack of men's flannel shirts, finding nothing of interest. "What about a winter jacket? Extra large."

"Sorry, no," Annie said. This wasn't strictly true. There were one or two boxes they hadn't opened. For all she knew, they could be full of men's jackets, size extra large.

"What about boots. Size 12." The look he gave her dared her to tell him they had no boots.

"Nonsense!" Vita snapped, stomping over and taking

charge of the situation before it got out of hand and Jack Hogan grabbed everything. "We gave you a pair of boots last month."

"They was no good," he blustered.

"They were good as new," she shot back. "All they needed was a little polish and a brush up. If you weren't so lazy, you'd be wearing them right now!"

He backed away nervously, keeping a wary eye on Vita, whose face was mottled red with indignation. "You got no call talkin' to me like that. I got rights, I'm entitled. This stuff is supposed to be free for anyone that needs it. Gimme any more trouble, and I'll sic the cops on you!" Sniggering, he lurched off down the stairs.

Undeterred by this show of defiance, Vita ran to the stairs and shouted, "Tell the police whatever you like. Don't come back. We don't want the likes of you here!"

At that point, for some reason, most of the clientele decided to leave, including Abigail Woodruff, who stopped only long enough to pat Vita on the shoulder and murmur that she'd done the right thing. The church shouldn't put up with riffraff.

Then her high heels clattered away down the winding stairs, and Vita turned to snap at the committee, by now collectively agape, "What are you staring at? Jack Hogan is nothing but trouble."

"But if he's in need, it's our duty to help," Ginger pointed out uneasily.

"Don't get snippy with me!" huffed Vita. "I'm perfectly aware of our responsibilities. That tramp frightens respectable people away and with good reason. He has a violent nature. I wouldn't be surprised if he didn't have a criminal record! You saw how nasty he got. And that disgusting animal around his neck! Who knows what he might try next time? Suppose he attacks one of us?"

"We can always call the police," said Annie helpfully.

"A lot of good that would do," snorted Vita. "Our reputation here would be ruined. That would be the end of the Belfry committee. Once it gets around town that you aren't safe coming up here at the church, we'd have no customers. As a matter of fact, we're lucky he hasn't tried anything before now."

"He got a little testy, but he actually didn't do anything wrong," Annie pointed out.

Vita sniffed. "This is your first time. You haven't seen what I've seen."

"What?"

"For one thing, he takes much more than any normal person needs. Probably sells everything on the side. He leaves here with bags of stuff. Sometimes two or three!" Vita tossed her head. "Today he showed up and look what happened. He drove everyone away."

Ginger cleared her throat. "On the other hand, charity begins at home, and Jack Hogan certainly needs our charity."

"Nonsense, the man's a common thief." Vita eyed everyone to see how they were taking the news. "The poor box was rifled last week. I saw him looking at it. There's no doubt he stole the money."

"That's not real proof," Ginger said. "There could be another reason he was looking at the poor box."

"Name one."

"It's right next to the men's room. Maybe he had to go to the bathroom."

Vita let out a snort of disbelief. "It's more likely he was planning to grab everything in the box, which is just what he did!"

"Oh, really," muttered Ginger.

"Yes, really! And what's more, he got away with it. Well, he'll be back again before long, and it won't just be the contents of the poor box he's after."

"What's that supposed to mean?" Sandy asked anxiously.

Vita narrowed her eyes. "He looks like a sex fiend, a pervert. Believe me, I know the signs."

"Oh?" Sandy's jaw dropped. "Like what?"

"Do I have to spell it out for you?" Vita asked impatiently. "I've seen men like him before, let's just leave it at that."

Annie kept her mouth shut. It was all too likely that Vita was speaking the simple truth.

They remained open another hour or so, but had few customers. By now the sky had turned dark and threatening as ominous, gray clouds scudded overhead.

Vita was suddenly in a hurry to get home. She was hosting one of her basket parties and had to pick up a food platter at the local delicatessen. One last straggler came in as they were cleaning up, a worn-looking woman with two small children. But Vita sent her on her way.

"We're closed. Come back next week."

The woman heaved a tired sigh, collected her children, and left. That accomplished, Vita wasted no time shooing the committee out and hurrying off to the car.

Annie got in her car. The wind had picked up. Out of the corner of her eye, she saw the church shutters rattle on their hinges. When she turned on the radio, she heard the weather report: Thirty-mile-an-hour gusts of wind were expected, along with bouts of torrential rain. Local flooding was more than likely.

Just then, thunder rumbled and rain fell in a downpour. The windshield immediately fogged up. She already had on the headlights, and she turned on the defroster, feeling a little depressed and wondering exactly what she'd accomplished this afternoon. It had been a huge waste of time. Thanks to Vita's interference, she'd gotten little or nothing out of Jack Hogan.

When she got home, the antique shop sign was swinging back and forth violently in the wind, and a crash of thunder overhead sent her leaping from the car and scurrying inside.

It was Kirk's night to stay late at the college, a staff meeting. So she wouldn't plan on him for dinner. Edgar now . . .

As it happened, there was a note on the kitchen table from Edgar Whittles.His handwriting was jagged and insistent, full of emotion. He'd had to go out on an urgent errand, but he'd be back and wanted to talk to Annie.

Uh-oh.

That didn't sound promising. It looked as if her worst fears about his visit to the police station had come true. Detective Jackson had pointed the finger of suspicion at Tom, or had dropped enough hints so that Edgar had figured it out for himself.

"Woof!" Claudius nudged her leg and demanded dinner. She filled his bowl and one for the cat, who seemed to be occupied elsewhere, doubtless breaking something expensive.

Claudius gobbled up his kibbles and when nothing more was forthcoming, went to snuffle at the crack under the back door. Outside, the wind and rain thrashed against the tavern clapboards. Trees waved violently, bushes bent over. A huge crack of thunder, then lightning flashed. The door rattled in the wind.

Claudius looked at Annie, then barked at the door.

"There's no one there," she told him. "It's just the storm." She hauled him back to the kitchen. Edgar was due home any minute. What to give that man for dinner? He probably wouldn't go for onion soup and a sandwich.

"Woof!" Claudius was back at the door. All hell was breaking loose outside, and he wanted part of it.

"Stop that!" She dragged him away again and gave him a slice of baloney, which he sniffed before devouring. God forbid she should offer him anything but the best baloney. Beef, no fillers. Or worse, pull a fast one and give him one of those "healthy" biscuits offered free at the vet's that no dog in his right mind would eat.

The front door slammed, and Edgar Whittles came in looking like a drowned rat. He was in a towering temper. His shoes squished and rain trickled down his neck. He'd neglected to wear a raincoat. He dumped his soaked jacket on a chair. "So," he said in an aggrieved voice, "you're home at last. Well, I want to talk to you!"

Annie gave him a blinding smile. "Why not go and change? I'll bring you up a hot toddy and make you a nice dinner."

Claudius, who'd gone to ground under the table, emerged at that point and bared his teeth in a facsimile of a smile. Butter wouldn't melt in his mouth. If any meals were being handed out, he planned to be first in line.

Before Edgar had time to start in again, she grabbed the dog by the collar and hauled him off to the bathroom. This time she put the rest of the toilet paper out in the hall closet. Thankfully, he went with hardly a complaint—just one look that told Annie exactly what he thought of all this.

"The same to you, only double," she muttered and slammed the bathroom door. All the same, she was getting sick and tired of shutting Claudius up every time Edgar set foot out of his room. That arrogant, pompous little man. He didn't appreciate anything she did for him. Not the carefully prepared meals served on her best china on a silver tray, and in his room, if you please. God forbid he should mingle with the hired help.

He struggled to untie his tie as he stamped off upstairs. "A hot toddy sounds good. Steak, medium rare, and a baked potato with sour cream. A salad with oil and vinegar dressing on the side. Some of that peach cobbler I had last night, and coffee, too. Two sugars and extra cream."

She heard his door close and wearily turned on the coffeemaker. Steak. She'd have to get that from the freezer and thaw it in the microwave. Then bake the potato. Well, he'd have his dinner in half an hour. If he didn't drive her to an early grave first.

She raced around the kitchen, trying to get everything done at once.

*   *   *

Another crash of thunder and Edgar shouted from the landing, "Where's my hot toddy? For God's sake, isn't that coffee ready yet?" A drumming of rain and a crack of lightning underlined his demands.

"Just be a few minutes," she yelled back. Peach cobbler. She doled a hefty portion in a bowl, took the steak out of the microwave—it needed another minute or two to thaw anyway—and when the peach cobbler was warmed through, took it out, and poured cream on top. By then the coffee was ready, and she made a hot toddy, put everything on a tray, and took it upstairs.

He swept a scornful glance over everything. "I hope it's edible. Are you sure the cream is fresh? I'm not risking salmonella!"

"It's fresh."

"Well, I'll have to take your word for it. But if anything tastes the least suspicious, I'm sending it right back!"

That didn't deserve an answer. She smiled and turned to go.

"Just a minute," he said. "As a matter of fact, I'm feeling quite hungry. Make that a large steak, and be quick about it. I have some important phone calls to make."

Restraining the urge to slam the door in his face, she managed to keep her voice calm. "I'll get right to it." She went back downstairs. The steak she'd already taken from the freezer was big enough for two people, let alone one. She chopped tomato and ripped lettuce, while Claudius howled his objections from the bathroom.

"Oh, shut up!" she told him, eyeing the kitchen light nervously. Had it flickered a minute ago, then settled into a dimmer glow? The last thing they needed was to lose power. Edgar Whittles would never let her hear the end of it.

Another crash of thunder shook the roof. A blinding flash of lightning lit the sky, and she almost dropped the salad tongs. That had been close. Right outside in the backyard, in fact. She peered out the window, looking for a downed tree and saw the tops of trees lashing back and forth in the wind. Then, just as she thought the wind was beginning to die down, everything went dark. The electricity was out.

Suddenly, the phone rang. Obviously, that still worked. Annie groped her way to it and said, "Hello?"

It was Vita Charlemagne and she wasn't happy. "You forgot to hand in your clothing tally. I need it for the committee accounts. I have to hand them in to the board early tomorrow morning."

"Oh." For a split second, Annie couldn't remember what she'd done with it. Tally sheet, tally . . . oh, yes. She'd put it in the table drawer in the belfry for safe keeping. "Can't this wait until tomorrow?"

"No," Vita snapped. "I'm working on the books tonight. What with the storm, I cancelled my basket party. Do you remember which garments, if any, you gave away?" The sneer in her voice left no doubt that she didn't think Annie had gotten rid of anything.

"Uh, we just lost power. Give me a minute to think."

By this time, Claudius's howling had reached deafening proportions. He was a thunder and lightning freak. Nothing got him more excited than Mother Nature's pyrotechnics. And as if this wasn't enough to drive her crazy, Edgar Whittles yelled indignantly from the landing that if he fell and broke his neck in the dark, he'd sue her for every red cent.

Annie dropped the phone, found some matches and lit a couple of candles. She took one up to Edgar, who told her exactly what he thought of New Hampshire fall weather. She endured another minute of his outraged ranting before informing him icily that usually the work crews got things back to normal in no time. She went back downstairs to pick up the phone again. "Vita?" It was too much to hope that she'd gotten tired of waiting and hung up.

"Well," Vita said in an annoyed tone. "Did you find the tally sheet?"

"No, we just lost power."

Vita sniffed. As long as her lights worked, she had no patience with other people's electrical problems. "I need those figures tonight."

"I left them over at the church."

"That won't do me any good. I said I needed them *tonight*!"

Annie sighed. "Then I suppose I'll have to go over and get it." The mere thought of going out in this storm set her teeth on edge. It had been a long day and was rapidly getting longer.

"You won't be able to get in. You don't have the key. I'll meet you there. Ten minutes, and hurry up about it. I don't want to wait around all night!"

All right. Anything to shut Vita up.

It took a good three minutes to remove Claudius from the bathroom—since there was no toilet paper, he'd chewed her Elmo body wash squishy to bits. She picked up the remnants of red netting and marched him upstairs to her bedroom, where he promptly jumped up on her bed. He knew perfectly well she was going out, and his glare told her she'd have only herself to blame for the consequences of her ill-considered decision not to take him with her. A chewed up pillow, books, or shoes. Well, she'd deal with that later.

Edgar was waiting in the front hall. "Where's my steak?" he demanded.

"The power's out. You'll have to wait until it comes back on."

"Just what am I supposed to do in the meantime? Go without?" As if this were beyond comprehension.

"Look, the electricity's bound to come on soon. I've lit some candles. Unfortunately, I've got to go out for a little while—"

"And leave me alone with that mangy cur? Not on your life!"

Claudius took exception to that, too. His accusing barks echoed down the stairwell.

Annie surrendered and went upstairs to get the dog. She'd have to take him with her. In a matter of minutes and feeling bullied, she snapped on Claudius's leash and led him outside.

He stood on the back step and sniffed the wind-driven rain. He quivered all over. He was raring to go.

Somehow, she got them both in the car without falling face down in the mud. Halfway across the driveway, he'd put on a burst of speed that had her practically airborne. Behind her, she heard Edgar yell, "Hey, wait a minute! You're not really going to leave me here alone in this storm!"

"It's all right," she yelled back. "Sit tight. You'll be fine. They're bound to get the power on in a few minutes." She slammed the driver's door shut and fended Claudius off as he leaped excitedly from the backseat to the front. "Sit down and shut up!"

He gave this the attention it deserved, immediately pressing his nose to the windshield and peering out intently. It was a wild night, and he didn't mean to miss any of it.

Meanwhile, Annie was fully occupied with looking for the car keys and wondering if it would start. Her old station wagon didn't like rain and tended to balk at going anywhere at the merest hint of moisture in the air.

True to form, the elderly Volvo with more than one hundred thousand miles on it took several minutes of coaxing before reluctantly rumbling to life and bearing them off down the road toward the other side of town.

Branches were down everywhere, and driving rain lashed at the car windows like the rattle of bullets. To add to her discomfort, Claudius decided to bark at anything that moved, and that included trees, bushes whipping back and forth in the wind, street signs. Nothing escaped his eagle eye.

White-knuckled and half-deafened, Annie hunched over the wheel and kept her eyes on the road. The lights were working on this side of town. Typical, she thought sourly. This side of the highway always got the best service.

To distract him from his incessant barking, she turned on the radio and caught the latest weather report, which was not promising. Several more hours of heavy rain were expected. Residents were to be on the lookout for fallen trees and downed power lines. Low-lying areas were in danger of flooding. Anyone who didn't have to go out should stay home. Those who did venture out should be careful.

The rear wheels skidded a little around the last corner. Claudius bumped her elbow accusingly with his nose, all but sending them into the ditch.

Annie clenched the wheel so hard her fingers hurt. She kept her voice even. "Look, we're almost there. I'll get us to the church, meet Mrs. Charlemagne, give her the clothes tally, and we'll go home. No big deal. We'll go straight home."

She dealt with several humongous puddles that sent spray flying a good twenty feet in the air and had the wipers flapping uselessly back and forth. Another gust of wind rocked the car wildly from side to side. Claudius erupted in another frenzy of barked complaints.

"Be quiet, please!"

He uttered a disdainful "Woof" and scrabbled at the window on the passenger side. Exciting things were going on out there, and he wanted to be part of it.

She sighed. What was the point of yelling at him, when he refused to pay the slightest attention. She concentrated on getting them to the church in one piece. The roads were covered with wet leaves, which made braking extremely risky. It was as bad as driving on ice. She let up on the accelerator. The rear wheels had skidded around that last corner.

Claudius stared at her and barked. Wonderful. Now he was criticizing her driving.

She kept her cool, but it took every bit of patience she

possessed to keep from screaming. "We're almost there. See the church spire just ahead over the trees?"

Unfortunately, they had to cross the bridge over Rusher's Brook to get there. In the past, the brook had been known to overflow its banks and flood surrounding land and houses, but there was nothing to be gained in dwelling on that. The Volvo rumbled over the old wooden bridge while Annie eyed the black water nervously and decided it was still a good half foot below the level of the boards.

Claudius jumped into the backseat, growled, and peered intently out the side window.

She pressed down on the accelerator. The sooner they got there, the sooner she could give Vita that tally sheet and the sooner she'd be rid of Claudius's backseat driving.

Unfortunately, just as they made it over the bridge, a loud crack of thunder sounded overhead, then a weird bluish light flared, and there was a booming crash yards ahead of them. Claudius tensed and started howling in her ear. Terrified, she stood on the brakes. The car skidded to a stop inches from a branch in the middle of the road and stalled.

Claudius woofed loudly, telling her what he thought of that. Someone would have to move the branch, and she was elected.

She shoved his nose out of her ear, got out with ill grace, slammed the door, and stood there, panting. It took another minute for her heart to flop back in its usual place, then she grabbed hold of the branch and tried to drag it off the road. It didn't move.

The branch, really a leggy tree trunk, weighed a ton and seemed to be covered with thorny twigs, but there was nothing to do but get a grip on it somehow and haul it away.

Working on the upper end, she managed to drag it sideways a foot or more, but that still left most of the tree obstructing the road. She'd have to move it from the other end.

Cursing under her breath at Claudius, snug and dry in

the car and still barking, telling her what to do and how to do it, she clambered over the branches and just kept herself from falling into a puddle.

The cold, driving rain was unpleasant, hitting her skin with the force of ice pellets. The faster she got the branch out of the road, the better, always supposing she was able to do it.

Determinedly, she wrapped her hands around the thick end of the branch, braced her feet, and pulled as hard as she could. At first nothing happened, then the branch yielded grudgingly, inch by inch. Claudius peered at her from the car and let out a few more deafening woofs. She was to get a move on. What was the hold up?

Annie glared at him and pulled harder as more dribbles of rain made their way down her neck. Another ten minutes of this and she'd be half-drowned.

The branch moved.

Even so, wrestling with the wet, slippery trunk was like wrestling with a hundred-headed Hydra. Branches extending in all directions, getting caught up on the road, snagging nearby bushes, making it all but impossible to roll it down in the ditch.

She wiped her hands on her jeans and tried again while Claudius glowered at her. It was just as well she'd managed to keep him in the car. The last thing she needed at this point was to have to chase him all over town.

On that thought, she redoubled her efforts and with another ten minutes of wrenching and heaving with all her might, finally worked the branch to the shoulder of the road.

She got back in the car, whereupon it took her a good ten more minutes of coaxing before the engine rumbled to life. A large dollop of cold rain fell on her left foot. She stared down in disbelief. The seal around the windshield was leaking.

Claudius barked demandingly. They didn't have all night. "Hold your horses," she snapped, and carefully eased the car forward. The engine sounded rough, but the car kept going, and she peered ahead, ever wary of more fallen branches.

Mercifully, they made it to the church without further incident. Of course, the branch and Claudius's antics had held her up. She'd kept Vita waiting a good half hour, which is exactly what Vita told her as she skidded to a halt in the church parking lot.

"Sorry," Annie muttered, trying unsuccessfully to keep the dog from getting out of the car. He barked, bolted past her knee, and she managed to grab the leash and hold on.

"Well, I'll get the bell tower door open, and you can get the tally sheet," Vita replied. Without further ado, she wrapped her raincoat about her substantial midsection and stomped off toward the church.

Just then, lightning flashed, and for an instant, the bell tower stood eerily white against the black sky. Above the tower balcony, the spire rose like a pointing arrow with its golden weathervane whipping crazily in the wind.

Another flicker of lightning—the balcony door was open, and Annie caught a glimpse of someone standing by the waist-high railing. No, surely there were two people . . . She held a hand over her eyes to keep out the rain. Claudius bumped into her, barking loudly, revelling in the wind and rain. Time was wasting. Were they going to stand around doing nothing?

"Wait a minute," she muttered, still looking upward, hoping for another flash of lightning. She was rewarded as one last roar of thunder and brilliant flash revealed a man up on the balcony, standing there, arms outstretched. It was Jack Hogan.

Vita had seen him, too. She gasped, "Look at that awful man up there! Of all the nerve, what does he think he's doing?" Her voice rose to a shriek. "You there—get off!" Outraged, she was on the verge of going up to the balcony and hauling him back down herself. But as it turned out, she didn't have to. Unbelievably, he took a sudden tumble over the balcony railing and plummeted downward.

Annie stared in open-mouthed horror as, a split-second later, he hit the pavement with a thud that made her stomach lurch.

For once, Claudius was mercifully silent. Vita, however, began screaming at the top of her lungs. Then Claudius lunged toward the fallen man, dragging Annie with him.

Oh no, she thought, holding onto the leash for dear life. Those filthy clothes, that horrible ratty fox hide around his neck. Jack Hogan was dead.

"Oh, no!" Vita shrank back, wringing her hands. "This is terrible! Is . . . is he dead?" Annie knelt by the body, trying to feel for a pulse.

"I don't know. Dammit, Claudius, let go!" She grabbed the dog's collar and heaved him away, or tried to. He'd sunk his teeth into the fox hide and wouldn't let go.

"What are you doing?" demanded Vita. "Don't touch him—he's probably crawling with vermin!" Belatedly, she fished in her purse for her cell phone. "I'll call the police."

Meanwhile, Annie still had to pry Claudius's jaws loose. She had the uneasy feeling that if she didn't, when the police arrived there would be hell to pay.

There was nothing else to do. She had to resort to brute force. Taking a deep breath, she got a good grip on the spiked collar and heaved with both hands. Claudius growled angrily, telling her what he thought of such tactics, but eventually, she dragged him off. And as Claudius let go of the fox hide, the body flopped over.

Unprepared for what she saw, Annie gasped. *His hand was bare. May's ring was gone.*

She rose to her feet, carefully avoiding the pool of blood beneath Hogan's smashed head. He was dead. Whatever he'd known about May's death was gone for good. Numbly, she put a loudly protesting Claudius in the car. He stared at her through the window with narrowed eyes as she walked back to the church. She tried the bell tower door. It was unlocked.

"I knew it," Vita was grumbling, as if Jack Hogan had jumped off the tower simply to inconvenience her. "First I get a busy signal, then the police don't answer. I'm going to write a letter to the paper about this!"

That didn't deserve an answer. Annie fumbled for the tower light switch and flipped it up. The brass wall sconce glowed to life. Immediately she started up the staircase, then stopped and listened, frowning. She'd heard something . . . the sound of a car starting up on the next street.

Down below, Vita shouted, "I got through. The police are sending an ambulance right away. Come back down at once. Annie, you're not to go up there!"

"Is there any other way in and out of the tower?" she called back.

"Well, the Fellowship building roof is right below the balcony on the other side, you could climb down from the fire escape if you had to, but I don't see what that has to do with anything."

"I saw someone else on the balcony before he fell."

"Nonsense, I saw the whole thing. There was no one else up there, just that dreadful man."

Her voice faded as Annie dashed up the rest of the stairway. The door at the top was unlocked, so either Vita had been uncharacteristically careless that afternoon, or Hogan had had a set of keys to the tower.

She stepped inside and turned on the light. The room looked much as it had earlier. Tables, boxes, and racks of secondhand clothes and household goods they hadn't yet found a home for.

Then something moved in the shadows at the far side of the room. The balcony door, swinging gently in the wind. She carefully examined the balcony floor. There were several footprints; it looked like more than one pair. But even as she came to that interesting conclusion, a torrent of rain came down, washing them away.

"Annie!" Vita's voice boomed up the stairwell. "The police will be here soon."

Somehow, she remembered to retrieve the tally sheet before turning off the light and going back downstairs. She handed it to Vita without a word, then walked across the shadowy parking lot to Hogan's body.

"You shouldn't have moved him," Vita scolded

Sirens wailed in the distance, growing louder as they approached. Flashing blue lights flickered in the sky beyond the roofs of the houses in the next block.

"That awful man!" Vita peered over Annie's shoulder. "How dare he jump from our church bell tower. It's blasphemous!"

Two of Lee's finest rolled up a moment later. The ambulance was not far behind. Vita explained their presence at the church bell tower with a hauteur only slightly marred by her trembling hands.

One of the uniformed cops went over to the body and said after a moment, "He's a goner. Cancel the Life Flight 'copter."

The other cop said to Vita, "Sure you locked up when you left this afternoon?"

"Yes, I'm not a complete fool. We have valuables in the church. Not the secondhand clothes, although once in a while we get some very nice things from Saks that look almost as good as new. You'd hardly know anyone had ever worn them. Let's see, what else? The coffeemaker, office supplies, and that new computer no one knows how to use."

"What about you, Miss?" the cop turned to Annie. "Did you see what happened?"

"Someone else was up there with him. He could have been pushed."

"Not that again!" snapped Vita.

"Are you sure you saw someone?" the cop demanded after giving Vita a warning look. "What did he look like?"

"He was just a figure. It was so dark, then lightning

flashed—that's when I saw him. But I definitely heard a car drive off a minute later."

"I didn't hear anything," Vita interposed firmly. She glared at Annie, who glared right back.

"I did hear a car! And there's another thing. Hogan was wearing an amethyst ring earlier this afternoon. Now it's gone."

This bit of news earned her a narrow-eyed stare from the policeman. "And just how did you discover that?"

"I looked at his hands."

"She moved the body," said Vita, looking like the cat that swallowed the canary. "I told her not to, but she wouldn't listen."

The policeman checked his notes and gave her a quick stare. "You're Ann O'Hara." As if she'd been concealing her identity all this time.

"That's right," she said half defiantly.

"Then you'd better stick around. Detective Jackson will want to talk to you. He'll be here any minute."

Just then, another car rolled up. Detective Jackson, and the look on his face when he saw Annie indicated his displeasure.

Everything had to be gone over again. Twice. He questioned Annie's reasons for being there. In fact, he asked the same questions two and three times, as if he thought he'd catch her in a lie. Had she made an appointment to meet the dead man? If the bell tower itself had been locked, how did she think he'd gotten up to the balcony?

That particular puzzle was answered a few seconds later, when a search of Jack Hogan's jacket pockets revealed a set of picklocks. Obviously, he'd had no need of a key.

"What did I tell you?" Vita crowed in triumph. "I knew that man was trouble, I kept my eye on him this afternoon. He was nothing but a sneak thief." She was about to launch into the poor box story, but Detective Jackson cut her off.

"Do you have any idea why he'd be up in the tower at this time of night?"

"He was crazy!" She glared at him. "On drugs, no doubt. Suicide while of unsound mind. Any fool can see that!"

The coroner arrived, and after the usual grim formalities, Jack Hogan's lifeless body was bundled into a rubber bag, loaded onto a stretcher, and borne away.

"Picklocks! Burglar tools!" Vita compressed her lips with outrage. "Hogan has probably been breaking into houses all over town, right under our noses. Well, I'm not surprised. The police are nothing but a bunch of incompetents. This isn't the first time they've bungled things. Last winter they helped dig a burglar's car out of a snowbank, the fools! I read all about it in the paper. During a snowstorm, the thieves backed up their car to the house and ransacked the place. The language they used was quite vulgar when the policemen drove up. It said in the paper that the air almost turned blue. By the way, that wasn't you, was it, sergeant?"

"No, madam," Jackson muttered. "That incident was regrettable, though understandable in the circumstances. The patrolman thought they were relatives of the homeowners. And it's Detective, not sergeant."

Vita uttered a snort that told him exactly what she thought of that, and he gave her a long, level look before turning away to confer briefly with one of the patrolmen.

When he was done, Annie cleared her throat. "Jack Hogan was murdered. Someone pushed him off the balcony. I saw two figures up there just before he fell. And the ring he was wearing, May Upton's ring. It's gone!"

"This is official police business," he informed her coldly. "I told you before, stay out of it." His tone of voice said he was prepared to consider real evidence, but had no time for hysterical nonsense.

"But what about May's ring?" she demanded.

"You're not even sure it was Mrs. Upton's. And even if it was, maybe she gave it to him. Maybe he left it back at the mill. Don't worry, we'll get to the bottom of this."

"I wouldn't bet on it," Vita sniffed.

Annie turned to Jackson, who looked grim. "When can we go home?" she asked

"Yes," piped up Vita. "I'm soaked to the skin." She sneezed. "I'm very sensitive to cold." Thunder rumbled and a sudden spatter of cold rain underlined her complaint.

"Okay, you can go," he said with reluctance. "We've got all we need for the time being. If anything comes up, I know where to find you." Somehow that sounded suspiciously like a threat. Annie frowned. *She was getting paranoid.* Why would the police possibly think she'd had anything to do with Jack Hogan's death? Suicide or murder. Either way, she had a witness to prove she'd been standing at the foot of the tower when he jumped off or was pushed.

"Detective Jackson," said Vita plucking at his sleeve. "Ordinarily, I'd be the last to speak ill of the dead, but I'm not one little bit sorry that we've seen the last of that man. The truth is we'll all sleep better now that he's dead." With that—Jack Hogan's epitaph—she stomped off to her car.

From the Volvo's front seat, Claudius barked demandingly. Annie shoved him aside and got in. Indignant, he flopped down and propped his nose on his paws with a snuffling sigh as she drove out of the parking lot. He should have known better. Just when things were getting interesting. The least bit of excitement and Annie could be counted on to run like a rat.

More rain fell, shining like diamonds in the flashing blue and white police lights. Vita's words rang in Annie's mind: "We'll all sleep better now that he's dead." Yet she couldn't shake an uneasy feeling that Vita was wrong. Jack Hogan was certainly dead, but they hadn't heard the last of him.

CHAPTER
14

When she got home, the lights were on and Edgar Whittles was standing in the kitchen doorway chewing on the last of the apricot tart.

She put Claudius in the bathroom—there was nothing left for him to chew—and hung her coat on the hall tree, her hand brushing against Edgar's jacket. It was wet, and when she looked down, she saw rain water from the jacket sleeves dripping on the hall carpet. What did he care that it was a nice, old oriental.

Annoyed, she dragged a length of plastic from the closet and spread it under his jacket, at the same time wondering how Edgar's jacket had gotten so wet. She glanced at him. His shoes were wet, and the ends of his trousers looked soaked. Edgar had been out.

He wiped his fingers on a napkin. "So you're back. Well, it took you long enough. What happened? Bad roads? You know, you should reorganize the pantry. It's a mess. I don't know how you find anything in there."

Ignoring the crack about the pantry, she told him what had happened at the church, adding at the shocked look on his face, "Lee is a small town. Not much violence happens around here. The police are doing the best they can."

To add to her annoyance, on the way home she'd passed the Shell station and had noticed a large, new-looking, bronze Toyota Camry just pulling in. Tom, behind the

wheel, had looked inordinately pleased with himself. Lydia
had been right beside him.

Obviously, the insurance money had already burned a
hole in his pocket. Tom had already traded in the Hyundai.

Claudius hadn't been much help. One sight of Lydia,
and he'd carried on for miles. He was heartbroken. The
one person in his life he cared about, gone forever. He'd
whined all the way home.

"Do you want coffee?" she asked Edgar.

"Hmmph," he said, ruminatively. "No, I didn't feel like
waiting all night, so I went out. Drove over to Dunkin'
Donuts. I got a couple of French crullers and coffee.
Wouldn't you know, the crullers were stale and the coffee
practically stone cold. They hadn't made any fresh for
hours." He gave a dismissive grunt. "Not that you'd expect proper service. The workers barely spoke English.
Lazy incompetents. They could hardly find the coffeepot
let alone use it. Hmm, I need a snack. That peach cobbler
will do if you've nothing better. And more coffee." He
stomped off upstairs. "With extra cream."

Damn Edgar! She counted to ten, then dumped a size-
able portion of peach cobbler in a bowl, microwaved it,
poured on heavy cream, and took it upstairs with a pot of
coffee.

He took the tray and said, "I probably won't sleep a
wink all night."

"You didn't say you wanted decaf—"

"It's not the coffee. I'm a light sleeper. That dog has a
bark that would peel the paint off the walls!"

"I'll make sure he's quiet. He won't bother you. You'll
hardly know he's here."

"I hope so. I've had quite enough excitement for one
night!" With that, Edgar closed the door firmly in her face.

From downstairs came an insistent, loud, questioning
bark. Claudius was already proving her a liar. She got his
leash and took him out for one last walk as Kirk arrived
home. She told him the news about Jack Hogan's death.

Just the bare facts, that he'd fallen from the church bell tower and that it hadn't been an accident. She didn't mention the possibility that it might have been murder.

"Hogan was certainly disturbed," Kirk said with a frown. "But I didn't anticipate anything like this. Suicide—well, that's too bad."

She resisted the temptation to tell him about the other person she'd seen on the balcony. She was too tired to deal with another skeptic at this hour of the night. "I'm going up to bed. Will you lock up?"

"Sure, no problem."

Claudius padded up the stairs behind her. Maybe it wasn't fair to lump Kirk with everyone else. Usually, he kept an open mind about things. Not like some she could name, including her nearest and dearest—her brother, Tom, for instance, who, upon hearing of May's death, had immediately jumped to the conclusion that Annie had killed her.

She frowned again at that unpleasant thought and let herself into her bedroom, deftly grabbing Claudius by the collar before he could decide to turn around and sneak back downstairs. "No, you don't!"

He watched glumly as she shut the door, then he grumbled and curled up on the rug.

Lord, she was tired. Taking off her clothes, she dumped them in a pile on a chair, pulled on a T-shirt, and climbed into bed. With a wide yawn, she leaned over and turned off the light and was asleep by the time her head hit the pillow.

But not for long. It seemed only moments later that she realized she was lying, wide awake, staring up at the ceiling. Everything was quiet, or as quiet as an old house could be. Floors settled and creaked. Shutters rattled in the wind and rain.

Or had someone gotten up in the night to use the bathroom? Flushing the toilet.

No, whatever she'd heard, it hadn't been water rushing

through the pipes. She pulled on her robe, tiptoed to the door and opened it a crack. And listened.

Had that cat broken something downstairs? Come to think of it, she hadn't seen Pumpkin all evening. She opened the door wider and listened again. Silence. Then a cold nose nudged her leg and after a moment's hesitation, she let Claudius out into the hall. He padded off downstairs, a black shadow slipping into the darkness. If she heard any indignant feline howling, she'd go down and rescue Pumpkin.

Another few minutes passed. Surely, by now, Claudius had found whatever the cat had broken. Please, let it be something she didn't care about. Maybe he'd tipped over something unbreakable this time, like that old wooden bowl filled with pine cones.

It was eerily quiet, with only the faint drumming of rain on the roof to indicate that the storm hadn't completely passed.

Then she heard it. In the distance, down at the main road, the faint, muffled sound of a car engine. Someone turning around at the foot of her driveway.

Headlights flashed through the curtains at the hall window, then disappeared. The sound of the car had stopped, too. She pressed the button on her wristwatch to illuminate the dial. Quarter after one.

She twitched the curtain aside and looked out. This side of the tavern overlooked the barn and the maze. She could barely make out the gleaming rows of yellowing stalks, standing tall. Ralph Goddard hadn't cut them down yet, and they seemed to sway slightly in the wind-driven rain. Had someone decided to try and walk through the maze at this hour of night? A bunch of kids, doubtless boozing it up. That would appeal to the typical adolescent mentality. The Halloween skull and crossbones maze, scene of a gruesome murder. Ha Ha.

She leaned closer and rubbed the glass where her breath had misted. The nearest rows of corn were clearer now. Involuntarily, she stepped back. Surely someone was standing down there, watching the tavern, looking up at the window.

Wondering what to do—if she called the police and it turned out to be kids, there'd be an unholy uproar. No, the kids would be long gone. She'd look like a hysterical female. The police reaction would be grim impatience.

Meanwhile, Claudius, who usually barked at anything that moved, hadn't let out a peep. So much for Bruno the Wonder Dog.

She peered out the window again and thought she saw the nearest rows of corn move as if someone were walking off at an angle toward the western edge of the field, bordering the road. Someone who hadn't wanted to be seen—

As if sensing her surprise that he'd been quiet in spite of all the strange goings-on outside, Claudius suddenly erupted in a cacophony of loud barks that shook the plaster from the ceiling.

Not to be outdone, Edgar Whittles commenced thumping angrily on his wall. A moment later, he stood in his doorway, glaring at her. "What the hell's going on? That damn barking's enough to wake the dead!"

"Sorry, I'll take care of it. I was just going downstairs for a cup of tea. Would you like one?"

"No! And if you had any sense, you'd get rid of that dog! First thing in the morning, I'm calling the dog officer. That dog is a menace!"

"There's no need for that," Annie said quickly. "I've been keeping him temporarily. I'll . . . take him back to his owners in the morning."

"See that you do or I'll have him put down!" Grumbling, he slammed his door. The light in the crack under the door went out, and she heard the faint groan of bedsprings as he climbed back into bed.

Down in the living room, she discovered the overturned wooden bowl by stepping on a pine cone. After muttering a curse and rubbing her sore foot, she kicked the rest of the cones aside and stood for a long moment by the window, staring out into the night. Faintly, from the direction of the road, she heard the sound of a car motor start up, then fade away as whoever it was drove off.

"Woof!" Claudius almost gave her a heart attack as he jumped up on the sofa and stared down the driveway. He stiffened as she scratched his large ears, but for once didn't shrug her hand away.

"What did you see?" she asked him.

He turned his head, his eyes gleaming a question. *Didn't she know? Hadn't she seen, too?*

From his perch atop the old pine desk on the far side of the room, the cat let out a grumpy yowl. He was annoyed at being awakened. He leaped down, landing with a thud that set the nearest lamp swaying, and stalked off to the kitchen for a midnight snack.

With Claudius at her heels, Annie went back up to her room and closed the door. Dawn was only a few hours away. Drunken kids in the maze or not, she had to get some sleep.

Claudius curled up on the bed at her feet and with a soft, snuffling sigh, relaxed. His breathing became even and soon he was dead to the world.

Unfortunately for Annie, her tired mind went busily to work, thinking up unpleasant scenarios to do with the cornfield, murder, and kids. She fell asleep around 5 A.M.

The morning dawned pale and watery, with the November sun struggling to shine through a sky full of clouds. Bone-tired, and feeling like one of the walking dead, Annie stood under the shower until she came back to life. By the time she dressed and went downstairs, it was after nine and the birds were chirping, flitting about the feeder in the cherry tree by the kitchen window. She groped her way to the coffeemaker. After two or three swallows, she'd just about decided she could face the day.

Unfortunately, Edgar Whittles was up bright and early. Red-faced with anger, he strode into the kitchen, waving a sheaf of papers. "What the hell's going on? Not only is her pocketbook missing, but so is May's will!"

"I told you, I had to look through her room to find your name and number," she said.

"Yeah, yeah, but her *will* is missing!" He repeated this louder, as if he thought she was hard of hearing or just plain stupid.

She sighed. "Wouldn't her will be at her lawyer's?"

"Of course, but she'd keep a copy on hand."

"Sorry, I can't help you. I wasn't looking for her will, just your name and number. But she had a storage locker downtown. She was going to close it and move the rest of her things into the carriage house. She was throwing money away, renting space downtown."

"I'm not in the least interested in your carriage house!" His voice rose to an angry shriek as he thrust the papers under her nose. "Look at this nonsense! May worked up an astrology chart for herself. Also, she'd been seeing some fool psychic. Both the chart and the psychic predicted her imminent death at the hands of someone she knew and trusted!"

For a moment, Annie almost told him she'd paid a visit to Prudence Cannell and learned more or less the same thing May had. But Edgar was bound to twist whatever she said into something conniving and evil. Especially when he found out about the beneficiary of May's business insurance.

So she said nothing and sat there drinking coffee while he continued to rant and rave. When he ran out of steam, she rose and said she had productive things to do, even if he didn't. Whereupon, he narrowed his eyes, sneered that she'd better get rid of that dog before he called the dog officer, and stomped back upstairs.

Under the table, Claudius yawned widely and shut his teeth with a horrible clicking noise. Propelled by anger she couldn't control, she leaped to her feet, grabbed his leash and before she changed her mind, loaded him into the Volvo and headed for Tom's house. If he and Lydia were setting up housekeeping again, well, for starters, they could jolly well take back their dog.

Claudius would be thrilled. Tom, she wasn't so sure about, since originally, the dog had belonged to one of Lydia's lovers. But that was Tom's problem, not hers. It was time for Claudius to go home where he belonged.

Delirious with anticipation, Claudius hurtled from the backseat into the front, sticking his nose out the window and snuffling. He whined expectantly. He knew where they were headed and could hardly wait.

At the center of town, they hit a red light and she stepped on the brake. He threw her a look of impatience.

"You're a damn fool," she snapped. Fine. If he wanted an owner who didn't think twice about dumping him on any stranger's doorstep, then he and Lydia were made for each other. Soul mates, in fact.

By the time she reached Tom's house, her neck was stiff and she was clenching her teeth so hard her jaw ached. Never mind, she was glad she was returning Claudius to his rightful owners. Delighted about it. Couldn't be happier. She'd never envisioned keeping him, anyway.

What would life be like if she'd kept him? If she were condemned to spend the most productive years of her life taking care of a dog who was almost smarter than she was. Or thought he was. Even if she were able, somehow, to get him to obey simple commands, a few basics like "come," "heel," and "stay," even if she kept him outside in the backyard most of the day, he'd still come inside at night, otherwise he'd bark and the neighbors would complain. They'd spend too much time together, and in no time, he'd drive her nuts, if he hadn't already.

As it was, only the knowledge that sooner or later Lydia would take him back had kept her sane.

She parked in the driveway of Pondside Luxury apartments, right next to the shiny new Toyota. Thirty-five thousand and change. Obviously, they were now living high off the hog. Doubtless, Lydia had talked him into it after a night of expert Kama Sutra moves.

Tom was out of his mind.

Grimly, Annie rang the bell. "Look who's here!" he cried, opening the door and giving her a big hug. "Come in." He turned and shouted, "Honey, we've got company. It's Annie!"

She looked around. It was a small, two story apartment, made smaller by a lot of furniture. She didn't remember that black leather sofa or that ornate credenza by the window. Spanish oak and way too big for the room.

The rug was new, too: ugly leaf green wall to wall carpeting.

"We're having a cook-out," Tom told her. "Want to stay?"

In November? On the lovebirds' deck? Definitely not.

Meanwhile, tail wagging wildly, Claudius raced from room to room, sniffing everything. Every few seconds he returned and nudged Annie's leg, only to dash off again. He trotted off in the direction of the kitchen. Suddenly, outraged high-pitched yapping ensued.

"Oh, I forgot Oreo!" Tom rushed down the hall to the kitchen and came back, carrying a little brown Yorkie with bright button eyes, who continued the outraged yapping from his arms.

Claudius ambled back, licking his chops. *That package of ground round meant for the cookout had made a tasty snack.* He eyed Annie, yawned, and ignored both Tom and the now howling Oreo. *Okay, he'd checked the place out. When were they leaving?*

"Claudius!" Lydia came tripping down the stairs and rushed to his side. Kissing and hugging him as if she hadn't seen him in a million years. "Did you miss me? Of course you did, lambie-pie. Want a brownie? Dance, Claudius!"

Immediately, he reared up on his hind legs, dancing around, pawing the air with his forelegs. Lydia smiled and gave him a brownie while Annie watched with growing outrage. Didn't Lydia care about his health? Chocolate could kill him!

Unfazed, he swallowed the brownie whole, dropped to all fours, and headed for the door. He nosed it open, ran out to the Volvo, and jumped in the front seat.

"Claudius?" Annie called to him, but he didn't come back. Instead, he stared at her expectantly. Her heart skipped a beat, then raced madly. *He didn't want to stay with Lydia. My God, he wanted to go home.*

Lydia, already absorbed in her adorable new puppy, held her arms out and took Oreo from Tom. "Does Mama's little darling want a treat, too? Of course you do." Her voice faded as she hurried off to the kitchen.

"Sorry," Tom said defensively. He avoided Annie's eyes. "Lydia wanted a small dog. Oreo will go better with her new decorating business. Claudius wouldn't fit in." He smiled. "He'd scare off customers."

Annie didn't smile. She wouldn't have left Claudius with her brother and Lydia if they got down on their knees and begged. If they were the last people on earth. They didn't deserve him.

She pushed past Tom and went outside. The air smelled fresh and clean, rainwashed.

She took Claudius home. Her heart was still thumping away like a mad thing. She was adjusting to the unbelievable fact that Claudius had made it perfectly clear that he had no intention of remaining with Tom and Lydia. No matter what.

He'd chosen her.

He was hers, or at least he'd decided to make his home with her. In which case, God help her, they were a family.

CHAPTER
15

Exhilarated, yet half terrified by the knowledge that she seemed to have adopted Claudius for good, Annie was almost home when she realized that was the last place she wanted to be.

Edgar Whittles would still be at the tavern, and at the moment, she didn't think she could deal with him. She had too much to do today to waste time listening to his never-ending complaints.

Her first thought last night after Jack Hogan had died, or as she believed, been murdered, was to pay another visit to the mill. May's ring had to be somewhere. It hadn't been on his hand. The murderer could have taken it, or, as Gus Jackson had pointed out, Hogan could have left it at the mill.

Well, she'd go over there later. She planned to make another stop first.

The windows of Heavenly lluminations looked much the same as they had the last time—filled with displays of New Age claptrap. The scent of peach incense assailed her nostrils as she stepped inside. The door bell tinkled behind her. She looked around. The shop seemed deserted, although soft music was playing in the background. Rhythmic cymbals and whining sitar to put you in the mood to get in touch with your inner oneness.

Maybe Prudence Cannell was in the back room, busy with scissors.

A sudden noise to the right, and the psychic poked her head above a rack of paperbacks. "What do you want?" she demanded.

"I thought we might have a friendly chat."

"There's nothing to talk about. I'm in business. You want to buy a book or a candle, fine. Otherwise, I'd like you to leave." Prudence darted down the aisle toward the counter. Annie grabbed her arm.

"May Upton was murdered. Before she died, she received threatening letters made up of words and phrases cut from a newspaper. The other day I saw a letter like that in your wastepaper basket. Now, if you don't want me to go to the police, you'd better explain exactly what you've been up to. If you didn't write those letters to May, you know damn well who did. *Don't you?"*

"I don't know anything." She eyed Annie nervously. "You don't understand. Go away and leave me alone!"

"If I leave here, I go straight to the cops."

"No, don't do that! If he found out I'd talked to you, he'd . . . I don't know what he'd do."

"Who? Your brother, Mike?"

Prudence nodded unhappily. "How'd you know?"

"It's hardly a secret. Your family's made the police log in the newspaper more times than I can count. Raging temper, abuse, threats, restraining orders."

"It wasn't Joe's fault. He loved Helen, but when he tied one on, he'd go crazy. Everything would have been okay if she hadn't written to May Upton. It all fell apart after that. May told her about the shelter, Helen left him for good and filed for divorce. Joe couldn't take it. He killed himself."

"That's too bad, but his suicide wasn't May's fault."

Prudence looked at Annie, her eyes filling with angry tears. "You don't know squat. If she hadn't meddled—"

"Things would be fine? Maybe by now your sister-in-law would be dead, along with both her kids."

"He wouldn't have touched a hair on their heads. He

wasn't like that. Sure, he talked big, but it was just liquor talking."

"Come on, you don't believe that."

She blew her nose. "Okay, I don't."

"So when did you start sending May those letters?"

Prudence rearranged the books again. Finally she mumbled, "A couple of weeks before she died. You've got to understand, it wasn't my idea. I wanted no part of it, but Mike was furious. He blamed everything on May. He swore he'd get even. Said she deserved it. Joe was dead and I was scared." She gave a miserable shrug. "I'm still scared."

"Was May's grim psychic reading part of the plan?"

Prudence's face flushed, then she nodded reluctantly. Annie felt a surge of satisfaction. This was proving easier than she thought. All you had to do to pry information out of people was act tough, lean on them a little, and not let on how little you really knew.

"Okay," said Prudence defiantly, "I let her think she was in danger. So what. I really saw what I told you, the coffin and flowers. Only, I got scared. Mike goes crazy when he gets mad, and I figured scaring May wouldn't hurt any. Might even do some good. She'd take off and Mike would forget about her. If she stayed here, writing that damn column, week after week, he'd go after her. Sooner or later, he'd kill her."

"She's dead, or didn't you notice?"

"Yeah, well, Mike didn't do it. He . . . was with me that night. We had dinner and a few drinks. He passed out on the couch." Her eyes flickered. She was lying.

"Let's say I believe that. Where's Mike now? I need to talk to him."

Prudence stared at her for a startled second. "Look, I told you the truth. Stay away from Mike."

"Or what? He'll get mad?"

"Whatever." Prudence stared at her sullenly. "Are you going to the cops?"

A familiar, loud barking erupted outside. Claudius, left

in the car for all of ten minutes, was making his displeasure clear. Annie sighed. Just when she was getting somewhere.

"Whether I go to the cops or not depends on your brother.
Tell him to call me or drop by the Thurston Tavern. Do
you happen to know where he was last night?"

"Right here. We'd just sat down to supper and the power
went off. I made lasagna. Mike likes my lasagna. I use real
riccota and mozzarella, no low fat. He doesn't like that,
says it tastes like cardboard. Anyway, after we finished eating, the power went off. Mike got real ticked. He likes to
watch the wrestling." She shrugged. "Two streets over they
had lights. Happens all the time. The electric company
promises it's not going to happen again, but it always does.
Some idiot slams into a pole on Main Street and we're
without lights for hours." She frowned. "Why do you want
to know where he was last night?"

"Jack Hogan was murdered."

"That's got nothing to do with Mike."

The door tinkled open and two women came in.

Prudence glanced at the customers, then back at Annie.
She lowered her voice. "So what are you going to do?"

"That depends. Tell your brother to give me a call."
Leaving Prudence to think it over, Annie bought a box of
organic wheatgrass dog yummies for Claudius and went
out to the car. He sniffed the box in a desultory manner
before deigning to eat one. His expression said he was
doing her a big favor. He was used to the good stuff, like
brownies.

Well, he'd seen the last of chocolate.

"Get used to eating healthy," she told him as she drove
toward the edge of town and the old mill. "From now on,
that's all you're getting." He twitched his large ears and
grunted a protest deep in his throat. "Too bad. You're the
dog and I'm the boss. I give the orders and you obey them."

Let him chew on that for a while. It was time they got
things straight. What he needed was structure, discipline,

a firm hand on the leash. Annie could see herself striding down the street with him, looking like one of those people with dogs who followed every spoken command, every flick of the finger without the use of bribed treats. She wasn't sure she was up to it, but for both their sakes, she was willing to give it a try.

The church was just ahead. As she drove past, she noticed several squad cars in the lot. What do you know, it looked like the cops were on top of things. But whether this was progress was another matter, entirely.

She put on sunglasses and slowed, trying to look invisible, and hoping they wouldn't recognize her.

Claudius, of course, had to screw things up by sticking his big head out the window and uttering a loud "Woof!"

Blue-capped heads turned. All the way past the church she tried to slide down in the seat as far as she could.

Thank God, Jackson was nowhere in sight. He'd probably have pulled her over and demanded to know if she was snooping. As it was, the cop nearest the curb was measuring the distance to the spot where Hogan's body had fallen and glanced up and gave the car the once over.

He was fairly good-looking. A little harmless flirtation seemed in order. She pulled over and parked in a spot reserved for the handicapped. Well, the yellow paint was almost all gone. You could hardly make out the little wheelchair.

The cop put away his measuring tape. Annie got out, leading Claudius, who grudgingly agreed to go for a walk. Everyone in town had a dog. The sidewalks were full of them, walking up and down day and night, pooping all over the place. This was country, where dogs were dogs and people didn't carry pooper scoopers.

"Hi," she said, flashing her best smile.

Up close, the cop was even better looking. A little young, though—late twenties. An admiring gleam shone in his baby blues. "Hi, yourself."

It didn't take much prodding to pry information out of

him. He grew serious as he talked about last night's tragic happenings. The terrible storm. A man had fallen from the church bell tower just as lightning struck a nearby pole, knocking out power over half the town. This probably had startled the poor man, who then fell to his death. Open and shut, really. Still, they had to tie up the loose ends.

She chewed her bottom lip. So that was the official line. Not a murder, and not even suicide. Jack Hogan's death would be explained away as an unfortunate accident. Obviously, Jackson had ignored her statement about the other person on the balcony. Which meant they wouldn't have to look for anyone with a grudge against Jack Hogan—just about everyone in town. Maybe that was it. The police had decided it was too much trouble to bother grilling everyone.

Vita Charlemagne and Edgar Whittles were right. The cops were a bunch of nincompoops. Calling it suicide, on the other hand, would open up an entirely new can of worms. The town social services agency would be on the spot: Why hadn't they intervened and helped the poor man? They should have seen how troubled he was. It's not as if he was a recluse. Fingers would be pointed. Editorials written. Blame apportioned, and in due course, heads would roll.

As far as the town was concerned, accidental death worked quite nicely, and it wasn't as if he was anyone important with relatives and friends to complain and stir up trouble.

After moving away from Claudius, busy sniffing his shoes, the patrolman nodded politely and went back to his measuring. She loaded the dog back in the car. The other policeman, snapping pictures of the exact spot where Jack Hogan's head had hit the pavement, gave her a suspicious look, hesitated, seemed to make up his mind, then crossed the parking lot to talk to the good-looking patrolman.

Time to be gone before things got sticky. She gunned

the engine and roared down the street. There was one more place she wanted to go before heading home.

The old mill.

She took the turnoff for Mill Road and drove on cautiously, slowing to twenty as the road, badly rutted from last year's frost heaves, gave her shock absorbers a workout.

The mill lay just ahead, but there was a police car sitting in the middle of the parking lot, and they already had yellow tape up, cordoning off the nosy public. She'd have to ask Gus Jackson if they found the ring.

Not that he'd tell her.

Well, there was more than one way to skin a cat. He might tell Edgar Whittles. In fact, he'd have to. The ring was part of May's personal effects, and Edgar had every right to know what had become of them.

She drove home feeling better than she had all afternoon.

Fifteen minutes later, when she pulled up her driveway and parked by the carriage house, she noticed that Edgar's big Toyota was gone. He was out. Well, she'd talk to him about May's ring later.

In the meantime, there was work to be done. The barn needed cleaning. The other morning she'd dumped the Halloween witches, ghosts, and cauldron in a heap near the door. Everything had to be put up in the loft.

First, though, she opened the shop. She'd put away the decorations and keep an eye out for customers. But she barely got started, when Claudius began pacing up and down, his tongue hanging out. He was thirsty. *When was she going to do something about it?*

She dropped the stuffed witch and took Claudius indoors for a drink. While he was spilling half of it on the kitchen floor, she decided to go upstairs to make Edgar's bed. It would only take a minute or two, then she'd start dinner. Onion soup and French bread with a salad.

Edgar's bed was a mess of tumbled sheets and blankets

but didn't take long to straighten. He'd evidently done some paperwork. Screwed up bits and pieces lay on the floor by the waste basket. She picked them up and dusted the bed-side table.

A white pad covered with scribbled figuring and words lay by the lamp. She couldn't help snooping when she moved it to run the dust cloth underneath. The numbers on the pad were preceded by dollar signs and there were dates, names of racetracks, people.

Fat Louie and Benny the Shiv.

How interesting, Edgar Whittles appeared to be a com-pulsive gambler. From the look of things, he didn't win very often. Too bad. She looked around. He'd dumped a pile of change on the bureau by a black leather laptop bag. A piece of blue and red bordered paper was under the bag, his boarding pass and airplane ticket receipt. He'd flown into Boston on United. First class, of course. The date, she was interested to see, happened to be the very day May had been murdered, not thirteen days later. So Edgar had lied about his whereabouts. Annie wondered what Detec-tive Gus Jackson would make of all this.

There was a spring in her step as she finished straight-ening Edgar's room and went downstairs to start dinner. A few words from her and Tom would be in the free and clear. May had been more valuable dead than alive as far as Edgar was concerned. What if he'd waited outside for her to come home, then begged her to help pay off his debts and she'd refused? He could have flown into a rage, struck her down, and hidden her body in the maze. That this had taken place after dark, and that portly Edgar would have had a tough time chasing May all the way to the brook, practically at the center of the maze, Annie decided to ignore. Desperate, he could have coped. He could have had a flashlight, and the maze wasn't all that difficult. He could have blundered in and out in say, ten or twenty minutes.

By this time, Annie had practically convinced herself that Edgar was guilty of his sister's murder. Jack Hogan's death, though, gave her a moment's pause as she made onion soup. There didn't seem to be a motive for Edgar to have murdered Hogan, but there could have been something. Maybe Hogan had spotted him the night he'd killed May. In that case he'd have had to get rid of the homeless man.

There was the time factor to consider. She'd been delayed a good half hour that night by the storm and the branch in the road, not to mention Claudius's incessant barking, practically driving her nuts. She'd taken the back roads, too, which had delayed her further. So there'd been time, if Edgar had gone by the main road, for him to arrive at the church before her and throw Hogan off the bell tower.

She added two cups of brandy to the soup, turned to put the lid on the pot, and found Claudius standing on his hind legs sniffing the contents with great interest. She shoved him away. "Down!"

He sat down and prepared to wait. There'd be leftovers. Better still, she might leave the kitchen for a minute.

The soup was simmering fragrantly on the stove when a customer drove up and wanted to browse around the shop. Annie put Claudius in the side kennel, where he protested vociferously. Even one of his favorite beef-biscuits failed to shut him up. Frustrated, she told herself he'd start the healthy diet tomorrow and gave him leftovers from yesterday's lunch: half a chicken pot pie.

The customer browsed a while, then bought some smalls—wooden spoons and an old potato masher. She left, and Annie went back indoors, taking Claudius with her. All she needed was a call from the dog officer, and what with the racket he was making, the phone was bound to ring any minute—at which point, a distraught Edgar arrived and waylaid her in the kitchen.

He was babbling, on the verge of panic. "Keep an eye out for strangers. Someone followed me from town! I'm going up to my room, if anyone asks, you haven't seen me."

"Oh, would that be Fat Louie or Benny the Shiv?"

"How did you find out?"

"I was cleaning your room."

"Snooping, you mean!" He was mopping his sweating brow. Then, forgetting his anger in the face of more pressing concerns, he muttered, "God, what will I do? It's terrible! They said they'd break both my legs! I don't know what to do. Yes, I do. I'm packing. I'll get out of town, they won't find me."

"I wouldn't count on that." Annie didn't know much about gamblers, but if she'd discovered Edgar's whereabouts by the simple expedient of dialing information, so could Fat Louie.

He mopped his brow again. "You have to help me! One of them shot at me downtown. The bullet whistled right by my head. I thought it might have hit the car, but I didn't see a hole. They're bound to try again!"

"It was probably a car backfiring."

"I know a gunshot when I hear it!" His voice rose indignantly.

"That doesn't make sense. Why would they try to kill you? Then you'd never pay off your debts."

Edgar hesitated and for a moment seemed to think her argument had merit. Then he changed his mind. "My death would be a warning to other gamblers. I'm going up to pack. You keep an eye on the door. If anyone shows up, say I've left. I had a business appointment in . . . Canada." He thought hard. "Yes, that'll throw them off the scent for a few weeks. Maybe even long enough for me to collect on May's estate."

Poor Edgar. If she'd had an ounce of compassion left, Annie would have felt sorry for him, but she didn't. He'd lied about being in New England when May was killed. He needed money badly, and she wouldn't put it past him to have murdered his sister.

"I'll call my broker in St. Louis," he said abruptly, hurrying away upstairs.

Annie stood there a second, then decided to check the rental car. If he'd really gone to Dunkin' Donuts, there'd be proof, a paper bag or even the coffee cup—if he hadn't tossed them out. There'd been no sign of either in his room or in the kitchen trash. If they existed, they might still be in the car. She went outside and walked around to where it was parked, its metallic bronze paint gleaming in the afternoon sun.

She peered in the passenger window. The front seat of the car was littered with several newspapers: *The Wall Street Journal* and *The New York Times*. Peeking out from beneath yesterday's *Times* was a crumpled white bag with the telltale orange and pink logo, Dunkin' Donuts. And there on the floor lay a squashed coffee cup. So he'd been telling the truth about going out for coffee.

Or maybe he'd been clever enough to have gone there this afternoon. But the cup bore a dried brown coffee stain on the side that looked at least a day old. Edgar could have been telling the truth.

On the other hand, he might have stopped for coffee on the way home after killing Hogan. Although Edgar didn't strike her as being subtle, the sort of cool customer who could carry something like that off, you never knew.

With a despairing sigh, she let herself into the house by the back door. Nothing about detective work was simple.

Suddenly, like the crack of doom, the front doorbell rang.

Claudius barked and went to see who it was.

White-faced, Edgar clattered downstairs. "Oh, God! You promised, not a word about my whereabouts." He turned and fled back up to his bedroom. The door slammed and a second later she heard the snick of the lock.

Meanwhile, the doorbell continued to ring as whoever was out there leaned on it. Claudius, not to be outdone, kept up his end of the din, and she had a devil of a time wrestling him to the bathroom. "Stay there and shut up!" she yelled and slammed the door. "Bark your head off for all I care!"

Ignoring the din, she went to the front door and opened it, leaving the chain attached. The dark-haired man outside on the front stoop, not surprisingly, looked somewhat taken aback at the ongoing racket. But only for a moment.

He narrowed his eyes and crossed his muscular arms across his burly, no doubt hairy chest. "Annie O'Hara?"

"Yes." He was big and mean looking. He could be Fat Louie or Bennie the Shiv, but she didn't think so. He'd ask for Edgar if that were the case.

"Mike Cannell." He glared at her, beetle-browed. "Stay outta my business! And stay away from my sister or you'll be sorry. Another thing, you call the cops, and I won't be responsible for what happens."

"Did you kill May Upton or Jack Hogan?" she demanded.

"No! What the hell's that got to do with me?"

"That's what I'm trying to find out."

"You think you're gonna pin that on me? Think again." He jutted his Neanderthal jaw. "Try it and see what happens!"

"How was your sister's ravioli last night?" she asked, hoping to catch him in a lie.

"It was lasagna, not that it's any of your business." Realizing they'd digressed somehow from the main reason he was there, he snarled, "Like I said, keep your mouth shut, and don't call the cops or you'll get it!"

"Get off the premises, or I'll do just that!" She slammed the door in his face and moments later heard his truck roar off down the driveway.

So Mike Cannell had had supper at his sister's last night. Still, that didn't mean he hadn't killed Jack Hogan. Heavenly Illuminations was only a few blocks from the church. He could have driven there, tossed him off the tower, and been back at his sister's in time for wrestling on TV, always supposing the power came back on. Which meant that he wasn't in the clear.

She went to the bathroom and found that Claudius had dragged towels from the linen closet and dumped them on the floor. She'd have to wash them all over again. This was getting annoying. It looked like she'd have to find somewhere else to lock him up everytime someone came to the door. The cellar, maybe. He wouldn't like that, but too bad. Yelling at him didn't help. Negative reinforcement got her nowhere.

She gathered up the towels and dumped them in the washer while he trotted off to the kitchen, doubtless planning more mischief. In the corner by the tub was a mess of spilled bath salts. She went to get a pan and broom. She felt like screaming.

"Who was that at the door?" Edgar gasped, rushing downstairs and immediately getting in the way.

"It's your lucky day," she said tiredly. "Someone threatening me, not you."

"Oh." This state of affairs seemed to take him completely by surprise. For once he was thinking about someone else. "Well." His look of astonishment faded. He perked up a bit. "As you say, it's not my problem. Just remember what I told you before. If someone comes looking for me, I've gone to Canada." He turned to go back upstairs. He was no fool. If he could continue to get Annie to run interference for him, all the better.

He paused in midstep to eye Claudius, who, ears pricked and returning from the kitchen with what appeared to be a loaf of French bread in his mouth, had obviously heard every word.

"What's that dog doing here? Damnit, you were supposed to get rid of him!"

That was the last straw.

She threw down the pan and broom with a clatter and rose to her feet. The fat fool. She wasn't taking one more word. There was no reason to extend anything but the merest courtesy to Edgar Whittles. He was a guest at the tavern—fine, she'd grant him that and nothing more.

"That's it," she yelled. "One more word and I'll toss you out on your ear!"

Edgar took one look at her furious face, scuttled back upstairs, and shut himself in his room once again.

Claudius continued chomping while giving Annie an ingratiating smile. She did some mental screaming and went back to straightening the bathroom. So there was no French bread for croutons. She'd use the stale loaf in the freezer she'd been saving for stuffing. They'd survive somehow.

Once the bathroom was in order and the towels were in the wash, she remembered the barn and the decorations. It was almost dark, but there was still time to finish cleaning up that mess. She didn't dare leave Claudius in the kitchen—undoubtedly he viewed bread as a mere appetizer—so taking him along, she parked him by the foot of the ladder beneath the loft. She tied his leather leash securely to an iron ring in the wall. "Stay there!"

He sat down and watched with interest while she lugged a stuffed witch up the ladder. She made four more trips, dumping various ghosts, witches, and plywood tombstones up in the loft.

As of the moment, oddly enough, she was feeling better. Yelling at Edgar had helped, and everything was more or less under control. Dinner was on the stove. In the larger scheme of things, toilet paper, towels, and a loaf of French bread weren't worth worrying about.

She'd treated herself to a tot of brandy while measuring two cups for the soup. No one could blame her for taking a tiny drink, not with what had gone on lately. People she knew and liked being murdered right and left. So she hadn't much liked Jack Hogan. In death at least, she was prepared to let bygones be bygones.

A worrisome thought occurred: where had Tom been last night? Tucked up in bed with Lydia? For once she hoped he'd been practicing every porno move Lydia could think up.

In which case, there remained the question of who had pushed Jack Hogan off that balcony. The same person she'd seen roaming around near the maze later on? Maybe not. It could have been Fat Louie or Bennie the Shiv, assuming Jack Hogan had had a gambling problem. This was getting confusing. In any case, whoever had been roaming around the maze last night probably hadn't been there with an innocent motive. And she didn't think it was kids, drunk or not.

Thoughtfully, she picked up the witches' cauldron and dragged it up the ladder. It was heavier than it looked. She set the cauldron down by the pile of tombstones and ghosts, tossed out the tissue and newspapers inside, then groped around the bottom. Might as well clean it out. Next year she'd stuff it with something more realistic looking. If she had the maze next year. That she hadn't made up her mind about

Hmm, she could feel something with the tips of her fingers. Rectangular, soft sided. Like suede.

She drew it out with astonishment. May's pocketbook!

Inside, she found the usual: wallet, handkerchief, keys, odds and ends. And there was something tucked in the zippered pocket just below the clasp. It was small and hard—May's amethyst ring!

How in heaven's name had it gotten here? It certainly hadn't been in the cauldron when she'd set up the decorations just before Halloween. She'd put the newspapers and tissue in herself. Someone had hidden the purse and ring here afterward, when May was killed.

Maybe not the ring, though. If she'd seen Jack Hogan wearing it, and she believed she had, then someone had hidden it here last night. The person who'd killed him.

She tried to remember the sequence of events Halloween night and the next morning. But the only thing that remained vivid in her memory was that awful moment she found May's body.

Still . . . she thought again and random bits and pieces came back to her. Claudius and the collar, now stored in the bottom kitchen drawer until she made up her mind what to do with it. By rights she should take it back to the hardware store. Lord knows it cost enough with that damn remote, and she knew perfectly well she'd never use it again.

Electro-shock therapy was basically heartless.

She took time out from this worrisome thought to toss Claudius an exasperated look and notice with alarm that he was chewing on his leash. In short order he'd have it gnawed through, and then, presumably, planned to take off. So much for trust and leather leashes.

She climbed down and promptly put a stop to that. He looked philosophical. You couldn't win 'em all, and it had been, at best, a long shot. Right under her nose, she was bound to have noticed sooner or later. With a grumpy sigh, he flopped down and brooded. It was all very unfair.

While they were heading back to the house, they had to pass Edgar's swanky rented Toyota. On impulse, she looked it over for bullet holes. Not that she expected to find any. Edgar had said he hadn't seen any.

What was that, right there in the back near the rear window? Probably nothing, but her inquiring fingers ran over the suspicious dark spot anyway and found a dimple. No, a hole. Small and round, exactly what one would expect to find if one were looking for a bullet hole.

CHAPTER
16

"We should call the police!" Edgar stood well back from the narrow window by the front door, peering out nervously at his rental car in the darkened driveway. He hadn't taken the news about the bullet hole in the car very well. He looked terrible, white-faced and trembling.

"Okay, I'll dial 911," Annie said.

"No!" He frowned. "On second thought, that's not a good idea. It would all come out, my reputation would be ruined—are you sure you saw a bullet hole?"

"Near the back window. It couldn't have been anything else. Didn't you say you thought you'd been followed from town?"

He peered out the window again. "Maybe not. There was a suspicious looking car about the time I heard the shot, but I think I lost them." Reassured that there was no sign of anyone resembling Fat Louie lurking in the driveway, Edgar scurried back to the dining room, where, moments ago, he'd divulged his unfortunate dilemma to Kirk Deitrich, hoping the psychologist could figure out what to do. Ph.D.'s were supposed to be smart.

Kirk was taking bowls of onion soup from the oven. Covered with melted cheese and croutons, they bubbled fragrantly. Still in the front hall, Annie sniffed appreciatively.

Her stomach grumbled, she followed her nose to the dining room. Just as they all sat down again, the cat stalked in and let out an ear-piercing yowl. He had to go out. Resisting the temptation to throw her plate at him, Annie pushed back her chair and followed the waving yellow plume back to the front hall. She opened the door a crack, looked around cautiously, then, seeing nothing untoward, inched it wide enough for Pumpkin to squeeze through. He disappeared into the dark.

When he'd come home earlier, Edgar had left his overcoat on the hall tree. It was double-breasted and black, expensive looking, and when she couldn't resist the temptation to touch it, felt like cashmere. Nothing but the best for Edgar.

She wondered if he'd left anything interesting in the inside breast pocket. That's where her ex-, Lennie-the-jerk, stashed incriminating evidence: other women's phone numbers, betting slips. The overwhelming impulse to check in Edgar's pocket was more than she could stand. She waited only long enough to make sure he was still safely occupied in the dining room.

She could hear Kirk talking. "Well," he was saying, "it sounds as if you might have a gambling problem."

"Nonsense!" Edgar denied stoutly. "Anyone could have a run of bad luck."

"Still . . ." Kirk said, trying to talk sense into him or at least suggest the possibility of a treatable neurosis—a psychologist's stock in trade, "No wonder they're trying to strong-arm you. Eighty thousand is a lot of money."

"Not necessarily." Edgar took issue with that, too. "It depends on your point of view. My company's worth thirty million. Compared to that, eighty thousand is peanuts."

"Good point," said Kirk. "But perhaps not relevant in the present circumstances. You said you had a cash-flow problem."

Glum silence. For once, Edgar seemed at a loss for words. There was a clink of glasses and a gurgle. Wine was being poured.

She patted the overcoat's inside breast pocket. Nothing. It was empty. She eyed his briefcase on the hall table.

He hadn't locked it. Well, well. It wouldn't hurt to take a quick look. She opened it, careful to make as little noise as possible. It contained several travel brochures extolling the beauties of New Hampshire: Happy couples skiing, toasting each other by candlelight in a quaint, country inn, picking up bargains at some out of the way antique shop. Thus confirming her opinion that Edgar wasn't in New Hampshire merely to bury his sister.

Underneath the brochures was a folded piece of paper. She held it under the hall light. Son of a gun. May's will, neatly typed, all legal and binding.

She was interested to see Andrew Carrigan's name scrawled at the bottom as a witness, along with that of someone else, a barely legible, feminine-looking, looping backhand with little "o"s over the "i"s, probably his secretary. She tilted it higher under the light from the wall sconce and scanned it, curious to see what May had done with her worldly goods. Good grief, a small bequest to herself—that she hadn't expected. A larger bequest to the local fund for abused women and children, a few thousand to the library. A good deal more to the Bide-A-Wee home for cats and dogs. Several paragraphs down, Edgar's name appeared. Fifty thousand. Not bad, but not quite enough to get him out of his present difficulties.

She refolding the will, put it back in the briefcase, and quickly searched the pocket in the lid, discovering a small envelope containing credit card receipts—doubtless saved for tax purposes. Our boy, Edgar, was nothing if not thorough. He'd filled up the rental car here in Lee the day May had died. Not only had he been in New England, he'd been right here in town. He'd needed money badly. He could have killed his sister.

In the dining room came the sudden noise of four paws hitting the floor along with the clatter of cutlery. "Claudius!

Cut that out!" Kirk yelled. "Well, let him have it. There's plenty more in the pot. Annie can fix herself another bowl."

The phone rang and Annie answered it.

It was Iris Buchman. *"Where are you?"*

At home, which should have been perfectly obvious, since she'd just answered the phone. "Right here," Annie said, frowning. What was Iris's problem?

"It's six-thirty. You were supposed to be over here a half hour ago! It's my bingo and board games night—for people over forty-five. I planned to grab a bite with some friends afterward, remember?"

Annie did, finally. Apologizing profusely, she promised to be right over. The showdown with Edgar Whittles would have to wait until later.

When she got to the sprawling fieldstone house on Ivy Lane, Iris waved her into the living room. She pulled on her coat. "I'll be back around eleven. Steve's gone to bed, so he shouldn't be a problem. Not that he ever is. I'm a worry wort." Looking harassed, she rushed off.

Annie peeled off her coat. The TV was on. Wide-screen, it took up half the wall. She made herself a cup of instant coffee and sat down on the couch. A boring sitcom rerun. She hadn't seen it the first time and wasn't watching it now.

Where was the remote? She looked on the table, moved a couple of magazines, under the couch pillows, and finally found it on the floor.

Claudius, already asleep on the rug, woofed softly. His eyelids fluttered, his legs moved, nails clawing fitfully. He was dreaming of chasing big, bad, yellow cats.

There had to be something on she could stand. The TV Guide channel scrolled interminably: *Hitler's Henchmen*— the ending was always the same—she'd seen it three times at 2 A.M. during anxiety attacks about the tavern roof falling on her head and no money for repairs. Game shows—she hated them. Idiotic sitcoms, talk shows with weirdos,

Hitler's Generals on the Learning Channel, followed at nine o'clock by *Hitler and the Occult*.

Heavens, Edgar was right. What was the world coming to?

The animal channel was showing *Emergency Vets*. Pets in trauma. Well, maybe she'd watch that. Except if they had to euthanize anything. Somewhat apprehensively, she pointed the remote. On screen, a Persian cat yowled and attempted to bite the hand that was attempting to minister aid and comfort. Claudius woke up and immediately became engrossed in the goings-on as the apprehensive owner conferred with the vet. The cat had had a run-in with a skunk. In due course, the cat was cleaned up and sent home, then a dog with ear mites was tended to. Claudius watched avidly. All too soon it was over. The next program was exotic pets, snakes. That's where Annie drew the line.

"Not on your life," she said. She switched off the TV. The screen went black, and she listened to silence. Only the house wasn't really silent. Upstairs, the floor creaked. Outside, a branch tapped on the window. It was pitch-black out there. She couldn't see anything, but it felt like eyes were staring in. She got up and closed the drapes and immediately the room was warm and cozy.

Safe.

She found herself shivering for no reason. This was silly. She frowned and finished her now cold coffee.

It was just after eight. Iris wouldn't be home for ages. Time dragged.

The branch tapped again. Just the wind.

There was a bookcase full of interesting things. Evidently Iris liked travel books. Hardcover, some paperbacks. On the end of the top shelf was a scrapbook.

She sat down and opened it in her lap. Lots of what looked like vacation snapshots: camping in the mountains, fishing, bicycling. Iris in a two-piece bathing suit, Iris in waders, triumphantly displaying her catch: a tiny brook trout.

Annie yawned and flipped a few more pages. The house

during remodeling: the kitchen with drop cloths everywhere and wires hanging from the ceiling. A man on a ladder, his face turned away as he wielded a paintbrush. She turned the page. In this shot he was hanging the chandelier Iris was so fond of, the one from the whorehouse.

Probably her first husband. Whatshisname. Annie thought hard, but couldn't remember. Not that it mattered.

She closed the scrapbook with another yawn. Maybe more coffee would help. As she went to the kitchen, the floor upstairs creaked again. Probably Steve getting up. Going to the bathroom.

Claudius parked himself expectantly on the rug in front of the stove. If she was eating, so was he.

Momentarily, Annie thought about fixing a freshly ground cup of coffee, but couldn't find the grinder. Well, more instant was fine.

The kettle boiled. Claudius trotted out to the hall and stared intently up the stairs. Steve must be up and about, she thought and was just stirring in sugar and milk when he shuffled in, scratching his tousled head.

"Hi, how about some coffee or a glass of milk?" she asked. But maybe he was hungry. "Or a sandwich, how does melted cheese or tuna sound?"

He frowned, making one of his rapid, nervous gestures, rubbing his head. "Mmm—n . . . no." He looked depressed. Perhaps something sweet would cheer him up.

She looked in the refrigerator while he sat down at the table with an air of staying there until his needs were met, until hell froze over if need be. Desperately, she examined various covered dishes. "How about bread pudding?"

He shook his head. Okay, she wasn't crazy about that, either.

"Ice cream, rocky road." She looked to see what effect, if any, the prospect of chocolate and nuts might have on his appetite. On second thought, maybe that wasn't such a good idea. What if he got hyper? He began mumbling under his breath.

"M . . . mm."

It was worth a try. She dug out a bowlful and set it before him. He picked up his spoon and picked at the ice cream. Tiny birdlike bites. At this rate it would take him all night.

He muttered something vaguely suggestive, which she pointedly ignored. He shot her a sly look. She ignored that, too. Silence seemed to work as he went back to eating. With a resigned sigh, she sat down opposite and drank her coffee. He nibbled ice cream and stared at her glumly. She stared back with an equal lack of enthusiasm.

Well, he still wasn't used to her presence; but things were bound to get better in time. Not that she had any intention of doing this for more than one more week. Iris would simply have to find someone else. Vaguely, Annie wondered how long bingo and board game season lasted, and if people played it all year round or just in the fall. Like deer season.

She smiled cautiously, hoping Steve wouldn't notice she was ill at ease. She wasn't afraid of him. It was the not knowing that bothered her. He was unpredictable. Door locks always had to be checked to make sure he didn't wander into the street and get himself killed like his poor dog, Caesar.

Plus she had to watch her back, or more precisely, her butt. Besides a penchant for making suggestive remarks, Steve was a pincher.

There was a brief commotion as Claudius, under the table hoping for handouts, decided none were forthcoming and crawled out. He flopped down on the rug by the back door.

Slowly the ice cream melted. Between teensy sips, Steve muttered about a woman who'd jumped in another man's pickup and run off for good. This seemed to be the cause of his depression. But when Annie asked when this had happened, he looked blank. He didn't know or couldn't remember.

She noticed with dismay that he was staring at her breasts. His eyes gleamed, his voice trailed off. Obviously he'd lost track of what he'd been about to say. He grinned.

She'd had enough.

"Stop it!" His eyes roamed avidly over her torso, the part he could see, between her neck and the top of the table. Annoyed, she stood up. "Cut it out!"

She stalked back to the TV in the den. Even *The Beverly Hillbillies* was preferable to this. A minute or two later he shuffled into the den and sat down in a wing chair. He became engrossed in the TV.

After a time, he grew agitated, mumbling, yet couldn't seem to take his eyes from the screen. She wondered if she should change the channel. It was just the news, but still—

Claudius trotted in and eyed the TV hopefully. If she wasn't watching the animal channel, maybe it was a cooking show. Something with meat. Disappointed, he yawned and curled up in a large, black furry lump. His tail covered his nose. One black eye squinted at the screen. Humans were running from a blazing fire.

Inexorably, one canine thought led to another. People food was often grilled over an open fire. He whined low in his throat and thumped his tail. He eyed Annie with a look of assumed adoration. A little honey usually worked wonders.

"Forget it," she said.

The sports scores flashed on. The Patriots had lost again. Nothing surprising there, except the inventive ways they seemed to achieve it week after week. Annie had given up rooting for New England's team a long time ago. Steve, bored with the box scores, got up and went up to bed.

Claudius woofed a complaint and looked up at her expectantly. He was starving. Dinner had been hours ago. He was wasting away to a mere shadow of himself.

"No more food. You had your dinner and most of mine, too, remember?" Then, weakening, she tossed him a wheat grass biscuit. But he turned his nose up. He wasn't interested in healthy snacks. "Suit yourself." She settled back to watch a movie; Christopher Lee as Dracula.

It was eleven by the time Dracula was dispatched with a wooden stake, Iris returned, and Annie was able to go home.

Kirk had left the light on by the back door. She let herself in, thinking how welcoming it all was. Home, hearth, a good night's sleep in the offing. Pumpkin, the cat, came in from his nightly ramble. He dropped a dead mole at her feet.

"Thanks," she said, picking up the tiny corpse with a paper towel and dropping it in the garbage. This was becoming a habit. Every time she came in the back door she risked stepping on something small and dead, a bird or a mouse—trophies, or else he brought them home hoping she'd cook them.

Of course, now that Tom and Lydia were again a loving couple, there was no reason for her to have custody of their cat. Pumpkin could be returned to the bosom of his family, and the sooner the better. Smiling, she opened a can of sliced veal cat food and dumped it in his bowl.

Claudius had gone upstairs on his nightly inspection. Having made sure everything and everyone was where it should be, he came trotting back, although not in the best of moods. He was hungry. That stupid cat was eating. He examined his bowl and found it empty. Where was his food?

"Sorry, this isn't an all-night diner," she told him, washing her hands at the sink. He nudged her leg and when that didn't immediately have the desired effect, nudged her again. "All right, you win." She offered another despised biscuit, and he promptly showed her what he thought of that by shouldering the cat aside and gobbling down the sliced veal.

"Bad dog!" she scolded, aware of his defiant gaze. She

got out more veal and, making sure there wasn't anything breakable within reach of the cat, fed him on the counter.

Then she turned off the lights and went upstairs to bed.

In the morning, over breakfast, she had a long, if unsatisfactory, talk with Edgar. After his initial outrage upon learning she'd had the gall to go through his briefcase, he calmed down and admitted he'd found May's will by chance in her storage locker downtown. Which, unfortunately, had contained nothing else of interest. He'd probably give the lot to the Salvation Army.

When Annie tossed the gasoline credit card receipts by his plate and demanded an explanation, Edgar resorted to bluster. So he hadn't been quite truthful about his whereabouts when May had died. It was understandable. He'd been in town on business, looking into real estate. He'd let Annie and the police think he'd been in Missouri because he didn't want to complicate matters.

May's funeral was the third topic of discussion. Edgar thought it should take place as soon and as cheaply as possible. May would want it that way. She'd never been one for pomp and ceremony, so he'd decided not to have a funeral at all.

"What about May's friends?" Annie demanded, frowning. "They'd like to say good-bye. You need to hold some kind of funeral ceremony, it's only decent."

"Nonsense, May always said she hated funerals." His eyes brightened as he came up with an idea. Free. Thereby obviating the need for the bother and expense of a burial plot. He gave Annie a smug look. "Actually, May told me her dearest wish was to donate her body to science, so I plan to make arrangements to give her to the University of New Hampshire."

By midmorning, Edgar closeted himself in his room and made half a dozen phone calls to wind up his affairs and hand his sister's remains over to the university's medical school. He appeared for a late lunch, chuckling and rubbing his hands with satisfaction.

"Barring unforeseen circumstances," he said cheerfully, "I'm out of the woods. Fat Louie's boss is prepared to call off the muscle and accept fifty thousand as partial payment on my markers. He hasn't exactly forgiven the remainder, but I've got ninety days to make good."

"Looks like your luck's turned," Annie said.

He tucked his napkin under his chin and dug into his lunch with gusto. "I've got a great plan. Don't know why I didn't think of it before. I'll just cancel the company Christmas bonus, and the savings will cover the rest of my markers. It's lucky I planned my vacation to coincide with the Florida racing season. Thoroughbred coats gleaming in the southern sunshine, thundering hooves racing to the wire ..." He sighed and said, "I can almost see myself winning the daily double."

"Well," Annie's voice broke in on his reverie. "I'll be back later. I'm off to the library for the presentation ceremony. I'm handing over the check from the annual cornfield maze proceeds."

"Wait a minute," he said, jumping up and grabbing his coat. "I'll come with you." No sense in sitting around waiting for Fat Louie to get word that the hit was off. Fat Louie's boss had assured him he was safe now, but deep down, despite his obsession with gambling, Edgar was a cautious man. And there was safety in numbers.

"Let's go in your car," he said. One potshot in his direction was more than enough.

"Fine." Annie was leaving Claudius at home. He was, of course, sulking. The breakfast she'd provided had been substandard again, generic dog food—no Iams, not even Alpo. "I'll go shopping later," she promised, looking down into those eyes that glared back with indignation.

She sighed. Why did Claudius always have to act like Claudius? "Be a good boy," she told him. He turned his

back. She'd cave in and hand out a treat or two. That was
what she always did.

But not today.

The door closed, and he dashed to the window in a state
of disbelief. The traitor, she was leaving with Edgar Whittles!

Aware of the fact that Claudius had not the slightest intention of being a good boy, and that even now he was
heading upstairs to chew her new winter boots, Annie turned
the nose of the Volvo toward the center of town.

It didn't take long to drive to the town hall, where the library was holding the program. It was to be twofold: the annual presentation by Annie of monies collected from the yearly
Halloween maze, and a video/slide show of local haunted
houses. Printed programs would be handed out at the entrance. Five dollars admission for members, ten for non-
members, who were encouraged to join the Friends of the
Library.

Refreshments would be served at the back of the hall—
cupcakes, cider, and chocolate chip cookies. They'd gone
all out with decorations. Wall sconces draped in skimpy,
black-dyed cheesecloth, stretched wide to resemble spiders'
webs. Black construction paper bats pinned to the webs.

The assembled crowd, thirty or forty people, took their
seats, and Annie presented the check for fifteen hundred
twenty-nine dollars and thirty cents to Vita Carmichael,
who accepted it graciously and announced that this would
go into the new book fund.

The scattering of applause died down.

Annie, a little embarrassed, smiled, and Vita looked
queenly.

Resuming her seat, Annie glanced around, noting with
surprise a few familiar faces in the audience: the Gander
brothers, Faith and Harvey Billington, even Prudence Cannell and her brother, Mike, who, upon eye contact, glared
malevolently.

Vita stepped up to the podium and announced that they

were in for quite a treat. In the past, reports of haunted houses in town had received scant attention. But this program would change all that. The committee had worked long and hard putting the program together. She beamed and said, "They conducted interviews and took pictures. I'm certain you'll enjoy the result."

She paused. There wasn't much applause since the hall was warm and the P.A. system inadequate. People were falling asleep.

"Well," Vita shuffled her note cards. "Let me introduce Akita Tanaka, our Japanese exchange student, who's been working on an arts project this past year. He will be running the slide projector and video machine."

The slim, dark-haired young man behind the projector stumbled to his feet, looked around with some confusion, and nodded. He sat down again.

"Lights, please!" Vita waved a commanding hand at Harvey Billington standing by the wall switch. The lights were duly dimmed and the first slide flashed up on the stage screen.

The legend read: "Local Haunted Houses."

This was the cue for Faith to step to the microphone. "The first house is the old Bartlett place." She nodded at Akita, who clicked the next slide. A blurry picture of a white clapboard Cape appeared. Akita, evidently misunderstanding as Faith described various ghostly apparitions in the house over the centuries, clicked away like mad, moving slides out of sequence. Three rooms whipped by with no sign of ectoplasm. In vain, Faith regrouped, shuffled note cards, and tried to catch up. The program proceeded at a breakneck pace through badly photographed views of fields, stone walls, streams, and thickets—evidently one ghost had a liking for the great outdoors.

Annie found herself nodding off. She forced her eyes open and stared up at the screen. Faith was droning on about the old mill, reputed to be haunted by a nightwatchman who'd fallen in the river and drowned.

Her part over, Faith scuttled to a chair and sat down.

"You'll notice," Vita resumed with a trace of complacency, "we've taken great care to try and keep precise locations of private homes unrecognizable. We don't want the owners pestered by curiosity seekers." About to nod at Akita to proceed, she realized he'd anticipated her. She frowned and sent him a sharp glance, whereupon, he fumbled with the projector and sent slides blurring backward at a dizzying rate.

The P.A. system let out an ear-splitting screech. Vita winced. "This particular house, the Thurston Tavern," and here, unfortunately, Akita had found the right slide, "is well known to the community. It's been an inn, a saloon, and town meeting place for more than three hundred years. In revolutionary times, both the Colonial militiamen and British forces often stopped by on hot evenings to slake their thirst. The militia used the field behind the tavern for maneuvers—today, of course, it's the site of our annual Halloween maze."

Annie listened with dismay. No one had asked her permission to use the tavern as part of the presentation.

Another view of the tavern flashed on the screen. The herb garden was front and center in all its scraggly glory. Vita consulted her clipboard. "The tavern has been a place of violence and death. Here in the herb garden, a duel is said to have taken place, and a man shot straight through the heart." She paused dramatically. "As we all know, unfortunately, the violence continues to this very day."

Of all the nerve! Annie was furious. To accept her hard-earned money, then turn around and practically call her home a den of iniquity!

Akita clicked on. A frontal view of the tavern. But there was something strange about it. It looked as if it had been taken recently. Very recently—in the last day or so. Edgar Whittles's rental car was visible in the driveway. But as usual, whoever had taken the photograph had bungled badly. Out in the street, another car had driven by. Barely recognizable, a bronze Toyota. The man at the wheel had dark hair, Tom. Lydia beside him, platinum mane blowing in the breeze, looking like the cat that had swallowed the cream.

Vita prattled on, making a few more scurrilous remarks about the tavern, then, mercifully, she went on to the old Lyman house. "Tragically, the scene of a series of deaths before, during, and after the great flu epidemic of 1918. The house functioned as the town poorhouse, then the work-house, where widows and orphans made up most of the population."

Annie got up and marched to the back of the hall for cider, where a knot of people had already gathered for the free eats, such as they were. Iris Buchman ladled cider into a paper cup and commented to Annie that she'd had no idea the tavern had such an interesting history.

"It's an old house. Comes with the territory," Annie said, trying to think of a way to change the subject.

"My house is just as bad," said Iris, patting Annie's arm comfortingly. "I used to hear strange noises sometimes, like a groan. It was a loose slate that had fallen down the chimney. It rattled when the wind blew. Never mind, this afternoon's program has really been quite interesting." Annie said glumly she supposed so, and Steve gave her a chocolate-smeared smirk from his seat in the back row.

Just then Edgar sauntered up and helped himself to refreshments. Taking his cue from Iris, he said, "Well, the program was . . . different." He chewed and swallowed a cupcake, then turned to Annie, frowning. "Is the tavern really haunted?"

"Nonsense," she said firmly. "I've never seen a thing. They made it all up." Edgar was giving every indication of taking the whole thing seriously—the coward. His hand shook as he held his paper cup out for Iris to fill.

Two or three more houses were displayed on the screen, including Wallace Horne's mansion on Main street. The ghost was a woman whose husband had come home from a journey lasting more than a year to find she'd had a baby in his absence. Incensed, he'd murdered her and the babe. Various visitors through the years had heard a baby's cry and seen a woman in black floating through the house.

At this point, Vita spoke a word or two about the Revolutionary graveyard behind the town hall, where a horse had been buried standing upright, facing its owner, a colonel in the New Hampshire regiment—a mark of great respect. The horse had been a stalwart through many a Revolutionary campaign. "If you decide to take a few minutes to look around the cemetery, we ask that you not take any rubbings. The stones are fragile. That concludes our program. At this time we will take questions and comments."

Abigail Woodruff's hand shot up in the air. "You had no right to put my house up there!"

"I beg your pardon?" Vita looked startled.

"You heard me," Abigail snapped.

"Well! There's no need to take that tone. We used no information that wasn't already in the public domain."

"That's not the point," Abigail retorted. "If this gets out, it will drive down the real estate value. No one wants to buy a haunted house!"

"If you're truly worried about the real estate market, I'll be glad to speak to you about this in private."

"Well, I should hope so!" Prepared to do battle, Abigail made for the front of the auditorium, and the last Annie saw of her, she was wagging an angry finger under Vita's nose.

As the audience trickled out into the waning sunshine, Annie headed straight for the car, followed by Edgar and further racket from the town hall. Heated words. She couldn't hear what was being said, but Vita seemed to be giving as good as she got.

Edgar, meanwhile, was taking his time getting into the Volvo.

"Hurry up," complained Annie. Maybe his life was coming up roses, but hers certainly wasn't. She still had a few chores to do before nightfall.

"Well," he said, eyeing the tilting old gravestones on the other side of the wall. "I'd like to take a walk around and see that horse's grave. What did she say his name was?"

"General, and you can drive back down here later. I still have my Hands and Hearts work—"

"Yoo hoo, Annie!" Jacob and Isaac Gander came hobbling over. "Wasn't the program wonderful! You're coming over to fix dinner for us, aren't you?" She nodded, and Jacob chortled, "Wonderful! Give us a head start so we can get home and unlock the door." The elderly brothers clambered into their Cadillac and drove off with a jaunty wave.

Edgar regarded their now disappearing car with suspicion. It was new and obviously loaded with every extra imaginable. "That's what's wrong with this country. Two old geezers living high off the hog! Free handouts, while the rest of us work our fingers to the bone to pay for their luxuries."

Annie spared a glance from the road toward Edgar-the-newfound-friend-of-the-common-man. Edgar in his cashmere Brooks Brothers overcoat and alligator shoes.

"It doesn't matter who gets elected," he complained. "The politicians are in bed with the AARP. They pander to the old bastards every chance they get."

Annie tuned him out, but all the way home he continued to complain about senior citizens and Social Security. She pulled into the driveway, got out, and unlocked the back door.

Complete disaster met her eye. Claudius had been busy. A chewed up boot. One of a pair she'd just bought from L. L. Bean for one hundred dollars, thank you very much. Two logs gnawed to kindling, and even the metal socket of a light bulb. She almost had a heart attack when she saw that and wondered if he was capable of eating ground glass. She didn't doubt it.

Noises came from the kitchen, where, thank goodness, she found the rest of the light bulb and Claudius, cleaning out the pantry. From the amount of ripped-open boxes and bags lying around, he'd already eaten most of the cookies and cereal. She snatched the last box of Oreos and told him firmly that he was a bad dog.

He wagged his tail and unrepentantly trailed her around the kitchen as she cleaned up the mess. If she was stupid enough to leave him home alone, she deserved everything she got.

After this, there was no question of leaving him here by himself while she went to the Gander brothers'. He'd eat her out of house and home. While she was wondering what in the world to do with the dog, Edgar, saying he wanted to check his E-mail and catch the latest stock quotes, dashed upstairs to his laptop.

The phone rang. It was Jacob Gander.

"Oh," she said. Why would he bother calling? She was going over there in five minutes. Maybe he wanted her to pick up something at the store.

"Just wanted to bring you up to speed."

"Up to speed?" she echoed. This sounded ominous.

"I went next door a few minutes ago to demand the return of Wallace Horne's antique mechanical card cheating device. Last week those crooks took it from the historical society without so much as a by your leave. Stole it. They had no right, no right at all. It was part of our permanent collection, which is exactly what I told them!"

"Cut that out! No, not you, Jacob. Claudius." She moved her foot. She'd just caught him eating her shoelaces.

"Annie, this is important! Get over here right away. I plan to go back over to the Woodruffs, and this time I'm wearing a wire. You wouldn't believe the threats they made. Once I get it on tape, I'll take it to the police and we'll see who's so smart. But the thing is, I need more than the tape. I need a corroborative witness for this to stand up in court, so you have to go over there with me."

In the span of less than half an hour, he'd managed to drive his brother home and get himself embroiled in what amounted to a knock down drag out fight over something as stupid as mechanical aids to cheating at cards, interesting though they might be. It was amazing.

She tried to talk sense into him and discovered she had an ally in Isaac, when, a short while later, she drove over to their house on Main Street.

"Damn fool won't listen!" Isaac declared, throwing up his hands in disgust as she walked in the door. "He's got a death wish!"

"Hah!" scoffed Jacob. Without further ado, he bundled Annie back out of the house and down the front walk.

"Should we bring Claudius along?" she asked with a frown. Claudius was trotting happily at her side, heeling for once—but there were all those expensive antiques at the Hornes', and he seemed to have developed a taste for wood.

At the sound of his name, Claudius's ears pricked. Surely she wasn't thinking of stashing him in the car!

"Let's take him with us," said Jacob, patting the dog on the head. "They won't dare try any funny stuff with him around."

They went up the mansion's brick front walk. The curtain in the drawing room window twitched. They were being observed.

"Nuts," muttered Jacob. "I wanted to take them by surprise. Wait a sec, let me get this switched on. It's voice-activated." He put his hand in his jacket pocket and turned on the recorder. "Okay, all set. Ring the bell."

There was no need as Abigail, still in a foul mood from her confrontation with Vita at the town hall, yanked open the door. *"Yes?"*

Hoping to forestall a shouting match, and since as far as Abigail knew, she had money and might be interested in buying the house, Annie smiled ingratiatingly. "Good afternoon, may we speak to you a moment?"

"Well—" Abigail eyed Claudius with disfavor. "All right, come in, but not the dog."

At which, Claudius promptly slipped past her and sat down, looking as if butter wouldn't melt in his mouth.

Abigail didn't have time to waste standing on the front step arguing, and after glaring at him for another second, snapped, "All right. But make sure he doesn't touch anything. If he does, you've bought it."

She led the way past a line of stacked, open cardboard boxes.

"They're about to make a getaway," hissed Jacob to Annie.

It was all too likely. Maybe Jacob was right about a few other things. What if Abigail and her husband had murdered her uncle and were now getting out while the getting was good? Presumably, if they hadn't disposed of his body already, they'd bury old Wallace Horne in the backyard. Perhaps the old man's corpse was stashed somewhere in the house. Downstairs in the cellar, maybe. They could have put him in a freezer. He'd keep for months, indefinitely.

"What do you want? If it's about the mechanical card device collection, just forget it!" Abigail folded her arms across her chest, annoyed and not caring in the least if they knew it.

"You've got it," Jacob retorted. "And we want it." He shifted so his jacket pocket was closer to Abigail. "You and your husband had a lot to say a little while ago. Would you care to repeat it, now that I've got me a witness?"

Abigail sneered, "She's your witness?"

"You're darn tootin'!" Jacob maneuvered closer. You never could tell with these new-fangled electronic devices, and he hadn't read the directions all the way through. He gave his pocket a brisk tap to get it going.

Claudius snuffled the bottom of the nearest stack of filled boxes, which he set to teetering slightly. Annie held her breath and hoped it was nothing breakable.

There was a short, icy silence, which Abigail occupied by tapping her elegantly shod foot. Naturally, Claudius transferred his attention to the shoe that wasn't moving. He drooled on the toe, then licked her ankle for good measure.

"For heaven's sake, get that disgusting animal away from me!" Abigail leaped backward, brushing off her ankle. "This is ridiculous! You might as well leave. We're up to our ears with packing—"

"I thought you were going to wait a few months and advertise a big sale," Annie said cleverly, sensing she had the woman on the defensive.

"Well, we were going to do just that, but after that stupid program about haunted houses—and the paper will carry a full account, thanks to that wretched Charlemagne woman—we've decided the best thing to do is to cut our losses and sell the house immediately. Once the word gets out, we'll never get what we should for it."

Annie gazed up at the ceiling. She could hear heavy objects being dragged around overhead, then soft footsteps descended the stairs. Someone was coming, reinforcements—no doubt, Nathan Woodruff.

"Do the right thing and return the collection to the historical society," she said hurriedly. If she talked fast, maybe she could persuade Abigail to part with it before Nathan arrived and threw them out on their ear.

There was another creak on the stairs, then silence. Obviously, he'd decided to stand there a while and eavesdrop.

God helped those who helped themselves, she decided, for the moment ignoring the flip side—God help those who got caught.

She whipped out the plumber's bill for her new hot water tank and waved it under Abigail's outraged nose, making sure she couldn't read Paul Kelleher's name at the top. "This is a copy of the receipt for the collection. It says right here that Wallace Horne has given it to the historical society in *perpetuity*. Which means *forever*! So hand it over right now or be prepared to face the consequences, and I warn you, they won't be pretty." Jacob, gaping at her with astonishment, had the sense to keep his mouth shut. Annie raised her voice, "Would you care to see the receipt, Mr. Woodruff? I'd be glad to show it to you."

Claudius stood up and shook himself, ready to go home. This was boring.

Nathan appeared in the doorway and glared at them both. "The hell with you! You're nothing but a pair of damn troublemakers!"

"Whatever." Annie put the plumber's bill back in her pocket. Claudius heaved a sigh and sat down again. This was going to take all day.

Meanwhile, Annie had noted warily that Nathan hadn't shown up empty-handed. He was holding one of this afternoon's blue programs. Belatedly, she remembered that he'd been there. He'd let Abigail do all the shouting, but he'd been there, all right, biding his time. So he'd certainly seen her donate the check, and he couldn't have missed those wretched slides of the tavern. They'd been blurry, but even a blind man would have noticed the peeling paint and leaky roof. It was going to be impossible to maintain the fiction that she was a wealthy woman, interested in buying the Horne mansion. Her cover was blown.

Claudius shook himself again and let out an encouraging bark. Were they going to stand around here all day?

The Woodruffs promptly scurried behind a large table and Annie jerked his leash. "Mind your manners, quiet!"

"So," said Jacob, gloating, "do I take it you're now willing to hand over the collection?"

"Oh, for heaven's sake, take the damn thing!" Grabbing a large leather case, Abigail shoved it at him.

Cradling it lovingly in his arms, he beamed. "Thank you!"

Leather? Claudius caught the alluring scent and at once leaped to his feet. "No, you don't!" Annie cried. She shortened his leash, winding it around her hand a half dozen times while he eyed her accusingly.

"And you!" Nathan shouted, glaring at her, "have an

almighty nerve! You couldn't even scare up the money for a down payment on a chicken coop. I made a few phone calls. The only thing you own is that Bates motel of a house you live in." Careful to avoid coming too close to Claudius, who was regarding him with open dislike, he stalked around the table to fling open the door. "Get out, both of you!" He stood back ungraciously as they swept past with heads held high.

Jacob was triumphant, clutching the suitcase with its precious contents, hardly believing his luck. Claudius was pleased, they were on their way at last and it was almost dinnertime.

But Annie suddenly had a disturbing thought. Hadn't the Woodruffs yielded too easily? They couldn't wait to get them out of the house. Why? Because they wanted to finish packing? Nobody liked packing, unless they were crazy. No, they'd kicked them out because they had something they wanted to do without witnesses.

They wanted to move Wallace Horne's body.

CHAPTER
17

By the time Annie took Jacob back home, the notion that the Woodruffs were only waiting until nightfall to move Wallace Horne's body had, in his mind, become a dead certainty.

But when he told Isaac what had happened, he flew into an uproar. "They're going to do *what*?"

"Move the body, of course," said Jacob, his eyes gleaming. He thought of having a quick snack, but that could wait. This was more important. He trained the binoculars on the Woodruffs' back door. He didn't intend to miss anything.

"I don't believe this. Jesus H. Christ!" Isaac yelled. "See what I have to live with?"

"Get real." Jacob was glued to the window, intent on the slightest movement next door.

"You're getting senile, like Uncle Ezra. The men in the white coats are gonna take you away."

Annie kept quiet, determined not to be drawn into this. Whatever the Woodruffs were up to, it was nothing but speculation on Jacob's part anyway. She went out to the kitchen and made their dinner, after which, she ran the vacuum around, and left them to their own devices.

She took Claudius and went home. She had an inn to run and dinner to fix. Edgar Whittles expected five-star accomodations for what amounted to peanuts. What he'd get was basic New England cooking made from whatever was handy. Just before five o'clock, she turned on the radio. Barry Manilow warbling about the Copacabana. Well, he'd have to get her through throwing a three-course meal together for Mr. Obnoxious. She had better things to worry about than the state of Edgar Whittles's stomach. While she was shoving an apple spice cake in the oven, the telephone rang.

"Thurston Tavern." She waited, but the person on the other end said nothing. "Hello, this is the Thurston Tavern. Is anyone there?" Still no answer, then a quiet click as the receiver on the other end was replaced.

Kirk Dietrich came in the back door and hung up his coat. "Who was that?"

"Wrong number," she said, wondering if it was true and hoping fervently that it was. She went back to the kitchen and checked the oven timer as the phone rang again.

Kirk was closer. "I'll get it," he called. A moment later, "Annie, it's for you."

She went back to the front hall and took the receiver. "Hello?"

It was Prudence Cannell. "I did the Tarot for you, and it looks real bad. The Grim Reaper turned up. Even worse, my brother's on his way over. He's been drinking."

"Well, what do you expect me to do about it?"

"That's your problem. I've done all I can. Mike's got a bad reputation. He's a mean drunk. You don't want to mess with him."

Claudius wandered in from the kitchen, where he'd been licking the mixing bowl. He sniffed Kirk's jean-clad legs, instantly learning where he'd been all day and what he'd been doing. Kirk patted him on the head.

"I hear you're staying. You know which side your bread's buttered on, don't you, old boy." Giving the dog another pat, he went upstairs, leaving Annie in the front hall, still trying to make sense of what Prudence was telling her.

"Hey, I've done all I can," the psychic grumbled. "Just

watch your back. Like I said, the death card came up twice. The cards never lie. What happens, happens."

"Forget the death card. Mike's your brother. If you care about him, call the police before he hurts himself or anyone else."

"I'm not getting mixed up in this."

"You're already in this up to your neck. You wrote those threatening letters to May."

Prudence gave a short, ugly laugh. "The cops already hauled us down to the station and gave us the third degree about that. Mike thinks you told them he killed her. He's out for blood."

With dismay, Annie realized it didn't matter what Mike thought. He didn't need a reason. He was mad and he was drunk.

Prudence was thinking out loud. "Maybe I'll leave town till this dies down. My cousin in Portland owes me a favor." This idea seemed to give her fresh courage. "If anything happens to you, it's not my fault. So I wrote a few letters to May, that's all I did. I didn't kill her and neither did my brother." The phone banged down in Annie's ear.

She stood there a moment, wondering if Prudence and the Tarot knew something she didn't, then dialed 911. In due course, and much to her surprise, she was connected to the officer on duty who said they'd have a car ride by the house. They'd keep an eye out for Mike, and if and when he showed up, they'd have a talk with him.

This was hardly reassuring, but there wasn't much Annie could do about it. She got the poker from the living room fireplace and put it by the front door in case Claudius decided the day's agenda didn't include protecting her.

About five minutes later, the phone rang again. This time it was Gus Jackson. "What's this about you wanting a patrol car to drive by the house?"

"Well, I didn't exactly—"

"What the hell's going on? No, don't tell me. I already

know more than I want to. Stay indoors. Don't answer the door if anyone knocks."

Claudius, sitting at Annie's feet, gave a worried snort. All these phone calls were annoying him.

"Was that the dog?"

"Yes."

He sighed. "Just do what I told you to." He hung up without saying good-bye.

Which was a good thing, Annie found herself thinking. Because she had something to take to the police station. A trip downtown to drop off May's handbag and ring was clearly in order. She went to the closet and got her coat.

Trotting to the front door, Claudius sat down and waited. Something was going on. It required action, of what type he wasn't sure yet, but he intended to get in on it.

Outside, the wind moaned around the eaves, and she frowned as a tree at the far end of the cornfield went over with a faint crash. Momentarily, she remembered the old maple and was thankful she'd had Ralph Goddard take it down.

Claudius began pacing up and down, snuffling at the crack beneath the door. She grabbed his collar and hauled him off to the downstairs bathroom to lock him in, but he wriggled free and ran back to the front door.

"You're staying home. Get in the bathroom."

He sat down where he was. Who was she kidding?

She pointed to the bathroom. "Get in there. Now!"

He yawned widely.

"Damnit, I mean it!"

He acknowledged her frustration by wagging his tail.

"I don't need this." She waited. He didn't move. She gave up. "Okay, but just this once."

Oh really? He was smirking triumphantly as he dragged her out to the car and jumped in.

"I hate you," she told him.

Engrossed in the scenery whizzing by, he ignored this lie. She didn't mean it. He was eminently lovable.

She hunched over the wheel and concentrated on the matter at hand. The sudden appearance of the ring and handbag in the barn had to be connected with the strange goings-on she'd seen the other night by the entrance to the maze. Which was exactly what she told the officer on duty as, fifteen minutes later, having parked in the lot behind the police station, she went inside and plunked the ring and handbag down on the counter.

Officer P. Morrison, a blond woman in her thirties with a hard face and mild-looking brown eyes, drew them through the opening in the bulletproof glass, a security improvement included in last year's fiscal budget, along with a request for semiautomatic weapons, which, not surprisingly, hadn't passed.

After placing May's property in a manila envelope, she handed Annie a receipt and went down the hall. A moment later she returned with Gus Jackson. He inspected the contents of the envelope and then hustled her back outdoors.

He wasn't happy. "Do you know what you just did?"

"Don't shout. I'm not deaf."

"Tampered with evidence in a criminal matter. That's a felony."

"That's ridiculous. I found them in my barn. I was storing Halloween decorations in the loft. I called you earlier and got one of your stupid recorded messages, so I brought them down here, like any law-abiding citizen."

He eyed her gloomily. "Okay, let's say you didn't do it deliberately, but the fact remains, that's what happened. We'll check the barn, take it apart, board by board if we have to, but any remaining clues are probably gone, destroyed when you moved the Halloween decorations. If and when we discover May Upton's killer, he or she just may get off because you screwed up the forensics. By the way, where was your brother the night Jack Hogan fell off the church tower?"

This last didn't sound promising. "If Hogan's death was a suicide or accidental, what does it matter where he was?"

"Humor me."

"Tom and his wife were separated. Now they're back together. They're having a second honeymoon."

"Isn't that convenient."

"Let's stick to the point. What about May's ring turning up in my barn? It was on Hogan's finger two days ago. Somebody planted it in my barn. The same person who pushed him off the belfry."

"Ah, yes. The mysterious person on the belfry and the ring you say you saw." He smiled. "We'll deal with them if and when we have to. You're probably wrong. You didn't see anyone but Hogan up on the belfry, and he never had May Upton's ring. He was a packrat. What you saw was probably a cheap ring he picked up at the dump."

"It was *May's*. I'd recognize it anywhere."

"Sure, and maybe you need glasses."

She wasn't getting anywhere. Obviously, he was more concerned over her having tampered with evidence than the discovery of May's ring. Disgruntled, and wondering if she'd really screwed up the police investigation, Annie stomped back to the car and got behind the wheel.

Claudius sensed her mood and whined as she put the key in the ignition. He gave her a worried look.

She scratched his big ears. "It's okay, we're going home. Nothing to worry about."

He stared out the window while she started the engine and zipped out of the parking lot. His expression said he wasn't buying a word of her white lies. The trouble was, she didn't, either.

The rest of the afternoon dragged by. There was no sign of Mike Cannell, thank God. She considered the options. This was a no-brainer: Either the cops had pulled him over and made him see the error of his ways, or he'd passed out somewhere. Either way, it was better to be safe than sorry, and since Claudius had parked himself by the stove in the kitchen, in case anything edible fell on the floor, she left the poker right where it was by the front door.

She opened the shop and four customers stopped by. Two from out of state: New York and Massachusetts, which, together with their Armani suits, Lily Pulitzer dresses, and Gucci handbags, meant money. The other two were from New Hampshire and wore the usual jeans and a jacket, but in any case, it hardly mattered where they were from or what they had on since she didn't have anything they were interested in. Then, just as she'd given up the ghost and was closing up, another car pulled in. This one from Maine, a woman looking for a set of country pine kitchen chairs. Happily, Annie had a set of six and sold them for seven hundred dollars.

Six o'clock. Iris was going out tonight, again. Annie put on a pot roast for Edgar and Kirk's dinner. A note from Edgar on the table by the front door informed her that he'd gone out to meet a real estate dealer. He was looking for a lakeside property. For a man who'd been paranoid just a few days ago, he was now acting as if everything was fine and dandy. Despite his sister's murder and Jack Hogan's recent demise, the heat was off as far as his gambling debts went—there'd been no sign of Fat Louie or Bennie the Shiv. Life had returned to normal.

She was still brooding about this when she had a brilliant idea. If she could reenact Jack Hogan's death at the church, she might be able to prove he'd been murdered. But she needed two people to help. Stooges. The plan was for one to be Jack Hogan, the other to stand in for Vita downstairs on the church porch, who might have seen more than she thought she had.

She dialed Vita's number.

"Yes?" Vita snapped. Evidently she was in one of her moods. This was going to take some work.

"It's Annie O'Hara. Could you meet me over at the church? I have several bags of canned goods and nonperishable food items for the food drive. I'd like to drop them off at the church tonight."

"I wasn't planning on going out." An annoyed sigh. "Does this have to be done now?"

"Well, yes. The food drive ends this week, and I have quite a lot to bring over."

There was a pause at the other end. Annie suspected that Vita had put her feet up for the night, but greed warred with sloth and in the end won.

"Oh, all right. I'll drive over and let you in."

A few minutes later, Annie had loaded half a dozen bags of canned goods, mixes, soup, rice, chili, and various other edibles in the Volvo, and was just closing the back, when Edgar arrived home. She explained that she needed his help for a half hour or so. At first he was reluctant to go anywhere near the church, but she wore him down, and soon they were on their way.

When they got there, Vita, already waiting for them, unlocked the belfry tower door. "I don't understand why this had to be done tonight. You could just as well have dropped off everything in the morning."

"I have an early appointment," Annie said airily. "By the way, there's one more thing I want to do while we're here."

"What?" Vita demanded.

"Hey," said Edgar, standing on the porch, arms loaded with groceries. "What the hell's going on?"

"As long as we were going to be here," Annie said, "I thought we could reenact Jack Hogan's death."

"Hmmph," Vita said. "Why would we want to do that? The man's dead. Good riddance to bad rubbish."

"What if he was murdered like May Upton?" Annie asked. "Someone's running around town killing people. What if he's not done yet?"

The frown on Vita's face deepened. The notion of a mad killer roaming the streets was something she hadn't considered. "What's the point? Reenacting Jack Hogan's death is impossible. It's not raining and it's dark. We can't see anything."

"We'll see all we need to," Annie explained. "Conditions aren't the same, but close enough. Besides, I'd like to be sure of exactly what happened—if he jumped, fell, or was pushed. Wouldn't you like to be sure?"

"I *am* sure," Vita snapped. "I didn't have to come over here. I'm doing you a favor, although God only knows why. I have better things to do than stand around wasting my time."

"That's right," Edgar said.

"Oh, Edgar!" Annie had almost forgotten about him. "You're Jack Hogan. Go up and stand on the balcony."

"I'm sure the vicar won't be pleased when he finds out what you've been up to," Vita said.

Annie didn't bother to reply. The groceries were a perfect cover, and she hadn't even bothered to call the rectory. The vicar was sure to be busy setting up bingo night over at the Elk's Hall. She went back to the car for the last two bags and set them down by the belfry door.

Vita grabbed a can and checked the label. "This chili says 1998. We can't give that out."

Annie snatched it back and stuffed it in her pocket. "The rest are fine. Trust me." Then she hurried up the stairs after Edgar, who was complaining that this was nothing but a waste of time. He was an important man. Time was money. He didn't have all day. "Well!" he shouted down at her. "Hurry up!"

She raced up the staircase. "Sorry, stand in the middle of the balcony, near the railing."

"Are you sure it's safe? The railing looks flimsy, and there's a lot of rust."

"The church has it inspected yearly. Besides, it didn't break when Jack Hogan went over it the other night."

From down below, Vita yelled, "Aren't you done yet?"

"Pretend it's the other night," Annie shouted back. "What do you see?"

"Nothing, it was pitch-black out."

"But we had lightning. You saw Jack Hogan, remember? You were angry because he was up here."

"He had no right trespassing on church property," Vita said.

Edgar sighed. "Can we go home now?"

"No, move over, more to the right." Annie edged him closer to the railing. "Wave your arms the way Hogan did, while I crouch behind you." She bent down as Edgar flapped his arms up and down. "Okay, Vita, what do you see now?"

"The same nonsense I've seen for the past ten minutes. Mr. Whittles flapping his arms like a duck."

"Keep watching." Annie pressed her hands firmly into the small of Edgar's back. He yelped and grabbed the thigh-high railing, steadying himself.

"Hey, what are you trying to do?"

"Pretend you just fell over." She examined the balcony, which wasn't large, really more decorative than functional. To the left, on the outside of the railing a set of steps led down to the Fellowship Building roof.

It had rained heavily the other night, but the police had treated Hogan's death as an accident. They might have overlooked something. She leaned over the railing and pointed her flashlight down the steps. Unfortunately, one thing she hadn't taken into account was her tendency toward vertigo.

It looked a long way down. She broke out in a cold sweat and started hyperventilating. Common sense said it was a mere ten or fifteen feet. Who cared. It looked like a hundred.

About to heave her leg over the railing, her shoe brushed something, and she aimed the flashlight in the corner. A few scraps of straw and a cigarette butt. She put them in her pocket, told herself there was nothing to be afraid of, climbed over the railing, and started downward, her heart in her mouth.

"What about me?" Edgar demanded.

"You're dead."

It was difficult managing the flashlight when her hands wanted to hold onto the fire escape with a death grip. Fear of heights was ridiculous, yet the more she told herself not to think about it, the worse it got. Eventually, and gasping for air, she lowered herself gingerly to the Fellowship Building roof. By now, Edgar had stomped off downstairs to join Vita on the porch.

Presumably Jack Hogan's killer wasn't afraid of heights. He'd raced down the fire escape, then across the roof and down to his car, conveniently parked on the side street. All of which meant that Hogan's death had been carefully planned in advance. Hogan had been lured to the belfry and murdered in a manner meant to look like an accident or suicide. Either way, the killer knew the police would jump at the chance to close the books on his death.

Annie felt her way across the slanting roof to the fire escape at the back. Moments later, her feet hit terra firma, and she let out a heartfelt sigh.

An examination of the side street revealed nothing unusual. A narrow road that went from left to right along the block was Withington Lane. A row of six small houses, one of them currently up for sale. The front yards enclosed by either picket fences or privet hedges, contained a few scraggly roses in the process of losing the last of their leaves, handkerchief-size patches of dead grass, and several nondescript flower beds. Behind them were small backyards, garages, and a few garden sheds. Beyond that were the houses on the next street.

But just across the way, all but one of the houses were shrouded in darkness. In one directly in front of the church, a flickering bluish light in a downstairs room. Someone was watching TV. Upstairs in an attic window, a pink and blue neon beer sign glowed. A teenager's room or perhaps a billiard room. In any case, no one who would have been looking out at the street the night Hogan died. No one who saw the killer get in his car and drive away.

He'd gone about his deadly business with impunity.

The weather had helped cover his tracks. The heavy rain had washed away all trace of his presence on the roof. Still, Annie examined the street near the fire escape. There was an oily sheen near the curb. Recent, not more than a day or two old. Perhaps the murderer's car leaked oil and the rain hadn't washed it away.

Unfortunately, despite a certain theory forming in her mind, none of this clever, deductive reasoning did any practical good. There was no real proof, nothing the cops were likely to listen to.

Even if she was right about the murderer's identity, she couldn't imagine a motive strong enough to make someone do this.

By the time she'd trotted around to the front of the church, she found Edgar pacing up and down, all by his lonesome. Vita had gone home in a huff.

"Well, did you find anything?" he demanded

"Maybe, maybe not." She gave him a tight smile and said they were going home.

By six thirty-five, Annie had settled him in the dining room, served up pot roast, and left for the Buchmans'.

She didn't know a whole lot about Bingo, but God, was Iris sick or what? There had to be more to life than matching numbers on little cards. When Annie got there, Iris was raring to go, already in her coat.

"Come on in," she said, ushering Annie through the long hallway down to the kitchen. "I've been baking. Everything smells wonderful."

She'd made apple pies for the Home for the Elderly. Several dozen pies were cooling on the kitchen counter. Annie was to wrap them in foil and then take them down to the freezer in the cellar.

"Steve adores apple pie," Iris said. "You'll have to keep an eye on him. He's liable to get into them and get sick." She smiled. "You've made quite a hit with Steve."

"That's nice," Annie said. One more white lie wouldn't hurt. Iris was a nice person. Why hurt her feelings.

"I almost forgot. The kitchen phone is broken. If you need to call anyone, use the one in the front hall. I called the phone company and they said they'd repair it, but they never showed up. One more thing, keep the cellar door locked. The stairs are steep. If Steve goes near them, he might get hurt."

"Hello." Speak of the devil.

Steve had wandered downstairs, noticing that his wife had her coat on. He started toward her, and in the commotion—Iris hadn't seen him and had turned away—her purse fell to the floor and popped open, the contents spilling out.

Annie helped her pick it all up: wallet, keys, handkerchief, cigarettes and matches, and a small tape recorder, a twin to Jacob Gander's.

Iris dropped it back in her purse. "It's handy. I always think of things when I don't have a piece of paper." She beamed. "Bingo awaits. Wish me luck, bye!"

The next half hour passed uneventfully. Steve announced he was hungry and shuffled to the kitchen for a quick bite to eat, and she paused in wrapping and freezing pies to fix him a bowl of corn chowder.

He ate halfheartedly, staring around the kitchen. He smelled the pies and that's what he really wanted.

"I like apple pie," he mumbled wistfully, his gaze returning to hers.

What the heck. One measly pie more or less wouldn't matter.

She went down the steep stone cellar stairs and got one of the pies that hadn't looked quite as perfect as the others. Surely Iris wouldn't mind if he had one piece. A big piece. God knows the poor man didn't have much to make him happy.

Steve's face lit up when she returned. "One piece," she told him, cutting a large slice. "How about watching TV in the den while you eat?"

He nodded and started for the den almost before she'd

put everything on a tray. When she turned on the TV and flashed the remote around, she happened to land on a monster truck rodeo, where trucks with beefed-up engines and huge tires whizzed around in mud, bashing into one another. Steve seemed entranced at first, then she noticed that he rubbed his forehead as if it was hurting. The sight of the trucks could have called up memories of his accident.

She aimed the remote and found cats and dogs. That seemed safe enough. A canine agility competition. Big dogs, little dogs leaping over obstacles, through tunnels and a slalom course. Steve relaxed in a wing chair and chomped his pie. Claudius flopped on the rug, eyes glued to the screen. They were in seventh heaven.

Annie went back to her chores in the cellar. Five minutes later the phone rang. She closed the freezer and traipsed back up the narrow stone stairs to the front hall.

It was Iris. "Thank goodness, you answered—there's a yellow pad on the table. I jotted down a number, then forgot to take it with me." In the background, Annie heard laughter and chattering voices. The bingo session was in full swing.

The number was right where Iris said it would be. It was a local number, and vaguely familiar. Annie repeated it to Iris and realized after a second that it was David Kelleher's number. The plumber. Life was full of coincidences. Iris must be having plumbing or heating problems. Hopefully, the toilet flushed. She'd given Steve a pretty big piece of apple pie.

"My pencil broke. Wait a sec—I've got a pen here someplace." Sounds of Iris scrabbling in her purse. "Okay, what's the number again?"

Annie repeated it, and Iris thanked her hastily, said she'd be home soon, and hung up. But Annie had barely put the phone down when there was a terrible crash from the back of the house. *The cellar* . . .

"Oh, God, Steve!" She flew down the hall to the kitchen. The cellar door was standing wide open, which was strange since she'd shut it securely and locked it. She looked down the stairs. It was dark. The light was off. Had she left it on? She couldn't remember. "Steve?"

No answer, but the TV in the den was still on, a commercial break just ending.

Claudius, where was he?

As if he had a sixth sense, he trotted in from the den. He was chewing something. She hoped it wasn't anything Iris cared about. It made a crunchy sound between his teeth, like a dog biscuit—but where had he gotten a biscuit?

"Steve?" She turned back to the cellar stairs, afraid to go down there, but knowing she had no choice. "Steve, are you down there?"

No answer, but a terrible stillness.

At the top of the stairs she paused. It was pitch-black down there. She flicked the switch, and nothing happened. The bulb must have burned out.

A frantic search of the pantry turned up some light bulbs, and she carefully groped her way down a few steps, and put in the new one. Immediately, the cellar flared into view. "Steve?" She caught sight of something small and shiny to the right of the first step, then she saw Steve's body at the foot of the stone steps and raced down the stairs. *He was all right. Hopefully, he hadn't broken any bones. He was all right . . .*

Only a miracle would make him all right. His head was caved in, and there was so much blood she couldn't tell where it was coming from. His eyes were open but sightless, and his right arm was bent under his body at an impossible angle. The wall behind him was spattered with blood.

Gagging sounds were coming from her throat. She swallowed bile and put a hand to his neck, but couldn't find a pulse. *Oh, God, he wasn't breathing.*

As luck would have it, Claudius chose that moment to come downstairs to see what was going on, and she had to grab his collar to keep him away. He wanted to stay where the action was. He whined low in his throat. "No.

Back upstairs," she told him, and somehow managed to drag him back up with her. She shut the cellar door with hands that shook, then ran to the telephone in the front hall.

It took two tries to get the number right. She waited, praying it wouldn't be the damned recording. Then, just as a real live human being—a man—said, "Lee police station. What's the problem?", a terrible scream echoed from the cellar. A woman's scream.

Annie's heart jumped in her mouth. Iris. She'd come home early and found her husband dead, but how had she gotten into the house? By the back door, probably—

She dropped the phone and raced back to the cellar. The door was standing wide again.

"He's dead!" Iris screamed from the bottom of the steps, where she was bent over her husband's body. "Damn you, you left the door open! I told you—"

"No, I'm sure I locked it when you called. God, I'm so sorry."

"Sorry? What good is that? You couldn't have locked it! If you had, Steve would still be alive!"

"I'll call an ambulance," Annie babbled, trying to do what she could. There was no way she could make things right. She concentrated on Iris's tear-stained face. She couldn't bear looking at Steve's bloody head cradled in her arms.

"Go ahead," Iris sobbed. "Not that it will do any good!" At the top of the stairs, Claudius began howling, his head back, fur bristling. "I can't stand this," Iris shrieked. "Shut that damn dog up!" She stumbled upstairs. Her coat was bloodstained, her face haggard, streaked with tears. "I'll get the ambulance. You wait with Steve."

Near the top step, she stumbled and grabbed the wall, luckily without falling back downstairs. White-faced, she brushed past Annie, who numbly did as she was ordered. Maybe Iris would find comfort in positive action, not that an ambulance would make any difference to poor Steve.

At the foot of the stairs Annie waited, the light overhead swinging, light and shadow flashing across the white-washed fieldstone wall. She called, "Iris, are they coming? Did you get through?"

No answer. Iris was probably still on the phone.

She looked around. There was a long, horrible, bloody streak on the wall by the last step.

She stood up, one hand on the wall well away from the stain, looking anywhere but at the lifeless body at her feet. Her mind was a frantic jumble of thoughts. God, she felt so guilty. She must have left the door open, but she had a distinct memory of having closed and locked it. It was a simple hook and eye, but Iris had thought it enough to keep Steve out. Evidently, she'd been wrong.

She looked around the cellar, anywhere but at the man at her feet. A collection of keys on a wall pegboard. They dangled like earrings, old keys, big and small, mostly brass. Some with big locks. Others with small, white tags. Hundreds of keys. One in a maple frame, a replica of the key to the Bastille.

"Annie!" Iris's urgent shriek from the front hall broke the silence.

"What?" she yelled, scrambling halfway up the stairs. A sudden bumping and scrabbling of claws, and Claudius barreled through the cellar door like a raging wolf. He rushed downstairs, all but knocking her over. He'd decided to check on Steve. Somehow she got one hand through his collar and the other around his neck to drag him away. He'd already started sniffing at Steve's pant legs, working his way up to the bloody head.

"No—oof!" His hind quarters bumped her into the wall shelf, knocking over a carton of old photographs and odds and ends. A stack of photographs tumbled out, the one on top a shot of a man in a fishing hat and waders in a stream, holding up a large fish.

He was smiling.

CHAPTER

18

The man in the photograph looked familiar. Some of the keys looked familiar, too. She'd seen several before. In fact, she'd sold them. She turned one of the tags over. Yes, August 6, last year. Eighteenth-century brass key, Boston. Even the price he'd paid: twenty dollars.

She remembered the sale. Three keys, part of a lot she'd picked up at auction. She'd cleaned them up and sold them to the man in the photograph, who must be Iris's first husband, Fred.

Annie kept a dish of hard candies by the shop cash register. If customers came in with kids, it kept them happy for a few minutes while their parents looked around and, hopefully, parted with some hard cash. The day Fred had bought the keys, he'd joked as he made out the check, saying he'd eaten too much candy lately. It wasn't good for his teeth. He'd gained weight since he'd stopped smoking. He had to go on a diet.

So they'd talked diets for a few minutes. She'd told him to cut out sugar and fat and he'd lose ten pounds right away. He'd laughed and said the trouble was that his wife was such a good cook.

He'd looked heavier than he did in the photograph, a good thirty or forty pounds, in fact.

Sirens shrieked in the distance, growing louder by the second.

It was creepy down here. She decided to go upstairs.

Steve didn't need her. There was nothing she could do for him, now or ever. No matter how long she stayed, he'd lie in that same crumpled heap, staring from his bloody blob of a face. He was definitely dead. He didn't need company, he needed an undertaker.

An hour ago, he'd been happily eating a slice of Iris's apple pie and watching TV. As her mother always said, it just went to show, you never knew. So it paid to make sure your underwear was clean and had no holes. You wouldn't want to lie on some hospital slab, dead, humiliated, while strangers cut off your holey underwear.

Annie hoped Steve's underwear was in good shape.

Of course it was. Iris was a marvelous housekeeper, another Martha Stewart. All those delicious apple pies, this beautiful house, a dream house, really—except for the deadly cellar stairs.

The air down here was cold and smelled of blood. It made her skin crawl. There was nothing more she wanted than to go upstairs, but there was something she could do for Steve. She could say a prayer for his immortal soul, always hoping that's what he would want. If he were a Buddhist, one of those Tibetans in the Himalayas, she could use a prayer wheel. She didn't have one of those, of course, but he didn't look like a practicing Buddhist anyway. He looked more like a white-bread Methodist, or a Baptist, a Christian, at any rate. You could never tell these days, though. People changed their religion at the drop of a hat. One minute they were devout whatever, then they got divorced or mad at their minister for some reason and became Presbyterians, Moonies, or lapsed Catholics, like herself.

On the other hand, Steve was never going to be a practicing anything again. Surely one Hail Mary wouldn't hurt. She crossed herself and said one silently.

The sirens' wail howled up the street, then stopped abruptly outside.

She went upstairs. If Iris knew about the Hail Mary, she

probably wouldn't be pleased, but it hardly mattered since Iris was already fit to be tied.

In fact, Iris was outside in the driveway, standing by the ambulance, talking to the paramedics. Annie couldn't hear what she was saying, but from the look of outrage on her face, it wasn't hard to figure out: Her husband was dead and it was all Annie O'Hara's fault.

More sirens as two cop cars arrived. Several cops jumped out and gathered around Iris and the paramedics, who were unloading equipment from the ambulance. Flashing blue and white lights flared eerily across their faces.

"Sorry." Annie stood aside in the kitchen doorway as two EMTs hurried past her with duffle bags and an orange stretcher.

Iris and the cops headed for the house. She was sobbing now, talking to the policemen in heaving gasps. "My . . . husband, Steve . . . is dead. He fell down the cellar stairs." She saw Annie and glared.

Everybody turned to stare at Annie.

"I thought I'd—" she started to say, but Iris interrupted.

"You left the door open! In spite of instructions not to. I warned you about the stairs. *Now my husband's dead. Are you satisfied?*" She broke off with a choking sob and leaned on one of the cops.

Both cops eyed Annie with expressions of deep disapproval.

"I didn't leave the door open," she said. "I locked it. I thought it was okay."

"Okay?" Iris shrieked. "How can it be okay if Steve's dead?"

"He must have unlocked it," Annie said. "The hook and eye isn't all that hard to work." But her protests only fueled Iris's rage.

"Steve didn't unlock it. You left it open!"

"I didn't leave the door open. And I didn't leave it unlocked!"

"We'll come in and take a look," one of the cops said,

with an air of stepping between two combatants. Iris tossed
her head, gave Annie a look that should have killed her
dead on the spot, and they went to the kitchen to check out
the lock. Then the officers tramped down into the cellar.

Iris stalked over and slammed the back door. "That damn
dog is shedding all over the place." Her voice was cold,
hard. Annie suspected she was focusing on Claudius to
avoid thinking about what the paramedics were doing down
in the cellar.

It was true, Claudius was shedding like crazy. Though
he'd been to the groomer's recently, she hadn't kept up
with the daily brushing he needed, and it showed. Several
clumps of thick, black fur had fallen to the floor.

She picked them up and put them in the trash as a sudden, horrible, thumping clatter sounded from below. The
steps were narrow and steep. Tight quarters. Steve had been
a large man, over six feet tall, more than two hundred
pounds. They were having trouble loading the body onto
the stretcher.

Claudius stood up and barked.

"Quiet," she said. "It's okay." She looked at Iris, who
was now blowing her nose. "I . . . noticed the key collection on the pegboard."

"They were my first husband's." Iris stuffed her handkerchief in her pocket. "People sent him keys from all over
the world."

"I saw his photograph in one of the boxes. He bought
some of the keys from my shop."

"Really," Iris said indifferently. She wasn't interested in
casual conversation.

"I only met him once, when he came into my shop. I
sold him three brass keys, eighteenth century. Made in
Boston." Annie was chattering out of sheer nervousness.
"He said he was on a diet, he'd stopped smoking and gained
a lot of weight—"

Iris stiffened. "I don't care what you talked about. *Steve
is dead, in case you've forgotten. And it's your fault!*"

"What can I say—" Thoroughly upset, Annie apologized again and wished she was somewhere else. The Gobi Desert. Mt. Everest.

Claudius yawned and sat down again. He was faking. He wanted to go down to the cellar, and only her stranglehold on the leash kept him where he was.

She looped it twice around her wrist as the paramedics trudged back upstairs with the heavy stretcher. They'd covered the body with a sheet. Blood was seeping through by his head.

One of the cops came back upstairs, leaving his buddy down in the cellar, presumably taking notes. This one took out a notebook and wrote like mad while Iris repeated her version of the night's unfortunate events: She'd left poor Steve in Annie's care for the evening and had gone out to play bingo, thinking her husband would be waiting for her when she returned. She'd been horribly wrong.

"Because Annie left the door open," she said flatly.

"The stairs are pretty steep." The cop glanced at the cellar door, the dangling hook. "Probably wouldn't keep out a little kid, let alone a grown man. Sure he didn't unlock it himself?"

"He never went down there alone," Iris snapped, thoroughly incensed. "He knew better. I told him a thousand times, 'Don't touch it,' and he never did."

"But you weren't here," the cop said. "You don't know what really happened."

"He never unhooked the door before," Iris huffed. Her eyes welled up and spilled over. "Why would he do it tonight? It's obvious *Annie* left it open. She disobeyed my instructions, and he's dead as a result of her carelessness. Criminal negligence!"

"Calm down, Mrs. Buchman." The cop turned to Annie. "Want to give me your version?"

"I was putting pies away in the cellar freezer. The phone rang. The one in the kitchen isn't working, so I had to come upstairs and go to the front hall to answer it. I heard this awful crash. I ran back and found the door open and the light burned out. I had to change the lightbulb. Couldn't see a thing."

The words were hardly out of her mouth when Iris started waving her arms, screaming, "Stop lying. You left the door open and he fell down the stairs. That's what happened."

This was getting old. If Iris and the cops didn't want to believe her, fine. Poor Steve was dead. It was a tragedy, but not her fault. Maybe when she calmed down, Iris would change her mind. Arguing with her now was pointless.

But Annie couldn't keep her big mouth shut. "I didn't leave the door open, and I didn't leave it unlocked; but I can't prove it. I had to find a light bulb. Then I screwed it in and saw Steve at the foot of the stairs. I realized he was . . . badly hurt. I tried to find a pulse. There wasn't any, so I ran upstairs to dial 911. Next thing I knew, Iris had come home and was screaming in the cellar."

The cop nodded. "Too bad, these things happen in old houses. The cellar stairs are steep and narrow, hard to navigate at the best of times. With the bulb burned out, it was a death trap."

This sounded eminently reasonable to Annie, but not to Iris, who pointed out that she'd lived in the house for several years without incident. No one had fallen down those stairs, and no one had died. She knew exactly what had happened, and no amount of bare-faced lies would change things. Fifteen minutes later, having run out of nasty things to say about Annie, Iris blew her nose again, wiped her eyes, and said she was quite exhausted. There were funeral details to work out, but she supposed that would have to wait.

"Probably not," the cop said. "Call Badger's Funeral Home. They'll pick up your husband's body from the hospital morgue. You'll have to go down and make further arrangements, of course."

At that point, the second cop came upstairs. They moved over to the back door and conferred for a minute, then the first cop asked Iris if she was all right. "Can we take you to a relative or friend for the night?"

"No, I'll be okay. It's just the shock of finding him like that."

Which seemed to wrap things up as far as Lee's finest were concerned. They told Iris how sorry they were, told her to call if there was anything they could do, and left.

The ambulance was already gone. Suddenly, the house seemed very large and empty.

There was an awkward silence. Annie opened the back door and looked at Iris. "Is there anything I can do? Someone I can call for you? You shouldn't be alone." She waited, hoping Iris had calmed down. They could talk things out. Iris would understand that it hadn't been her fault.

But Iris glared at her, her face distorted with anguish. "Don't you understand? Thanks to you, I'll be very busy making funeral arrangements for my dead husband!" More tears welled up in her eyes and spilled over. She wiped them away with a hand that shook. "Just take your damn dog and leave. I'll go down to the hospital to spend a little time with Steve before he's taken to the morgue."

"Oh." Annie hadn't actually thought of what they would do to Steve. Her brain seemed to have stopped functioning the minute he'd fallen down the stairs.

They'd do an autopsy. It was the law in cases of sudden death, so the logical place to take him would be the hospital morgue. A doctor would have to certify that he was dead, then perform the autopsy—

"Get out!" Iris shrieked.

She did.

All the way home in the car she kept hearing sirens screaming in her head. Twin images: Steve dead, crumpled like a bundle of old clothes by the blood-splattered wall. Iris, hysterical with shock and grief.

Annie tried not to think about that. Her mind fastened on other things as she drove through town. Inconsequential things. Anything to keep from remembering.

The blood.

The disgusting metallic smell.

And Iris, white-faced, screaming. Her hands and dress smeared red.

Stop it! Okay, what had she seen at the top of the stairs once she'd screwed in the new light bulb? That tiny glint. Something shiny, probably metal. She'd been looking down the stairs to keep from falling. The stairs were almost like a ship's cabin, with drawer pulls screwed into the sloping ceiling, so you could hang on while you went downstairs. That's when she'd seen that shiny thing. Just to the right, about ankle height near the edge of the riser. It had barely registered, because once she saw Steve, she couldn't see anything else.

Blood all over the place, seeping from his nostrils. His eyes staring—

She shivered. Claudius looked at her and whined.

"It'll be all right." She patted his head and went back to brooding, while he settled down on the front seat and thought about what was in the refrigerator that he could talk her out of once they got home.

It was not going to be all right, she told herself. Steve was dead, and she'd been accused of letting it happen. She was probably lucky she hadn't been charged with criminal negligence right then and there. If Iris had had her way, she'd have been clapped into handcuffs and hauled off to jail.

Suddenly, all she wanted was to get home, crawl into bed, and pull the covers over her head. Not that it would do any good. She knew in her bones that things were going to get worse. Something very bad was going to come out of all this, worse than even poor Steve's accidental death. If that was possible.

Hadn't the psychic, Prudence Cannell, said so? She'd done the Tarot. The Grim Reaper had come up twice, and the cards never lie.

By coincidence she passed the shop, Heavenly Illuminations, on the way home. The windows were dark, the "closed" sign on the door. No lights in the apartment upstairs. Prudence must have been serious about leaving town.

For some reason, Annie felt abandoned, as if the rats were leaving the sinking ship.

It wasn't until she'd pulled into her driveway and switched off the engine that it came to her—the shiny thing she'd seen. A protruding nail head or even a scrap of aluminum foil from the pies she'd wrapped. But the odd thing was that it had vanished the last time she looked, when the second cop came upstairs after the paramedics had taken Steve away. Whatever that tiny bit of metal had been, it was gone.

It didn't matter. Probably just some foil.

The very next day things went from bad to worse. First thing in the morning, nine o'clock, Vita Charlemagne called. Bad news spread fast. She'd heard about Steve Buchman's death.

Her voice was icy. She was blunt, direct, and very much to the point. "I'm sorry, Annie. I have the agency to think of. Iris Buchman is threatening to sue Hands and Hearts, citing negligence as the cause of her husband's death."

"I didn't do anything wrong, it was an accident," Annie explained, trying to keep calm. "No one's sorrier than I am about what happened, but it's not my fault!"

"That's not the point. You represented the agency. We've been disgraced. You'll have to go."

"If I were in any way to blame, the cops would have arrested me. They didn't, and I don't appreciate your insinuations that I did anything wrong!"

"And I don't like being hit with a million-dollar lawsuit! Let me tell you, Annie O'Hara, I wasn't born yesterday. I have no idea why you did what you did. Furthermore, I don't care. Under the circumstances, the only thing to do is terminate your connection with us and hope Iris agrees to settle out of court—"

"Don't bother," Annie yelled. "I wouldn't work for your agency if you crawled on your hands and knees!" She slammed down the phone.

Who cared what Vita Charlemagne thought or did.

The morning paper had arrived. She shut the door in Claudius's indignant face and dug it out from the bushes where the paperboy had tossed it. Unfortunately, she had to step over a small, feathered corpse. Pumpkin had been at it again.

Wonderful. Great. Death followed her around like Typhoid Mary.

She grabbed a trowel and gave the bird, a little chickadee who should have known better than to mess with a tomcat, a decent burial under the rhododendrons. She put a small stone on the grave, then straightened and stood there with a sense of shock, thinking hard. *Somehow, it was all falling into place.*

Of course, it was possible; and it would explain everything that had happened in the past few weeks. Mayhem, murder.

It was hard to believe. People didn't do things like that. Strangers, maybe, but not neighbors—people you knew, or thought you did.

She swallowed hard, wondering if she should go to the cops. Did she have enough evidence? Any evidence?

No. She had squat. If she made accusations without proof, Gus Jackson would laugh in her face.

She went back in the house as the phone rang again. This time it was Jacob Gander. He'd already heard about the accident over his police scanner. "Terrible, Steve Buchman's dying like that. Weren't you helping out over there?"

She explained the whole sorry mess.

"Come over for lunch," he urged. "You didn't do anything wrong. It's plain as the nose on your face that it was an accident. I wouldn't worry about Iris Buchman. She'll probably get a nice fat insurance settlement—double indemnity. She'll be on easy street."

"I don't know. I feel terrible about it."

"Don't worry, there are no flies on Iris. She'll make out just fine. So, you're coming for lunch. You don't have to cook. I'll whip up something. Bring Claudius." He wasn't taking no for an answer.

Shortly after noon, Annie drove down to Main Street, plastered on a smile she didn't feel inside, and rang his doorbell.

Jacob swept her inside. "You look like you've lost your last friend. What you need is a good meal and a stiff drink."

She found herself and Claudius bundled down the hall to the living room. She was not to be allowed to set foot in the kitchen, she was told. They were preparing everything. After all, what were friends for in times of trouble?

Claudius greeted Isaac, who was sitting on the couch. He wagged his tail so hard he knocked Isaac's day's dose of pills off the coffee table.

"Good boy," Isaac laughed, bending to pick up the scattered pills. "Damnit, move your foot." Claudius licked Isaac's ear.

Annie frowned, aware suddenly of a burning smell from the kitchen. Lunch.

While Jacob took her coat, she checked the stove. Nothing was actually on fire, but the casserole was history.

"Is it ruined?" Jacob asked. "Maybe we could scrape the top layer off."

"I don't think so." She dumped it in the garbage. "Let's call out for pizza."

"So," she said, a half hour later, when they'd finished a Domino's special, "have you heard anything further from the Woodruffs?"

"Ha! They filled in one hole and dug another," Jacob said triumphantly.

"They what?" It was the last thing she expected to hear and made no sense at all. If the first hole had been a grave and they'd put Wallace into it, why dig another? They weren't serial killers. Or were they?

"Filled the first one in and dug another behind that big spruce," Jacob said. "I told you they were criminals. Nathan Woodruff's eyes are too close together. A dead giveaway, the first thing FBI profilers look for."

"Ridiculous!" Isaac sneered. "They're probably just what they say they are—honest people minding their own business, which is more than can be said about you."

"If you can sleep easy with a pair of cold-blooded killers right there on the other side of the hedge, then fine." Jacob sniffed. "But I'll have the last laugh when the cops catch them."

"All you've got is a bunch of what ifs. What if they killed Wallace Horne? What if they stuffed him in the freezer? What if they dug a grave in the backyard? You don't have a lick of proof that they've done a thing. The truth is, you don't know the first thing about the Woodruffs and you're not likely to." Isaac shrugged and poured himself a glass of Cabernet.

"I know what I saw and it's mighty suspicious." A flat statement of fact. Jacob was standing his ground. "Nathan Woodruff barely got that second hole dug, when he started yelling for Abigail. She came out, and I saw them carry a small trunk into the house. He must have dug it up out of that hole."

"They dug up a trunk and took it into the house?" jeered Isaac. "Ha! They weren't burying Wallace Horne, they were digging him up? That makes a lot of sense."

"Well, it's obvious, isn't it? They had to move the body once they knew I was on to them." Jacob's eyes gleamed. "Of course, they chopped the old boy up and stuffed him in that trunk. By now they've probably disposed of him in the furnace. Smoke's been coming out of the chimney all morning. Never mind, they can't get rid of everything. There's bound to be some evidence left, a tooth, a piece of bone.

"There was that notorious case in Connecticut, remember? A man bludgeoned his wife to death, and hid her in the freezer till he could rent a chipper. Late one night, he drove to a nearby river and fed her into the chipper. Pointed it down toward the water so the current would carry everything away. He thought he'd committed the perfect murder. No body, no evidence." Jacob grinned. "Just like the Woodruffs. But the cops turned up a tooth and enough of what was left of his wife for D.N.A. to prove her identity. Even then, he might have gotten away with it, but a passing motorist saw someone on the bridge with the chipper that night, and the killer had been dumb enough to use his credit card to rent the chipper. Plus, evidence still remained on the chipper, in cracks. He didn't get it clean enough."

"Enough is enough!" Isaac yelled, glaring at his brother.

"If we called Henry Lee, he'd know what to do," Jacob said thoughtfully. "That forensic pathologist who worked on the chipper case. Isn't he in New Haven?"

"I don't care where he is!" declared Isaac, thoroughly annoyed. He banged his wine glass down on the table so hard it spilled.

"Have another drink," Annie suggested.

"Best idea I've heard all day," he said, glaring at Jacob. He raised his glass. "To the divine grape. Gift of the Gods. The Romans may have been a tad barbaric, but they knew how to build roads and a little something about making wine."

The doorbell rang suddenly. Claudius barked from the kitchen. Isaac frowned. "Who could that be?"

"Holy Rollers, Jehovah's Witnesses—some damn bunch of nuts hell-bent on saving my soul," Jacob muttered, shoving back his chair.

"I'll get it," Annie said. As she went to the door, Claudius trotted in from the kitchen. He had the empty pizza box. She planted a knee in his face to keep him inside and opened the door a crack.

The Woodruffs stood there, holding a small trunk, and

obviously wondering why she was peeking at them through a crack. "You're not going out!" she told the dog. With considerable effort, she dragged him behind her and poked her head out. "Yes?"

Both Woodruffs frowned. Nathan shifted the trunk in his arms and said, "We'd like to see Mr. Gander. Jacob. If you don't mind."

"Oh." She opened the door wider and let them in. As they squeezed past, she managed to slam the door shut just in time. Claudius glared accusingly at her and woofed a protest that echoed deafeningly in the hallway.

"We'll just go on in, shall we?" Abigail darted after her husband, already hotfooting it in the direction of the living room.

What in the world was in the trunk, Annie wondered as Claudius nudged her with a cold nose. He'd smelled pizza on her fingers. Maybe she had some in her pocket.

He drooled.

She took a wheat grass biscuit from her pocket and offered it. He shook his head. Not on your life. He wasn't a vegetarian.

With a sigh, he trotted off after the Woodruffs. Jacob was in the living room. He could always be counted on for a delicious tidbit handed out under the table.

Annie got to the living room in time to hear Nathan Woodruff saying, "We thought we'd stop over and show you this." He set the trunk on the rug.

"Tired of digging up the backyard?" asked Jacob.

Nathan smiled and patted the trunk lid, which Annie noticed was rather dirt-encrusted. "Turns out all that digging was well worth it!"

"Why is that?" sneered Jacob.

"Because we found what we were looking for," Nathan said, flinging the lid of the trunk open to disclose a folded blanket. "My wife's uncle Wallace has enough money to indulge his taste in fine silver. But he became somewhat eccentric and decided a few years ago that he didn't trust his burglar alarm system. He buried this, the best of his silver collection, in the backyard."

Jacob sniffed. This was more trickery.

"Considering all the trouble you were taking," Nathan said snidely, "keeping an eye on things, we thought you deserved to see what we'd found. Without the aid of your binoculars."

"Oh, stop it," Abigail said. "Go on, show them what we found!"

Nathan was hoping to rub it in a little more, but allowed himself to be persuaded to remove the blanket. Once he did, a gleaming array of silver was revealed. Eighteenth-century. American, Annie judged, as he held up a teapot.

Paul Revere. Her mouth went dry. Her fingers itched to hold the lovely silver teapot. The surface was etched in delicate swirls and lines. The top sported a tiny acorn, the handle was ebony.

There wasn't a doubt in her mind. It was priceless.

Nathan smiled. "Would you like to hold it?"

She took it with trembling hands, turning it up to the light. Simplicity and elegance of form, purity of function. Lovely old soft patina, made by a master hand. At last she handed it back to him with a sigh of regret.

"The entire set is here," he said with pardonable satisfaction, considering everything. "Sugar, creamer, slop bowl, tray, even tongs, and a pot for hot water."

Jacob was still pretending he didn't much care what they'd had in the trunk. "Humph." He peered at the sugar bowl Abigail showed him. "You'll sell it." There was a hint of accusation in his tone. They'd sell it at auction to the highest bidder, and old Wallace Horne would never see a penny.

"My uncle knows we dug it up. In fact, he told us where he thought he'd buried it." Abigail put the sugar bowl back in the trunk as Nathan closed and fastened the lid. "We'd better go," she snapped, eyeing Jacob icily, "before I forget I'm a lady!"

They left.

CHAPTER
19

An hour or so later, Annie was back at home with Claudius, who was about to be groomed, whether he liked it or not. He eyed the brush in her hand with suspicion.

"This will hurt me a lot more than it does you," she said.

He realized at once that this was another lie, meant to keep him docile. Like a cow. The gleam in his eye should have told her he had no intention of cooperating, but Annie didn't see it.

"Stand still," she said, patting his back and taking a firm hold of his collar just in case. She had a fifty-fifty chance of success, depending on his mood—then she made the mistake of releasing the collar for a second to get a better grip. When she managed to grab the collar again, he was already in motion. He dragged her across the kitchen floor, tearing a large hole in the knee of her jeans.

"You must think I'm a complete idiot!" she yelled. "I'm not letting go no matter what you do." But in the end she did. It was either that or be dragged all over the house.

No one else was home to help, so she gave up and let him go. "Fine! I was going to brush you and get rid of that dead fur, but you'd rather look like something the cat dragged in."

He turned around and eyed her with suspicion. His tail wagged slowly.

There was a silence.

She inched closer, and he made no attempt to run off—

she couldn't catch him if she tried. He yawned and awaited further developments.

She crawled closer, pretending interest in a nearby chair leg. He shifted his feet, suddenly wary. But not quite enough. Before he had a chance to take off again, she caught hold of his collar, hauled him off to the cellar, pushed him inside, and slammed the door.

The barking from the other side was deafening.

"You had a chance to be good and you blew it."

He barked all the louder.

She turned on the kitchen radio. A talk show about hunting season, amusing stories about people shooting one another. She turned the volume way up. Let him think that over.

Meanwhile, she started dinner. White bean soup. Dessert would be poached pears and corn bread. She'd already soaked the beans and was just chopping carrots and celery, when she remembered she'd be eating alone. Kirk had to lead a seminar in Durham and would be back late. Edgar Whittle was in Laconia, looking over property for a summer home. Nothing suited him, and Annie suspected that in the end, he'd decide New Hampshire wasn't chic enough.

He'd mentioned Martha's Vineyard, hinting that he might fit in better with the East Coast upper crust.

Claudius finally fell silent, but she decided to let him contemplate his sins a while longer. She'd let him out later.

By seven, she'd settled herself in front of the fireplace with an old Agatha Christie.

She never quite knew when she fell asleep and began to dream. It seemed real, yet part of her mind knew it wasn't. She was in the church belfry with Vita, piling a huge stack of clothing. They kept slipping and fell to the floor, and she kept picking them up. A boot fell ...

Annie sat up straight in her chair. Footsteps. Soft, secretive. They came closer. The floor creaked in the hall.

Against the faint light from the kitchen down the hall, she saw a silhouette for a second. Then the intruder stepped into the room. It was Ralph Goddard.

She'd expected him, but not now, not so soon. The straw she'd picked up on the church belfry. In the past few days, he'd been out harvesting in his fields. Driving his tractor, baling hay. Bits of straw were bound to have gotten caught in his boots.

He'd killed Jack Hogan, but she didn't know why.

His eyes were on her face. He smiled. "Well, well, look who's here."

She forced herself to her feet. Her knees were shaky. "Did you want something? I didn't hear you knock."

"I didn't." His grin widened. He was carrying a thick rope.

She took a deep breath, her eyes flickering to the door, measuring the distance. If she was fast enough and her legs cooperated, she just might—

"Forget it," he said. "Too bad it's gotta be this way, but things got out of hand."

The back door closed, and quick footsteps approached down the hall. Feminine footsteps. "Ralph?"

Iris Buchman appeared in the doorway. "Oh, there you are. Good." She eyed Annie dispassionately for a second, then looked at Ralph. "What's the hold up? I thought she'd be dead by now."

"I don't like slip-ups," he said. "We take time to get it right. There's too much at stake to screw things up. Gotta look like suicide, remember?"

Annie swallowed. "Why?"

"Little Miss Nosy Parker," Iris said, strolling into the library. She snapped on a pair of rubber gloves. "Like your good friend, May Upton."

"May?"

Iris was obviously enjoying this. "The old bitch discovered Steve and I killed my first husband for the insurance. Unfortunately, after his accident, Steve tended to babble. I shouldn't have left him alone with May, but I figured she'd think he was talking nonsense. I had to let a few months pass before getting rid of him. Enough time so people would forget my first husband dying in the fire."

Annie already had figured out that much. All that talk about careless smoking had been a cover story. Iris had cleverly managed to blame her husband for his own murder.

"Worked like a charm," said Iris. "Steve burned down the cabin while I visited friends in Laconia, who'd vouch for my presence that evening. Then he had that stupid accident." She smiled at Ralph. "Luckily, Ralph's been very obliging. I had no intention of spending the rest of my life taking care of a drooling halfwit."

"What about his dog getting hit by that car last month?"

"Ralph, again. A big disappointment. Steve jumped out of the way in time. All he hit was the dog."

Annie frowned. "And no one suspected?"

"Oh, May did, and she wouldn't keep her big mouth shut, so she had to go." Iris was philosophical. One murder more or less didn't matter.

"What else?" Annie asked, determined to hear it all. The longer she kept them talking, the better her chances that Kirk or Edgar might come home.

"Sure you want to hear it?" Ralph smirked.

She felt very stupid. "The tree—you dropped it where we were supposed to stand, and the other night, that was you hiding May's pocketbook and ring in the barn."

He nodded.

"When Ralph cut down the tree," Iris explained, "we weren't after you, just Tom. He showed up, drunk, the night we killed May. Ralph chased her down in the maze. She tried to hide, but he caught her by the bridge and held her head under the water. Tom was stumbling around the driveway, waving a six pack. He spotted Ralph's truck, even walked part way into the maze looking for him before he passed out. At first we didn't think it mattered. Who'd listen to a drunk? Later we decided it was too risky. He just might remember seeing the truck, seeing Ralph. We couldn't take the chance."

"But Tom didn't do anything." Annie was stunned, sick. "It's horrible, killing for no reason—"

"Hell, I'd say three million bucks is plenty of reason,"

Ralph chuckled. "Accidental death. Double indemnity. Two policies. Iris makes out like a bandit."

"It's a shame we have to get rid of you," said Iris. "Without you, we couldn't have murdered Steve so tidily. You're so . . . gullible. So willing to be used."

"How—"

"Did we do it?" She shrugged. "Simple, really. I pretended to go to bingo. A few weeks ago, I recorded twenty minutes of bingo high jinks with my pocket recorder."

Annie stared at Iris, remembering Steve's knocking her purse on the floor and the small tape recorder falling out. *She'd had it right in her hand. She'd picked it up and given it back to Iris.*

"When I called from my car, I played the tape into the cell phone. You thought I was already over at the Elk's Hall. Ralph slipped in the back door. Gave some biscuits to the dog to keep him quiet, then rigged a wire across the top of the cellar stairs and screwed in a burned-out bulb. The wire was insurance, in case Steve got difficult. Luckily, all it took was a good push and the stone wall and stairs did the rest."

Annie couldn't bear to listen anymore. She edged toward the door.

"Stop right there," Iris produced a small gun from her pocket.

"Let's get this over with," Ralph said. "We haven't got all night." The way he was slapping that rope against his thigh gave Annie some incentive to listen some more.

"Wh . . . what about Jack Hogan?" *Please God, let Kirk or Edgar come home—*

Iris shrugged. "He happened to show up Halloween night, just about the time Tom did. He followed Ralph to the maze and saw him kill May. God, it was almost like Grand Central Station."

"Yeah, Hogan was a nobody, a schizo." Ralph smiled in a comfortable, folksy way that made Annie's blood run cold. "But he coulda made trouble. He grabbed the old girl's hand. Wanted that ring real bad, so I gave it to him. Figured it'd shut him up, but he started talking and holding those damn signs up all over town. Some of 'em were too close for comfort, so we got him up to the belfry and shoved him off. Piece of cake. He hit the parking lot like Humpty Dumpty, and I got away over the roof to the next block where Iris was waiting with the car."

He smiled again.

It wouldn't be long now, she realized dully.

"We'll rig something simple," he said. "Suicide. Cellar oughta do just fine. I'll throw the rope over a beam, put the noose around your neck, and kick over a chair. It'll be over before you know it."

Oh God, she wanted to scream, only there was no one to hear, and her throat was frozen.

"Let's go," Iris said, poking her in the side with the gun, urging her toward the kitchen.

The cellar door was twenty feet away now, fifteen . . .

"No one will believe I committed suicide," Annie gasped.

"Move." Iris poked her in the side again.

It was like getting slapped, hard. Annie's hands clenched into fists.

"Don't think anyone will believe you committed suicide?" asked Iris, amused. "Why not? It's perfect. You're sorry you caused poor Steve's death. You can't live with your guilt, so you take the only way out. We'll write a note and leave it for the police to find. Along the lines of, 'I didn't mean to hurt anyone. I can't bear the disgrace. Sorry—etc., etc.' " She laughed.

"As soon as the uproar over your suicide dies down, we'll arrange something for your brother." She dug the gun into Annie's back. "Drunk driving accident."

Her mouth dry, she said, "Go ahead, shoot me. Who'll believe a suicide with a bullet hole in the back?"

"She's got a point," Ralph said. "The gun could be trouble. Let me handle this."

"Oh, for God's sake." Iris shoved the gun back in her pocket. "Just kill her."

Ralph didn't waste time. He looped the rope around Annie's neck and grabbed the cellar doorknob. Everything seemed to happen at once. There was a huge, black, snarling blur as Claudius burst out, knocking Ralph flat. Iris began screaming and frantically scrabbled for the gun.

Annie yelled, "Claudius, help!"

Iris screamed louder as the growling dog charged, knocking her down the cellar stairs. From the racket she put up, it appeared she'd broken her leg.

Annie lost sight of everything in the whirling tangle of dog and man—swinging fists, scrabbling claws, snarling, kicking, and yelling. Then Claudius seized Ralph's arm in jaws of steel. He sank his teeth in and hung on like grim death. Ralph didn't have a chance.

Meanwhile, Iris came crawling painfully up from the depths of the cellar. She looked like hell. Her hairdo was history, and one eye was almost swollen shut.

The gun, Annie thought, panicking. *Iris had dropped the gun. Where was it?*

"Hold on," Iris told Ralph, by now wedged in the corner trying to pry the dog off what was left of his arm.

"Jesus, get the hell over here—get this dog off me!"

Annie got down on her hands and knees, peering under furniture and feeling all over the floor for the gun.

God, she couldn't find it. Iris would get it first.

Ralph kicked and yelled to beat the band, but Claudius chewed all the harder.

Then she spotted the gun. The metal barrel gleamed dully from under the kitchen table. Iris had seen it too, unfortunately. For a split second, Annie stood there like an idiot. Iris was closer. She'd get there first, even with that broken leg—

Damn, no she wouldn't. Annie threw herself under the table, punched Iris in the face, and grabbed the gun.

Then she crawled over to the phone and dialed 911.

CHAPTER
20

Finally it was over. Iris and Ralph Goddard had been driven away in two police cars, and Annie went downtown to the station to give a statement. She brought Claudius with her. It had taken a beefy cop a good ten minutes to pry his teeth loose from Ralph Goddard's arm.

She sat on a hard oak chair in front of Gus Jackson's desk. He took down her statement, listening and asking questions.

The room was small and bare, a few utilitarian pieces of furniture. Some framed citations on the wall. The air smelled of pipe tobacco. There was a pipe in the ashtray on the desk and he had five o'clock shadow.

So he smoked a pipe and needed a shave, she thought. What the heck, who cared.

She needed to think clearly, only at the moment it was impossible. Her head was throbbing. It felt as if someone had stuck it in a vise. She'd banged it under the table when she'd fought Iris for the gun.

"Ralph Goddard admitted killing May Upton as well as Steve Buchman?" Gus raised his voice, and Annie realized he'd repeated his question.

"Yes," she said.

"Iris Buchman actually told you she and Steve murdered her first husband, Fred Cohen?" He looked at her, hardly bothering to hide his disbelief.

"Yeah, for the insurance."

There were more questions. Somehow Annie got through it, though she couldn't help wondering what would have happened if Claudius hadn't been in the mood to play Bruno the prison guard dog. Presumably, Iris and Ralph would have strung her up in the cellar, and the fake suicide note would have silenced any skeptics.

"The thing is, we have a problem," Gus said.

"What?"

"The case has to be proven in court, and they're denying everything. All we have is your word that they attempted to kill you."

"What about the gun?"

"Iris has a permit." He shrugged. "She got it after her first husband died. Said she was afraid to be alone without some kind of protection."

Annie swallowed a hysterical desire to laugh. Iris needed protection? The woman was a black widow spider.

"They killed four people and almost killed me. If it hadn't been for Claudius, I'd be swinging from a beam in my cellar."

He shrugged. "We need proof. Iris says you made the whole thing up because she accused you of negligence in the matter of her husband's death."

"Oh, I just wanted to get even. Is that it?"

"That's her story."

"Well, she's lying. What about Jack Hogan's signs? They're probably still at the mill. The last one he painted was all about May's murder. That's why they killed him. He was blabbing and showing that sign all over town, and they got scared. Search the mill. The sign has to be there."

"Maybe, maybe not," Gus said. "We'll check it out, but it's still circumstantial. Hogan didn't actually mention either of them by name in the sign, did he?"

"No, but he wrote something about a woman's head under water, a woman drowning. He must have thought Iris and Goddard were demons. He talked about witches. It was Halloween. I'd put those witch figures all over the lawn, remember?" She swallowed hard. "Goddard said he took May's ring after killing her. He gave it to Hogan to shut him up."

Silence. Then Gus said, "What it comes down to is two scenarios: yours and theirs. They say you asked Iris to stop by. You're supposed to have called her. You wanted to apologize. She says she agreed, reluctantly, to come over—but her car wouldn't start. Ralph Goddard happened to be at her house. He'd been cutting brush, so he gave her a ride."

Annie almost burst out laughing. It was unreal. The case against Iris and Ralph was disappearing like fog. "So they get away with four murders?"

"Not if I can help it, but I could investigate Iris for a month of Sundays and still not come up with anything. She's smart and resourceful. If she's guilty, she's done a damn good job of covering her tracks."

"I don't believe it. Two people come into my home to kill me, and you won't arrest them. What about the rope they were going to hang me with? Doesn't that count as a murder weapon?"

"Goddard admits the rope is his. He says he used it to take down a dead tree in your yard. He left it behind by mistake and thought he'd pick it up tonight when he gave Iris a lift." Gus raised his eyebrow. "Did he take down a tree for you?"

"Yes, but he was trying to kill Tom at the time." The words were barely out of her mouth, and she could tell he didn't believe her.

He smiled. "By dropping a tree on him? That's a little hard to swallow."

"It happens to be the truth!"

"Okay, let's say you're right. What's the motive?"

"Tom was there when they killed May. He was drunk and passed out, but they knew he'd seen Goddard's truck."

"Again—your word against theirs—unless your brother remembers what happened that night. As it is, a good defense attorney would tear the case to bits."

Annie sat there, stunned and furious. Iris and Ralph Goddard actually getting away with four murders was unthinkable. The more she thought about it, the angrier she got.

"All right," she said, "what about Iris's tape recorder? She said she didn't go to bingo last night. She recorded twenty minutes of a previous session and held it up to her cell phone so I'd think she was at the Elk's Hall. Check her purse. The recorder should be there. That's proof."

He shrugged. "Unless she got rid of it. Look, we'll conduct a thorough investigation, see if anyone remembers seeing her at bingo last night, but don't count on anything."

"What about the insurance money Iris gets with Steve's death? Ralph said she'd get three million. Plenty of motive for murder."

Another shrug. "You said yourself it was an accident."

"That's before I knew they'd killed him!"

He leaned back in his chair. "Too bad Steve's dead. He's the key to the whole thing. If we could question him, we'd get some answers, always supposing he'd make sense."

"Wait." Annie remembered something. "He was watching TV, a news show. There was a fire, flames, and fire trucks. He got very upset—"

"It doesn't matter. He's dead."

"And Iris is three million dollars richer," Annie reminded him indignantly.

"There's no law against collecting insurance. People do it every day of the week. Hey, don't get mad. I'm just telling you the way it is. Unless we come up with something concrete in the way of proof that they can't argue away, the case is dead in the water."

She wanted to scream at him that this was insane. The cops were supposed to lock up murderers, not think up reasons to let them go. She thought hard. "The cellar stairs at Iris's house. They rigged a wire near the top step in case they had trouble shoving him downstairs. They didn't need it, but I saw something. I thought it was foil from pies I'd wrapped. But when they brought Steve's body up, I didn't see it. It was gone. Iris went upstairs earlier. She told me to stay with Steve's body while she dialed 911. She stumbled near the top step. She could have removed it, if it was part of the wire."

"All right," he said. "Let's say it wasn't foil from the pies that you saw. It could have been a metal screw eye to hold the wire across the steps. In which case, even removing it would leave evidence. A hole—well, two holes, since the wire would have been stretched across the step and fastened on both ends. Don't hold your breath, though. They're not stupid. Chances are they've filled in both holes by now."

"But there'd still be evidence, whatever they used to fill the holes."

He nodded. "Freshly applied, even painted over, it'd be hard to explain away. And it just might be enough to earn them a good long stretch in jail. Maybe. If we get lucky."

"And if we don't?"

"They both get off scot-free, and you'll be up to your neck in trouble for accusing them of attempted murder."

Finally, he was through questioning her and she went home, still furious. Hell could freeze over before Gus Jackson would get any more help from her. The phone was ringing when she let herself into the house, but she didn't answer it. She wanted to wait until she'd calmed down before talking to anyone.

She tossed her jacket on a chair and stood for a moment, listening to the silence and wishing she weren't alone in the house. Common sense and logic said there weren't any intruders. The only people she had reason to be afraid of were still locked up, though not for much longer.

Fear was a terrible thing. If she wasn't careful, it would take over her life.

No, it wouldn't, she decided. As long as she had Claudius, she had nothing to fear. And he deserved extra treats because of his bravery and quick action. Never mind the or-

ganic wheat grass biscuits. There was a bag of beef-basted
bones in the pantry, saved for special occasions; and if this
wasn't a special occasion, she didn't know what was.

For once, he accepted the bone in a gentlemanly manner, leaving all five fingers of her hand intact. It just went
to show that he could be the Cary Grant of dogs if he felt
like it.

"Sit," she said. When this didn't immediately have the
desired effect, "Sit!"

He displayed his teeth in a doggy grin, ignored the "sit"
commands, and flopped on the rug to chew his bone. When
he was done, he curled up for a nap.

A cold rain started falling outside. She stood by the window, watching the last of the leaves fall. The view was
colorless, but beautiful; black silhouettes of trees against a
gray sky. Arching branches glistening with rain. She wondered what the view was like down at the jail.

Moments later, Tom arrived in his old red Hyundai. He
must have had it repaired. He hadn't traded it in when they
bought the new Toyota. Or, more likely, the dealer hadn't
wanted it.

She let him in. "Hi."

"I just heard the news!" he cried, sweeping her into a
bear hug. "It's all over town. Thank God, you're all right.
Claudius came through." He laughed. "Who'd have thought
the mutt had it in him? You must have been terrified."

"I thought I was gonna die. The funny thing is, I don't
think I'll ever be frightened of anything ever again."

He looked a little surprised at that. There was a pause
while he poured himself a cup of coffee. "So they arrested
Goddard and Iris Buchman?"

"Not exactly."

Claudius opened one eye, noticed Tom, and wagged his
tail.

Tom gave him an absent pat on the head. "What do you
mean, not exactly?"

"The cops are questioning Iris and Goddard. The case

is circumstantial at best. If they hire a good lawyer, they'll probably get off."

"Christ!" he said, stunned.

She had to laugh. It was either that or cry.

"Four people murdered," she said, "the biggest thing to happen in town in years, and they might not even be charged!"

"That's unbelievable," Tom said, shaking his head. "I don't get it. Iris does away with two husbands, making it look like accidents, then Jack Hogan's death's listed as an accident, maybe—or suicide. But what about May? That sure as hell was no accident, and the cops know it."

Annie sipped her coffee, thinking. She said slowly, "What with all the uproar, the insurance company's bound to think twice about paying off on Steve's policy. In the end, maybe they'll face at least one murder charge, May's, along with assault and battery and attempted murder for what they tried to do to me." That seemed reasonable. "What do you think?"

"If they get off there's no justice."

"My sentiments, exactly."

He fiddled with his empty cup. Their eyes met.

"So, how are things with you?" she said.

He shrugged. "Not so hot. It turns out you were right."

"About what?" But she already knew. Poor Tom.

"Lydia said it wasn't working between us. The insurance money's gone. She cleaned out the bank account and took off."

"I'm sorry." This wasn't really true, and he knew it, but why kick a dead horse. On the other hand, why not. "I did warn you," she reminded him.

"So you did," he said with leaden irony.

She eyed him, sitting there looking miserable. She ought to feel at least a shred of sympathy, but she didn't. Tom walked around with a sign on his back that read "kick me," and as usual, Lydia was only too willing to oblige. He deserved whatever he got.

"You must be lonely, rattling around the apartment all by yourself."

He drained his coffee cup and set it on the table. "I haven't got time to get lonely. I'm only home at night."

"Never mind, I have a present for you."

On cue, the cat, Pumpkin, leaped on the table and inspected the butter dish. She picked him up and dumped him in Tom's lap. "Here, he's yours. You don't have to thank me."

"I don't need a cat."

"Oh, yes, you do." She got the cat carrier and set it on the floor by his chair. "He was Lydia's, his name is Pumpkin. He needs to be fixed and he might need shots. She used the vet out by the highway. Oh, if you have anything breakable, I'd put it away."

The next morning, Annie overslept. And no wonder, she thought as she made her way groggily downstairs. Coffee and breakfast.

Scrambled eggs.

Contemplating the sofar unsatisfactory outcome of everything that had happened, she made the eggs, dumped on salt, pepper, and catsup, took one bite, and gave it to Claudius. She'd make do with toast.

The phone rang. She let the answering machine get it.

After the usual beep, Gus's voice said, "Good news, Annie. We got what we need on Iris and Goddard. They filled in the holes by the stairs, but did a sloppy job. The putty shrank some, even painted over you could see where the holes were. Also, we found the recorder. Unfortunately for Iris, her bingo tape was still in it. There's no way any jury in the world would buy an innocent plea with evidence like that." There was a short pause, then he said cheerfully, "So, I'll see you around sometime."

She let out a long sigh of relief. Thank God. Her world was right-side-up again. As for seeing Gus Jackson sometime. Well, she'd see. Maybe, maybe not.

The morning paper.

It was still raining, so she pulled on a jacket and felt a slight crackle in the pocket. She drew out a folded piece of paper. Son of a gun. Prudence Cannell had given it to her more than two weeks ago. She'd told her to read it in seven days.

What with everything else, she'd forgotten about it. Well, it was probably nothing.

She hesitated, then unfolded it.

Four words were scrawled in black ink. A prophetic warning: *Stay away from stairs.*

Direct and to the point, but in the light of all that had happened, it was too little, too late.

In due course Iris Buchman and Ralph Goddard were arrested and charged with four counts of murder. The local paper carried a full-page spread along with photographs of the accused: Iris, looking slim and fragile in black, already dubbed "the Black Widow." Ralph Goddard, burly, angry, ducking his head away from the camera.

Claudius's furry face took up most of the top half of page two, along with Lydia, who'd rushed over to the tavern when she heard that the press was doing a big story on the scandalous goings-on. "The dog's mine. I'm just boarding him here," she'd told the reporter.

So he'd taken her photograph—it made a good human-interest shot. The dazzling blonde, identified as a well-known local interior designer, with her arm around the big, black dog. Much better, actually, than the uninspiring, and smaller shot on page three of Annie, the alleged assault victim, tense looking and resentful—who was quoted as saying that she didn't care to be interviewed.

When the paper came out and she read the story, Annie discovered it still made her angry. Lydia's horning in on Claudius's big moment.

"I need the publicity," Lydia said a short while later as she came across Annie walking Claudius down the driveway. Without a by your leave, she grabbed the leash and began petting him. "The newspaper publicity was a godsend. My business is just getting off the ground. Every little bit helps." With a smile like a rattlesnake, she cooed, "I can't take Claudius back, you understand. Not right now."

"Not ever," Annie said. "We're not playing that game again. God knows I've gone the extra mile, taking in your castoffs. But no more. Claudius is mine. He's not going anywhere."

"Well! I should have known. And after all I've done for you. I'm the best friend you ever had. Never mind lending you *my* dog, who just happened to save your life. Plus defending you all over town when everyone was saying you must have had something to do with May Upton's murder. You owe me!"

That didn't deserve an answer.

Instead, Annie took Claudius's leash away from Lydia and walked him back to the house without a backward glance.